SCARS OF FIRE
Dragon-Mage Book Two
by Raina Nightingale

AREAER NOVELS

Return of the Dragonriders
DragonBirth
DragonWing
DragonSword
(Available as omnibus)

Legend of the Singer
Children of the Dryads
Sorceress of the Dryads

Dragon-Mage
Heart of Fire
Scars of Fire
Healing of Fire*

Novellas and Standalones
The Gifts of Faeri
Kindred of the Sea
Gryphon's Escape
Promise of Fire

KAARATHLON NOVELS

EPOCH OF THE PROMISE: Dawn
Unseen
EPOCH OF THE PROMISE:
Vision's Light
EPOCH OF THE PROMISE:
Wings of Healing
EPOCH OF THE PROMISE:
Darkness Bright*

Other Novels

Kingdom of Light

*Not yet available

SCARS OF FIRE
Written by Raina Nightingale

Paperback ISBN: 978-1-952176-24-1

Summary: Camilla and Radiance have escaped from the Wood Elf slave-masters of Ilesh and done the unthinkable, but she still has to find her brother a safe place to stay – and overcome her fear of her own wild magic – before she can pursue vengeance.

Cover art and design by Raina Nightingale.
Maps by Raina Nightingale.
Interior Design by Raina Nightingale.
Illustrations, chapter headers, and scenebreaks by Raina Nightingale.

Published by Raina Nightingale
www.enthralledbylove.com

Preface

I first imagined *Dragon-Mage* when I was eight, perhaps nine years old. I knew who Camilla and Radiance were: I saw the moment when their souls recognized and the Fire made them one. Since then, I've tried to write the *Dragon-Mage* series a great many times. This is probably the only time I've consistently re-written a story, without it changing so much in the re-writes as to be unrecognizable, apart perhaps from a few nearly superficial elements, like a similar-looking main character, or some similar names – you get the idea.

But it was never right. It was never the story it was meant to be. Eventually, I got the feel for what that would be, and started abandoning my attempts half-way through book one, or maybe on chapter three. Even when I realized I needed to remove the love interest character, who was there only because that was the "pattern" I learned – somehow or other – that Epic Fantasy had, and that Camilla simply had no room in her life and no interest in such things, I still did not have it *quite.* But I was closer.

Then, one day, I saw a scene from book three. I even wrote the scene down because it was so vivid, even though I rarely *write* scenes out of order. And that was when I really started to get it. That was when I started writing *Heart of Fire,* and it *flowed.* It *fit.*

This is probably the most epic of my Areaer series, though as always it will have its slow, almost cozy moments strung throughout. As I say, the slice of life moments are just as important, and they're the only reason that those exciting moments of challenge matter, or that anyone can rise to the challenge and win, so they're *epic* too and belong in epic stories!

The slow moments are probably strongest in *Scars of Fire,* as Camilla must fight a battle within herself against her own fears. But I found it intense, and I find it rather fast when I re-read it, so I hope you enjoy!

Enjoy!
-Raina Nightingale

PS. Book three will be *Healing of Fire.* And when *Healing of Fire* comes out, then you can learn the name for book four. :D

Table of Contents

Map of Ellenesia

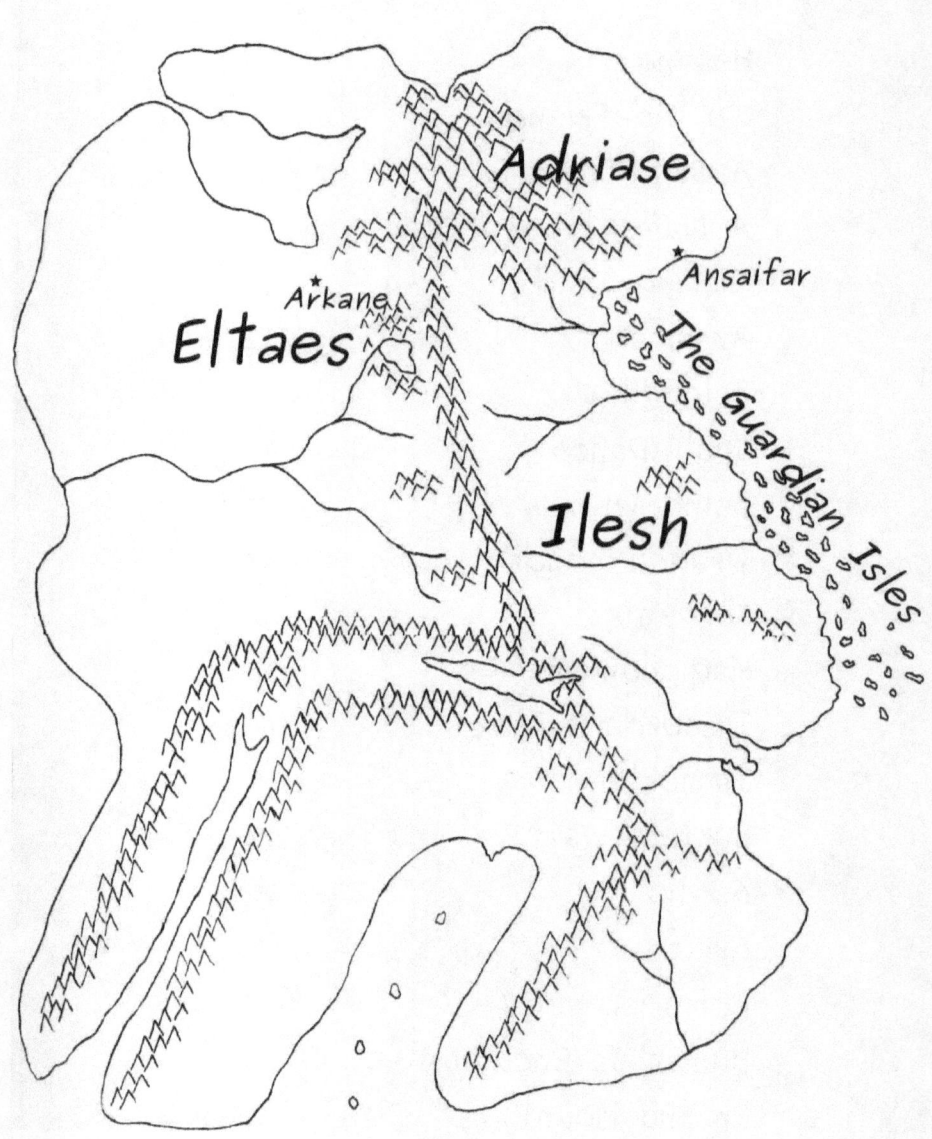

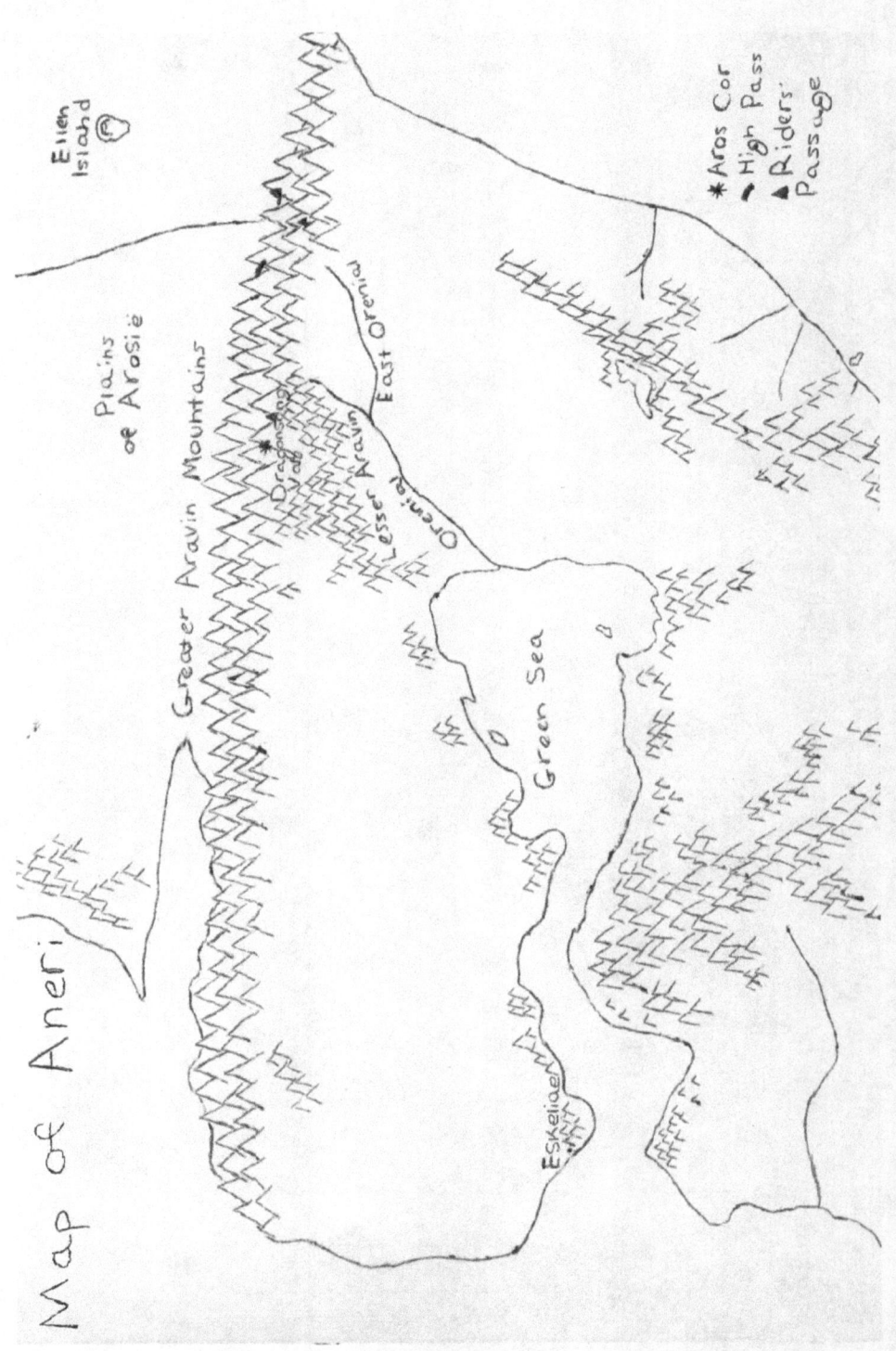

Map of Aneri

Ellen Island

Plains of Arosie

Greater Aravin Mountains

Dragonsflat

Lesser Aravin

East Orenia

Orenia

Green Sea

Eskelier

* Aros Cor
High Pass
▲ Riders' Passage

Healing

The Nightmare Lord, the Dark Prince, sat on his throne in Eltaes and ground his teeth – not that he usually had teeth, exactly, but he had to put up with it since if he abandoned this body it could fall to pieces and he might not be able to re-possess it. He could not believe what he felt. It sheered through the magic that was an extension of his being like agony, and he could not believe any but another Otherborn could conduct or direct that much power without being burned to a crisped, smoking corpse by it, yet this power was distinctly mortal.

For a moment he wondered if it was that Obsidian Guardian, Nelexi, and if the Obsidian Guardian had even more powers than had been shown over the ages or if one as old as Nelexi developed new powers – for though not strictly mortal, the Obsidian Guardian had once been mortal and was nearly mortal – but then he felt through the pain a mark that was definitely no Obsidian Guardian.

A mortal dragon and rider were the conduit and will behind this power, and he could not believe what it was doing. It was taking a half-undead dragon and shredding his spells of death and control into pieces, at the same time as it infused the life of dragonfire past his dark magic into the dragon's heart. In fact, that was *how* it functioned. And the dragon was already past his recall.

Quickly, he summoned the rest of the host back to him, drawing them through the spell of undeath into his presence, utterly angered. *No* one should be able to do this! He had seen other mortals do things he would not have expected, but nothing on this scale, certainly nothing involving so much sheer power. He doubted even the hated Guardian of the Volcano could do this. How *dare* a mere mortal elf-twisted dragon and her rider be able to manage it! For this dragon was clearly one of those warped by the elf magic. That piece of work should *never* have produced *this*.

Dark flames erupted throughout the hall, shredding the undeath-bound slaves with torment. Several of the bonds severed, slaying and freeing the slaves, but the Nightmare Lord did not care. He had a few to spare, and fear and agony fed the Nightmare. Consideration for others and compassion were concepts that did not even exist within his darkness.

At least, he thought, at least that mortal pair who dared to do what no Guardian, what no Otherborn, could ever do had probably died. It could not be possible for mortality to conduct that much power without the body being burned to ashes – or even vapor.

Camilla sat in Radiance's saddle, watching as Ben struggled into the air. He staggered when he walked and looked disorganized, but he flew even worse than he walked. He could barely take off, and he could not stay in the air for farther than two and a half lengths of his own body. It had now been a couple days since the attack when he had been freed, and they were trying to move slowly northward along the shore, towards Ansaifar, the Sea Elf city. Part of Camilla was glad that it was Alian with them, since she liked the red dragonmage better than the purple one, but another part of her wished it was Serrose with them. Serrose had far stronger magic and, therefore, healing powers, though Alian's healing powers seemed amazingly strong for his – or her – magic, she thought. Alian had a human form, which was male, and a dragon form, which was female.

Her own arms throbbed. They were incredibly sore and painful, and just beginning to itch, but she dared not itch them. The power of the magic that had freed Ben had apparently burned off most of the skin from her fingers almost to her elbows on both arms.

It was frustrating being unable to do almost anything. She could not saddle Radiance. She could not drink on her own, and she needed help to eat. She even needed help to mount Radiance, and she had to watch herself the whole time she was on dragonback to make sure she did not try to steady herself with her hands. She was bound into the saddle and in no danger of falling off, but there were some instincts it was hard to repress, even when acting on them caused searing pain. It was as if her body just could not understand that, no, she was not at risk of dying by falling.

Curse them. Curse it all. Curse the Dark Prince of Eltaes. Curse the Nightmare. And curse that dark elf, that Aishaena, if she is behind all this and betrayed us! she thought. For the thousandth time, she half-heartedly tried to stifle those angry, bitter thoughts. Radiance had told her that they did not help *her*, Camilla, to heal, and they certainly did not help Ben to heal from his long imprisonment of mindless slavery.

Yet they came to her so naturally, and she could not really cast them out. They made sense. Why should she not wish curses on such horrible things – things responsible for the wretched misery Ben had been made to pass through, for his present state, a grown dragon once able to soar on the winds now able only to stagger along? But somehow, for some reason, anger and curses did not help that healing, did not help Ben to focus on the light, not to remember the darkness, and to learn again all that he had once been and more. So she tried, as well as she could, to stifle the thoughts, but she could not keep herself from thinking them.

There were other things Camilla did not know what to think about, and Sylvara was one of them. The silver-rider had long been Camilla's enemy, regularly reporting her to the elf slave-masters and getting her punished by them. Now, there was no denying the fact that Sylvara was trying to be as kind and considerate and helpful as she knew how, and Camilla could not adjust to it. It was hard for her to even accept it.

How could Sylvara have changed so much? She knew that it was genuine. The dragon-sense could not be deceived. But she still had a hard time knowing how to respond. Camilla's first impulse, when Sylvara waited on her, ready to do *whatever* would make Camilla comfortable if she could, was to hiss in Sylvara's face and growl at her to go away and stop conniving and scheming, but she knew Sylvara *wasn't* conniving or scheming, or, if she was, it was not a dominant motivation; it could not be more than a very deeply buried side-current.

There were even occasional moments when Camilla felt like being kind towards Sylvara, but those feelings never lasted for more than a second before Camilla instinctively withdrew and pushed them away. She did not think she could *ever* forget what Sylvara had been, and she was not sure she wanted to. If Sylvara could change this easily into something nicer, could she not also change back? Additionally, being waited on and served galled Camilla. She thought she might have found it pleasurable if the elf slave-masters had been forced to serve *her*, their former slave, but Sylvara had been a snitch and something possibly even more deplorable than the slave-masters, and that very conniving aspect of what she had been made Camilla reluctant to accept her service.

Furthermore, Camilla was boiling with frustration at her *need* to be served, which only added more irritation and anger to the mix. She *hated* relying on or needing someone who had been such a scheming, deceiving enemy – not that she exactly relied on or needed Sylvara. Alian took care of many of their needs, and her brother, Lavilor, was incredibly helpful and caring, and his compassion actually made Camilla feel *good*. Despite the fact that she utterly hated needing to be hand-fed and watered, Lavilor and Radiance often contrived to make the process into a huge, ridiculous joke that had her doubled over in laughter. It made it take longer, but while Camilla felt that time was not something they had to spare, it was Ben's inability that was slowing them down, not her own more recent and superficial injury.

Both more and less pressing than her problems with Sylvara – more because it was a greater, more upsetting, more primal issue, and less because it was not a voice constantly speaking to her, a face constantly looking to her – was the problem of what had been done to Ben, and so many others, possibly including her own mother, and could – *maybe?* – be done to her. How was it possible? Why was it allowed by the universe? It upset her so much. The problem of how it was that other's personalities and lives could be so violated had bothered her for a long time, but it was even more emotional and pressing now that she was bonded to a dragon who had been a victim of such violation. She chaffed at his pain, at what he had suffered and gone through, and it made her bile rise that such a thing could *ever* happen. But thinking about that did not help either of them. He needed her love, her emotional support and union, not her agonized thoughts and philosophizing about what happened.

As Camilla looked around her for something beautiful that might take her mind off her dark thoughts, the blue of the sky or the shades of the sea, her eyes roved over Ben's stumbling form, his ribs prominent, his bones jutting out, and anger flooded through her again. At the same moment, Alian – in dragon form – stepped closer to her and Radiance, catching her eye. It did not help. Alian was nearly the same color as Ben, and glowing with health, even if she was not really a dragon. She swung her huge red head over the dragon and rider, and said, "Camilla?"

"Yes?" The word came out as a fair growl, but not because Camilla was upset at Alian.

"You and Ben should both feel encouraged. He's putting on weight quite quickly, and his coordination skills are improving extraordinarily."

"I suppose," Camilla grumbled. What Alian said was true. Ben had been barely able to crawl after he had dropped out of the sky that night when her magic had freed him. Nonetheless, none of it improved Camilla's mood. Right now, all she wanted was to find some way to torture whatever creature was evil enough to do this to anyone …

Camilla tried to force the thought down and keep her emotions under control. Alian would not approve, and while she did not have the same extent of empathy that a true dragon did, she did have some, and Camilla was more than a dragonspeaker; her thoughts and feelings could be radiated not only to all dragons but to all humans as well. She was fairly certain the dragonmages picked up on more than they ever let on, though they only scolded her about it when she let her emotions so out of control that she practically screamed them at everyone, including other humans, who usually were not the most sensitive. Even more importantly, it would not help Ben anymore than any of her other angry thoughts.

There's something very wrong with the world. I hate evil. I must hate evil. I want to hate evil. It is in my nature to hate evil. If I love, I must hate. It goes against all I know of love not to hate. Yet hatred does not help me love. It does not heal those I love. It does not soothe or nourish or complete them. It does not make me happy or good at loving, yet because I love, I must hate. And I've been told that hatred is from the Nightmare and its fear, and is the Nightmare within me, and it seems to be so, yet it is also because I love.

Camilla fixed her eyes on Ben and tried to stop thinking about how wasted he looked and how much she wanted to find some way – magical or physical – to torture the Wizard-King of Eltaes. It was a daunting prospect; how did a mortal first defeat, and then torture, an entity powered by supernatural darkness? Nonetheless, Camilla was determined that she *would* not only attempt to kill the Lord of the Northern Horror, but would succeed at doing so, and while that was more important than torture, she still entertained the thought. But just at this moment, Ben was collapsing on the ground, having tried to fly again. It was his own urges and instincts that drove him to attempt flight so often. He was not a hatchling, but had been an adult dragon, soaring in the skies, before his captivity, and Camilla thought that captivity had only honed his urge to fly *free* once more.

It's okay, Ben. You're doing better, much better. Give it a rest, and maybe you'll do better this evening or tomorrow morning. It doesn't help to scramble so much. You're free now. Feel the sun on your scales. Feel the sand between your toes and under your tail. Feel the breeze against your face and wings. Take a dip in the sea, and feel its salty waters swirl around you and reach your skin between your scales, if you want. You're big enough it won't wash you right away, even if you can't swim or run.

Camilla was somewhat surprised when after making a few more attempts to fly, Ben chose to take her advice. He flopped over, and rolled himself in the sand and surf, rubbing his wings in the sand and making the waves splash around him. He arched his neck back, and scratched its ridges deep into the wet sand. He wriggled with sheer delight, clearly enjoying an activity that was unaffected by his coordination problems, and the surging of the waves, first pulling back, then rolling against his side. His delight was so strong that Camilla felt as if she would be knocked down by it at first, just as she would be if she ventured into the bigger waves, but then she laughed out loud.

Ben lifted his head and looked into her eyes. The waves reflected off of their jewel-like facets. His tail slapped the waves. No words came across their bond, but Camilla understood perfectly. His healing had begun in earnest, now. Happiness and contentment washed through his soul like the waves washed over his scales. With it, a feeling wholly new washed through her – or was it wholly new? Hadn't she been a nurturer to Radiance? But, no, this was different. Radiance had upheld her even more than she had upheld Radiance, if it was possible to speak of such things regarding two who were, in many ways, more one than two. This was different. She liked it, and it numbed the pain and frustration of not being able to do anything for herself, but it felt strange, too. Finally, she settled for just saying, *I love you, Ben.*

He rolled all the way over, and lashed the shore with his tail, sending up a spray of sea-water and sand. Again, Camilla laughed.

This was much better than hating. It was much happier, and it was doing much more good. Yet she *hated* and she *needed* to hate. Perhaps, she could settle for learning to only think about the evil and the hatred it deserved when necessary, and focusing on the good, the love that healed, the rest of the time. *I love to heal. I hate to destroy. I love you all, and I always will, but I should only hate when I'm focusing on fighting and destroying, and most of the time it's not the time for that.* Nonetheless, there was a way in which Camilla felt more comfortable hating. For some reason, she felt out of place, clumsy, exposed when she didn't hate.

To Old Friends

Flameheart and Nelexi flew broad circles over the Sea Elven fleet they had rescued from marauding black dragons. The sky around them was blue, with wisps of cloud in it, and below them the sea rippled with blues and greens. Flameheart sensed that her dragon friend was distracted, and wondered what could possibly distract her. It was not the blue of the sky or the shades of the sea; if it was, Nelexi would be sharing it with her rider.

"No, you're right. We've just flown within fair speaking range of some old friends of mine."

Several thoughts clamored in Flameheart's mind. *Old friends of you? You did not mention old friends still living on Ellenesia that I remember – Fair speaking range? Can't dragons speak without effort across any distance?*

"I did, but it was on the way here, while you were feeling sick. Remember when I told you about the situation on this continent? About the dragonmages? As for speaking range, the dragonmages are like dragons, but not. They can speak telepathically, similar to us, but they're affected by distance."

I thought that was a long time ago. Longer than anyone but obsidian dragons and maybe elves live.

"It was not quite that long ago, though it might seem so to you, but the dragonmages are also long-lived. Yet I did not know for certain that they were still alive when I told you about how I found and woke them, but I suspected as much."

I remember now. You said they are creatures unlike any that have ever been made before, made directly by Shallim-Araldor when a bunch of people were killed by an evil Wizard-King. What are they telling you?

Nelexi took a moment to respond, and Flameheart could almost feel too many thoughts moving in the dragon's head at once. *"A lot of things. A great many things have happened in Ellenesia since I chose you, and many of them are so wild and significant I hardly know where to begin. We had not really thought the dragonmages were a viable race, having been created singly and for a specific purpose, but it seems that they may be. Many of them were strange in ways that seemed not to allow for young. Yet one pair has laid eggs, which have now hatched.*

"Human Dragonriders have come out from the closed elven lands of Ilesh. One is a dragonkeeper and more than a dragonspeaker – able to speak to humans as the dragonmages speak, though it is not yet clear whether she can speak to humans she knows without regard to distance, as dragons speak and as dragonspeakers speak to dragons.

"Furthermore, she is a mage like no other. According to the report, she had a fair magic potential prior to bonding to her dragon, Radiance, but since

bonding she is expressing a kind of magic that may be as unique as we thought those we've called 'dragonmages' to be. You don't know enough about magic to know all of it or all the signs of her magical potential. She has recently used what must be dragon magic – or earthfire magic – to free a dragon from the bonds of the Wizard-King, and has bonded to this now-living dragon as well as Radiance. However, he is struggling and weak, and she burned herself badly."

And we are going to them next?

"Yes, but I will stop in Ansaifar first. It should not cost us very much time, and you will greatly appreciate it."

Flameheart knew she did not understand half the import of the things Nelexi had relaid, but her body thrummed with the dragon's excitement, and she could not imagine what it must take to so excite a creature as old and wise and powerful and experienced as Nelexi. *What is this dragonmage's name?* she asked.

"Alian. His – or her (for this one is male in his human form and female in her dragon form) – mate is called Serrose."

Flameheart caught the sliver of another thought. She did not think Nelexi was trying to keep it from her, but was simply preoccupied and neglecting to share it with her. If that was not the case, Nelexi would know her intentions, and that she was not trying to pry into what the Obsidian Guardian could not share with her. *You're thinking something else, aren't you?*

"Yes. That perhaps the Dragonrider with all the magic – Camilla, rider of Radiance – is the dragon-mage. She is bonded to Radiance as it seems no other dragon and rider have ever been bonded, though I will have to see for myself. I will have to see her magical imprint for myself, too, and shall as soon as I can speak to her and hear her as dragons speak to and hear one another. But the creatures with the dragon and humanlike forms need a better designation among those who speak and think not as dragons do, especially if they are to become a race."

Though her head hurt from the crash course Nelexi was giving her on Ileshian, the Wood Elf language and apparently the only language known to these Dragonriders, once slaves of the Wood Elves, the prospect of seeing land greatly excited Flameheart. She did not like sleeping on a ship or in the saddle. She did not like crossing from the ship to Nelexi or the other way around on the dragon's wing; it felt too precarious even though, somehow, she had managed not to fall into the sea yet. Just as importantly, she had been getting sicker and sicker, eating only what Nelexi and she could find or catch while traversing the sea and landing on an occasional island, and while the food the

Sea Elves gave her had greatly helped, it had not helped a lot, and she expected to be able to get better food in their city.

Also, it would be nice to get a new saddle, one made of new supple leather that had not been ruined by being submerged in the sea during the fight with the obsidian dragons. There were times Flameheart still felt a little bad about it. Nelexi was either impossible to kill, or nearly impossible, and despite the fact that the dragon insisted that it would not be easier for her to fight the Nightmare without Flameheart, there were times when Flameheart only half believed her.

When the Sea Elf city, with its tall towers, its twisting spirals carved as if to resemble waves, some of them in blue or green stone instead of white, its curving streets and its gardens, materialized below her, she could hardly contain her excitement. She did note, however, that this city – Ansaifar – looked a bit different than the one on Galen looked. It was not huge, but there was a decidedly different feel to the way the buildings had been arranged and the way the stones were carved.

"It might be because the stone they used was different, or it might be more because of the tastes and preferences of the different elves who built them," commented Nelexi, *"but we're going to wait to descend until the ships dock. Otherwise, I would land some distance away and let you go in and explain, a little like we did on Galen but with less caution and more boldness, since the Sha'adhri and the Nations of the Sea are no longer at war. As it is, it will still be a long time before Sea Elves can see dragons and not think of danger and burning ships, so I would rather let those we rescued first tell them what happened. Then I will land somewhere there's enough space for me but you can easily get in."*

You could just speak to them and let them know who we are and what happened.

Nelexi chuckled *very* softly. *"You must know this, but that's likely to scare them more and be less effective."*

I do know that, but I still find the idea attractive to imagine. She could hardly contain her excitement while Nelexi hovered, keeping her distance, far enough that she would not be an imposing presence over the city and that Flameheart could discern a few of the details of the city only by relying on her vision. Flameheart's stomach did flips while she waited. The ships seemed to move *so* slowly.

Finally, the ships sailed slowly in and anchored next to the white docks, and the Sea Elves who had come out to see the fleet come in and those on the fleet spoke below them – not that even Nelexi could *hear* from this height – and then they visibly began to get more animated, some of them expressing concern and some expressing excitement. Nelexi clearly felt the waves of emotion, and passed her awareness onto Flameheart.

It was then that she began to descend, gliding down with an occasional wingbeat. Flameheart's stomach fell, but her heart rose. This was her favorite kind of flying!

As they neared the ground, the cheers erupted in earnest, clearly centered around them. Nelexi glided to the side and landed on the wide beach near the port. The Sea Elves gave her plenty of wingroom. Flameheart recoiled a little from what she knew was coming. The Sea Elves were apt to treat her as something between an exotic animal and a heroine, and neither way of treatment pleased her.

The leading edge of the crowd curtsied to the dragon and rider. It might not have been considered a crowd by city-dwelling human beings, but it certainly seemed like a crowd to Flameheart, who was from a clan of tribes that roamed the Plains of Zharda in Galen. She found the mere idea of a city, or viewing one from above, repulsive, unless it was a Sea Elf city, which were rather different from human cities, not nearly as crowded either with humans or with buildings, and more a place for congregating, a sort of year-long meet, than a place for living, for most Sea Elves lived mostly in their ships upon the sea, a way of life that made sense to Flameheart, for her people roamed the plains in much the same way, even if she did not enjoy the sea at all.

Flameheart felt Nelexi urging her to speak, but she could not pluck up the courage to speak to all these people. She thought the words would die on her lips, if she could even speak past the lump in her throat. *No, you do. You don't mind all this attention, and you can speak to them as easily as I can.*

"It is not our habit to speak to those whom we do not know and are not Dragonriders casually like this, and it is a little harder than you think for me to make myself easily heard by Sea Elves, but I will do so if you cannot," said Nelexi.

After eating a good meal tucked against Nelexi's side, Flameheart was soon hopelessly bored with preparations. Nelexi had herself measured for a new saddle, and then told Flameheart that, since it would take some time for the Sea Elves to craft the saddle, she would continue wearing the ruined one until they returned. She was getting itchy in it, but she could tolerate it for a few more weeks, and she certainly did not expect Flameheart to get it on or off in its present state.

I could ride you bareback, Flameheart said. *I did before, and I'd do better and be more comfortable now.*

"Yes," said Nelexi, *"but if we have to fight for some reason, I would prefer we have the saddle."*

What if it breaks? asked Flameheart. *That would be worse than me clinging to your scales bareback.*

"It's enchanted by the Light Elves for me. I doubt that will happen."

With that said, Flameheart climbed into the stiff saddle and fumbled with the straps to secure herself. Nelexi lifted off into the air to the cheering of the Sea Elves and commented to her rider, *"I can't say I enjoy their attitude towards me, but it is a wonderful thing to see the Sea Elves and dragons seeing one another as something good, as friends, instead of as enemies. I love it when the Nightmare's plans turn against it like this, for now fear is undone and trust is being built as would have taken much longer otherwise, but things don't always turn around this quickly or this simply. We must never lose heart."*

Nelexi banked rather sharply and flew southwest over the bay. Flameheart put a hand over the satchel of fresh food to remind herself it was real.

A couple days later, Nelexi told Flameheart, *"Here we are. I can feel them below me,"* and glided down. The Obsidian Guardian's excitement was contagious, and Flameheart wondered again what could be so strange and new and wonderful to cause excitement in a creature like Nelexi. Of course, Nelexi was always sharing with her the wonder and excitement and joy of the world, a world that Flameheart understood as never before was so wide and awesome and *real* that it would never get old – one could always discover new beauty in the blue of the sky or even the shades of blue-green on a wave – yet this was a different kind of excitement from that wonder and delight.

Flameheart leaned out over Nelexi's shoulder, hoping to get a glimpse of where they were landing and what they would be seeing. It was an almost instinctive action by now, but totally useless on this wintry day.

The sky was speckled with clouds around them, though Nelexi flew mostly in open sky between two layers of cloud. Even if the sun sometimes showed – to Flameheart's almost wild delight – through a rift in the clouds above them, there was no way she would be able to see the fog blanketing the land and sea below them, and rising up in huge frothing pillars that looked like they might turn into storms around the mountains ahead of them.

Nelexi's eyes could not see through all that cloud anymore than hers could; it was her dragon-senses that told her she was near. Perhaps, she was even in communication with those strange creatures she had described, in particular with the individual she had described in some detail to Flameheart only a few hours earlier – if it was hours earlier. Flameheart could not always tell the different between a few hours and half an hour, especially when the sky was overcast.

Then they entered the lower cloud layer, and Flameheart felt moisture beading on her face – exposed today, since the air was wet from all the clouds and would not be likely to cause windburn – and on her hands and cloak. When she moved her hand on Nelexi's scales, she felt moisture there, too. *Does this go all the way to the ground? How will you land safely, if it does?*

"Yes, the cloud pretty much goes all the way to the ground. Don't worry about my landing. I know exactly how far I am from the earth at all times and without effort."

A part of your magic?

"Largely, yes, but some of it is also experience. Both my heart and my wings know. Regardless, it is no issue. I have done this thousands of times before in far more turbulent weather and I've never landed wrongly. Flameheart, I haven't even forgotten to lighten myself in such circumstances. One of the only times I've ever done that was when I was so excited to finally bond with you, and then your fear threw me off."

By now, Flameheart knew – *felt* – that there was no need for an apology.

Finally, Flameheart saw the ground as a slight variation in the shade of the clouds around them – pointed out first to her by Nelexi. It grew rapidly more visible, as the dragon shifted her wings, slowed, and landed in front of what appeared to be one gold dragon and two silver dragons, both quite small, a large red dragon, and four riders – but Flameheart knew one of the human-like creatures was not a Dragonrider at all, but something as dragon as it was human and neither dragon nor human. Nelexi had described him so perfectly, Flameheart knew him by his stance – or perhaps, she knew him by Nelexi's recognition. That was when she realized that she also knew which female was Camilla, the dragon-keeper and dragonspeaker, the dragon-mage, the one whose magic startled Nelexi.

A Sand Volcano

Camilla stood on the sand and watched the *huge* black dragon descend out of the clouds. Her wings almost glowed red-orange, not quite like coals. Camilla tightened her hand around the hilt of the magesword as her whole body tingled. She had felt it since about the same time that Radiance and Alian had both told her, as well as they could, who was coming, but it only grew stronger as Nelexi, the Obsidian Guardian, glided closer. It was magic like no other, and yet it called to her. It burned in *her* blood.

She recognized it, primal and deep and unspeakably beautiful – and like the fire in the vision she had had after freeing Ben. That fire *lived* in this creature.

Feelings she could not ever begin to sort out, and that she did not want to admit she did not understand and control, warred in her as the obsidian dragon glided down and landed. The ground *barely* trembled as she landed, and Camilla *knew* there was more magic involved. This being's very nature was magic, all her actions interwoven so flawlessly and perfectly with it that there was no telling the magic from what was not magic.

Then Nelexi spoke into her and Radiance's minds, together, with a voice like raw fire. *"Camilla, all nature is magic. You but see only a very small bit of reality – of nature and of magic, as do I. There never is any true telling of magic from nature."*

Camilla had never really thought about that before, but she knew that her own magic had told her that all along. *Nelexi, are you like me?* This dragon spoke to humans *and* dragons much like she did, and this dragon's magic – well, it was not really a surprise that a dragon's magic was like her own given Serrose's and Alian's speculations about Dragonrider-mages and bonding to the elf-twisted dragons making or increasing the magic of humans, though this dragon was not much like Radiance or the other dragons.

"In some ways, I am. In other ways, I am not."

The enigmatic answer bothered Camilla, but what could she say? She could not really challenge it; it was obvious. At the same time, she knew Nelexi meant something other than what was obvious – or did she? *Can you teach me?* she asked.

"Patience, human," said the dragon, and bent her neck, lowering her nose low to the ground. Even Alian in her dragon form was dwarfed against the dragon's bulk. The two greeted as long lost friends. Camilla heard only a faint hum and a glimmer of meaning here and there from their greeting. She wondered at it. Had Alian not said he had been in contact with Nelexi for several days now? What had they not shared, could they not share until they were in nearly physical contact?

Camilla pulled herself out of her own thoughts to pay attention to the dragons. Ben was staring at Nelexi with an emotion Camilla could not describe, and did not think she had ever experienced before. Lavilor was almost clinging to her, and as she took one step forward he whispered to her, "She's huge! I didn't think ..."

"I know," replied Camilla. "She is huge. And look how her wings and that stripe along her spine almost glow in the fog!"

"It's beautiful. I think I like her," said Lavilor.

At that moment, Nelexi raised her head from her greeting with Alian, and Camilla saw a small dark-skinned girl – her skin almost black against the fog, brown only by comparison with her dragon's scales – step out from behind Nelexi's foreleg. Her small form made the dragon seem even huger, even though her shoulders already towered above them and the edges of her form melted away into the fog. It was hard for Camilla to conceptualize a living creature so huge, even when it stood before her.

She's shy! thought Camilla, considering the girl, when Nelexi spoke to all of them. *"Greetings. I am Nelexi, Obsidian Guardian of Areaer, and this is my rider, Flameheart Kario from the Plains of Zharda."*

Along with her words, images flashed through Camilla's mind of skies and mountains taller and steeper than she would have imagined possible, of volcanoes and storms, and then, bright against that background, of sweeping wide, flat plains with a few ever-so-gently rolling hills and scraggly bushes and copses of trees, the grass green-yellow, the sky a startling blue, harder and drier and more brilliant than she had ever seen before.

Flameheart stepped forward and curtsied. "Hello," she said slowly and with a thick, clumsy accent, but her voice now betrayed excitement mixed with her shyness. "I ... will be very happy to meet you."

Alian, who had stepped back a few paces, turned on her haunches to face Flameheart without blocking the view of the others. "Hi, Flameheart," she said. "Nelexi has told me a lot about you. It is lovely to meet you, her new rider. I don't know if you saw me transform earlier through the fog. Would you like to see me transform back?"

"After talking to Nelexi so long it's not very strange to talk to dragons out loud," said Flameheart, slowly and haltingly.

A set of very awkward introductions followed.

That night, Camilla lay awake staring at a single constellation that appeared through a rift in the clouds. The stars of the Dolphin – the constellation her mother had once shown her and told her was her father's favorite – were blurry through the mist, but she could still see it. It brought tears to her eyes, reminding her how much she missed her mother, and her father who she knew had loved her but whom she would never see again, at least this side of death, but those thoughts and feelings were not enough to distract her from something else that lay heavy on her.

Ever since she had freed Ben, she had felt strange, and it was becoming impossible to ignore how strange she felt, just as it was impossible to ignore the itching of her burned arms. She wanted to believe that the power was hers, that her determination and the purity of her desire to be free and to make others free had provided the power that had done what everyone else thought was impossible. In a sense, she believed it was, but she also felt as if it *wasn't hers*.

Nelexi's presence had reminded her, not because the fact it was Nelexi's power as well would have been upsetting to her sense that it was her power – in her idea of a perfect world, everyone with that determination to be free would have that power – but because Nelexi's magic had reminded her of the magic of that night, and thus of what she thought and felt about it, and she was absolutely determined that her life and magic and power and actions and victories should be chosen by herself alone.

She was not some plaything of higher powers, not some creature to be chosen, for however lofty an end, however much she might desire that end, by someone else. She wanted her power, her magic, to come from herself alone, not from someone else, not even from the thing, however beautiful and entrancing, she had sensed in the vision and in Nelexi. She wanted the freedom to make her own destiny, and she wanted that freedom for everyone else.

A part of her wanted to fight all reality to make her vision come true. She believed that she was right and that what she wanted the world to be was good, and even that she could stand against all existence to remake it so. Yet ... yet ... the Fire, the Earthfire, the Heartfire, was so *so* beautiful.

The song of its flames even now haunted her dreams and seemed almost to speak to her again in Nelexi's magic. What could she ever want more than to be united again with that Heartfire? What was that dark girl's name again? Flameheart? Oh, how she wanted to be one with the Heartfire again ... could that wonder exist in a world where all her magic came from *her* alone?

Not unless she *was* the Heartfire, and if she were the Heartfire, she would be the Heartfire, not Camilla ... it did not really make sense. But the Wizard-King was evil, the dark magic and power could *not* exist ... and yet it did. Ben *had* been enslaved.

She, Camilla, had to destroy at least that, and she would not be the slave or servant or property of *any*thing or *any*one else. It was just wrong! It was evil! No one should be effectively slave or property of anything else. Everyone must be master of her own destiny. Anything else was evil, the very essence of the Northern Horror.

So why did she want so fiercely to be united to this Heartfire, this magic, this power and essence something a little like a will, that was so far beyond her and transcended all her understanding and all that she was? She was *no* slave, and there was not even any slavery in this desire of hers …

With that thought muddling into the river of her mind, Camilla fell asleep.

The next few days were rather awkward, but not nearly as awkward as having Aishaena, the Dark Elf, with them had been – or even as awkward as being around the dragonmages, especially Serrose, had been at first. Flameheart was clearly shy and spoke very awkwardly, but she also had a kind of connection to the dragons, and Camilla was certain that Ben benefited a great deal from her attention and kindness, even though the two could not speak to each other.

That irked Camilla. She hated accepting that Flameheart could do what she could not. It had been quite enjoyable to discover that she could be a nurturer, and she could not stand that someone else, who was not even bonded to the dragon or a dragonspeaker, could be that for him better than she could. At the same time, she felt drawn to Flameheart herself. But though the other girl seemed shy, she did not seem particularly adverse to Sylvara, though Camilla could sense that Flameheart felt something towards herself that Camilla had never felt before. It was not very strong, but it was there, and Camilla thought it might be related to the connection between her and Nelexi, between her magic and the dragon's. As Flameheart became a little less shy and quickly more comfortable with the language, they spent a little more time talking.

It made Camilla happy to see how well Flameheart and Lavilor got along. Both of them were shy and reserved at first, but they quickly became friends, and spent a great deal of time together. They threw themselves into building sand constructions with a will and exuberance that both made Camilla's heart thrill and sting. Slavery had stolen so much from her and her brother – and her mother and father – and it made her so angry she almost thought she might start sprouting flames, and intentionally tried to dampen that image lest it actually happen, and it made her feel so sad.

Yet it made her feel just as happy to see him playing and having fun, enjoying the things that had been stolen him. There was such bright, innocent joy in his and Flameheart's games that it infected Camilla, too. She thought it helped Ben as well. He was stronger every day.

One day, she decided to join Flameheart and Lavilor on the beach. Ben was playing in the water not far away, flapping at the waves with his wings and lashing at them with his tail. Flameheart was giggling ecstatically, as she and

Lavilor worked on building a volcano. "Have you actually seen a volcano?" Lavilor asked her.

"Yes. I did. Nelexi took me to see the volcano she came out of. A long, long time ago, she flew into it and came back out. That's why she can breathe lava, and why her wings and stripe are that glowy red."

Camilla stepped in and sat down between the two of them on one side of their work area. "What was it like?" she asked.

Flameheart screwed up her face as if remembering – or trying to remember some part of the language she had not quite gotten yet – and said, "It was ... well, I liked it but also not. It *glares*. And I would have been scared if I wasn't with Nelexi. It doesn't smell good either. I'm not really sure how to describe it. But it's ... it's ... fascinating? It feels like a friend ... or as if it would be a friend if it knew you ... no, it seems like a friend but one's that very ... different. I don't know how to say this."

Camilla listened intently, and she was never sure if she was not also listening with that other part of her, that part of her that heard and spoke as dragons hear and speak, even though she was not trying to eavesdrop. She knew that Flameheart did not feel like she did about freedom and power, free will and destiny and greater beings. She wondered if she should talk to her about it. Her thoughts of a few nights before, and her feelings from the night she had rescued Ben, returned to her, mixed with a tinge of something else, something she thought came from Nelexi and Flameheart.

Lavilor interrupted the silence after Flameheart was done speaking before Camilla could get too woven into her darker and more confused thoughts. "Why don't we just build the volcano?" he asked. "At least Flameheart can tell us if we've made it right!"

"Sure," said Camilla. "Tell me what to do. But make sure it's something I can do! My hands are still pretty bad, so I'll have to work mostly with my feet."

Flameheart and Lavilor instructed her in what they were doing, correcting her about how to build the sand, or what kind of wetness was best to use where and how, and showing her where to put it – and often offering insights and suggestions on how best to work with her toes.

They utilized her feet quite well, having her compact the sand where desired, while they worked on other places. It was an interesting experience, especially because of the way she had to go about it, and Camilla enjoyed the challenges of the endeavor, as well as working with her brother – and Flameheart – on such a game.

It was nice that it did not matter that she was temporarily crippled and considered least, since the only purpose was to relax and have fun. She tried to quell the voice that rose up in her, saying, *Look how many wonderful things you are even now just discovering, that you should have had from childhood. Think how cruel are the elves!*

It might be true, but thinking those thoughts would only be allowing the elves to continue to steal joy and fun from her. It would not make this experience any funner. It would not heal anyone. It would not help Ben.

Into her thoughts spoke, like a current of fire through the earth, Nelexi's voice, like the voice of the Heartfire itself. *"No, Camilla. It is not the elves you would be allowing to continue stealing from you the life and joy you ought to have. It is the Nightmare you would be granting that power. It is the Nightmare that seeks misery and hate and despair."*

Camilla stopped in what she was doing, and her eyes stared into empty space. *It is the elves who* did *these things to us, and they are not witless tools, like a shovel or a broom. They* chose *it.*

"That is true. All choose – though not always in ways we would understand or expect – whether to succumb to the Nightmare or to be what they are made to be in the Heart of the Heart of Fire."

"Cam, what's going on?" asked Lavilor.

"Talking to Nelexi," Camilla answered, half in a distant tone of voice, half in a growl. *Whatever,* she replied to the dragon. *Go away and don't stick your nose in my thoughts. I try not to do this to other people. You should be able to as well. And I don't see the world the way you do. I don't believe what you do.*

For a moment, Camilla felt the irony of her response, the weight of the Obsidian Guardian's power and knowledge. But she did not believe in the idea of the Obsidian Guardian, and she dismissed the feeling. She was a power herself, and she would never cringe before anyone or consider herself less than.

"Very well, Camilla, but I don't want you to bow before me or anything. I don't think you understand these things you refuse to acknowledge, and that's half the reason you won't acknowledge them."

Half? Only half? thought Camilla, *Maybe. It very well might be,* and she returned to the volcano building. Nelexi did not continue to intrude on her thoughts.

Eventually, they had the volcano built. "I don't know how this will work," Flameheart said.

"But we won't find out if we don't try it!" said Lavilor.

"We can always try again if it doesn't work. That's how you learn," commented Flameheart.

"Okay, what do we do next?" asked Camilla.

"Pour water in it over here! Did you miss that?" asked Flameheart. Lavilor said something similar.

"I ... a little. I've never played with sand before, and I was sometimes distracted."

"Well, let's get the water!" said Flameheart. "I think there's an empty water-skin we can fill up with sea-water!"

Camilla laughed. "There are some things the sea is good for, right?"

She had heard Flameheart talking earlier about the miseries of her flight with Nelexi over the ocean.

"Of course." Flameheart tossed her a cheeky grin. "The beach. The sand. The wetness of it. But any water would do for this." She shifted her head a little, surveying the sea, the sky, and the beach. "Playing with the sand is so fun. I hadn't thought."

Inferring that Flameheart meant that she had never played with sand until a few days ago, Camilla asked, "Was that because there was no sand where you grew up, or because you were a slave and they didn't let you play very much, or let other people who were supposed to be working play with you?" Bitterness colored her voice a cold and angry green.

"I'm sorry you were a slave," said Flameheart with a genuineness and kindness that made Camilla's heart flutter with something she had never felt before. "But, no, there's just no sand where my people come from. Not where I lived. I really miss the Plains, too."

While they poured water in the opening in the mound that was supposed to send it into the volcano proper where it would trigger an eruption once they had poured enough of it in, Ben rolled over, his brilliant red form looming out of the waves which splashed about his paws. *Can you tell them I prefer the other game – the one where they build the sand castle and village, and I try to destroy it by focusing the waves and overwhelming their sea wall?*

Images of Ben's games flashed in Camilla's mind as he spoke to her. She had seen and felt them before, as bits and pieces of his fun playing leaked into her awareness through their bond, but she had not seen them so clearly and strongly yet. She marveled at how much better he was getting, and thrilled that this provided an adequate distraction from his obsessive need to fly and soar like an adult dragon, and focused his energies and mind on something that was not too much and did not hurt him, but did challenge him and develop his body and coordination. She realized that he, too, had never known such fun before.

The next day, they played the other game.

A Name from a Tale

Camilla tried to hold as still as possible while Alian and Flameheart – Sylvara had helped in the past, but Camilla still did not feel comfortable with her – unwrapped the soft bandages on her arms. The last time they had been unwrapped for a breath of the air what had been left of her skin had looked utterly horrible. Camilla was certain it was beginning to heal now, but it still itched like crazy. If anything, it itched even more. Often, it itched so terribly the itching was almost a torture, preventing her from sleeping.

She gasped when the wrapping pulled gently away, causing far less pain than it had last time, and revealing her ruined skin to all their eyes, including their own.

Or what *had* been ruined skin.

It was very tender, under-skin, but it was a soft, shiny skin that was decidedly unlike anything anywhere else on her body – and unlike anything she would expect a healing burn or other wound to look like. It shone as the rest of her skin did not, smooth as the rest of her skin was not, and it was a markedly different color – gold, shot through with the faintest highlight of lemon and lime. And spaced fairly regularly, but not in a perfect pattern – it couldn't be! It couldn't be! Those looked just like tiny scales climbing from the surface of her skin, gold like Radiance's! She uttered another soft cry.

Beside her, Flameheart breathed in a rapt voice, "That's no scar! What is it?" Lavilor looked over her shoulder.

"The true dragon-mage," said Alian, his voice if possible even more rapt, hushed with something Camilla could not identify. She wondered if the scales – no! what did it mean?! *she* had scales?! – were related to the unrelenting itches. A moment later, he straightened and spoke in a more ordinary tone of voice. "Perhaps the damage the elves did by refusing to heal you may be completely undone by this. This is one of the most extraordinary things I have seen in my lives."

Camilla did not miss his phrasing. He believed himself to be a new creature created by some Lord of Light at the death of a rider and dragon who had assaulted the Wizard-King of Eltaes, hoping to defeat him, but instead suffering defeat. The Lord of Light had saved the dragons and riders from being enslaved by the Wizard-King in death, and had created new beings in that moment, possessing both bodies of each dragon-rider pair, and all their combined memories, before placing them in a cave to later be awakened.

Camilla only half-believed it. She hated powers and forgers of destiny like this Lord of Light. It was utterly unfair for these new beings to have such destinies. Nonetheless, their abilities were real, and so were their memories, and whatever had caused that could hardly be less extraordinary than what was happening to her.

She thought back to the experience she had when she had sustained this injury, to the Heartfire, and wondered if the Lord of Light – or whatever it was that had rescued the people Alian had been, if they were not he, and created him – had touched her also. It terrified her, if she admitted it, nor could she help realizing that the terror she felt of this was *partially* quite different from the terror she experienced at the thought of the power of the Wizard-King, what he had done to Ben and countless others, what he *could not,* must not be able to – and, yet, whispered an insidious voice, did she *know* he could not? – do to her and Radiance, a terror and a thought she scarcely ever so much as barely admitted or acknowledged, and which she fought to keep from surfacing in her mind.

Both would control her destiny, would have power over whom and what she and Radiance were, yet the control and the power were wholly different. For the one was beautiful and entrancing, calling to her soul, and something in her soul longed to answer it, and that calling and longing was part of the terror, whereas the other was only fear and torment and despair, and her entire being rejected it in wholehearted accord.

Returning her mind to the situation at hand, Camilla asked, "Do you think so?"

Alian held her gaze with his green eyes. "Do you think otherwise? This is certainly no *scar.*"

Camilla quirked her lips up into a smile. "I suppose."

"We let her skin air now, right?" asked Flameheart.

"Yes, definitely," Alian said.

"Then it's awkward you calling *her* a dragon-mage," – she inclined her head towards Camilla, as she was holding the wrapping gently – "at the same time you refer to your kind as *dragonmages.* It's an awkward – uh? name? word? – anyway."

Wait! thought Camilla. *It's magic! It's my bond with Radiance! This isn't, can't be, the work of some great Power. Burn – no! don't – Alian for trying to make me think that by implying it and comparing it to what happened with him! It wasn't expected, of course, but we know that I and Radiance are exceptionally close magically! That I regrow extremely damaged parts more like her isn't even that much more remarkable than other effects of our bond, if it is at all! It's just because she and I are one. I don't need any greater Power and I won't have any part with it!*

"You have an idea?" asked Nelexi, while Alian was still staring at her as if he

did not understand why she had said what she had or what she meant, and while Camilla was acting like she had not even heard her and was instead glowering at Alian with a fierceness that Flameheart found mildly unnerving, and which she did not understand. It had not been there a moment before and she could not think what had caused it. Trust Nelexi to always pick up on her thoughts before anyone else could, though. She did that to Nelexi more often than was desirable ...

Yes. I had it last night, Flameheart responded.

"*Ah! I remember. That half-dream,*" said Nelexi. "*I approve.*"

At the same time, Alian's and Camilla's eyes flicked to her. "Do you have a better idea?" Camilla asked. She was clearly still glowering mad, but not at Flameheart. At least, Flameheart did not think her anger was directed at her, and she was glad for it, since she did not trust Camilla not to sear the object of her anger in one flash. The same question lit Alian's eyes.

"Yes, I do. There was a story I heard from some people that gives me an idea." She remembered meeting those people, hearing their stories. It was during the time when Nelexi had been showing her Aneri, and they had been visiting a people who lived in mountains not far from the sea. It had been an interesting place, both like and unlike her own home. "We could call you were-dragons."

"Were-dragons?" asked Camilla. "Why?"

"Tell us the story!" said Lavilor, who was waiting next to Camilla.

"*Go ahead,*" said Nelexi. "*I will try to help you with the language if you have problems. I will also help you remember. You'll do fine.*"

Flameheart swallowed hard and then began, "I can't tell it well. I don't know if it's true or not, but I remembered it last night, and it reminded me of you, Alian. There ... in the story there were great eagles who sometimes hunted and killed humans, usually babies, to feed to their ... babies. There was once a pair of eagles keeping their egg, and the father eagle was killed by the humans. Without him, the mother eagle had to leave her egg during the hottest part of the day to hunt food. Just before the egg was going to hatch, she snatched an infant human girl to give living meat for her baby. But when she found her nest it had been disturbed and her egg was no longer there. So instead she cared for the human girl." She paused, her concentration taxed to the uttermost in remembering this tale and re-telling it, when she had both first heard it and was now re-telling it in a language different from her own.

"The human girl grew strong and healthy, but she was different because she was fed and cuddled by a mother eagle and because of the mother eagle's prayers that her last child would not be helpless and crippled, unwinged, in the eagle world. One day, when she was growing, she fell out of the nest and transformed into an eaglet. Afterwards, she could always change between being an eagle and being a human girl. She learned to fly and live as an eagle. She taught the eagles and the humans to stop fighting and she mated an eagle. All her children were girls and were-eagles, able to be either humans or eagles. Some of her children's and children's children and children's children's children mated humans and some mated eagles. The boys are always whatever the father is, but the girls are always were-eagles."

Flameheart relaxed, exhausted by the telling, and was about to sit down when she remembered – just in time – that she was still holding the wraps for Camilla. She handed them to Lavilor, who folded and held them very carefully, and sat down on the grass. *Nelexi?* she asked. *Do you know if it's true or not?*

"Other than that the Arathalese and the eagles do in fact not kill each other, and that the Arathalese are the only people I know who tame and hunt with eagles, I don't know and I offer no opinion."

"How interesting," said Alian. "I do think that is more fitting than what we have been calling ourselves. I, Serrose, and Camilla were discussing once the potential problems with calling ourselves dragonmages, quite apart from the fact that she is clearly the dragon-mage. We will have to share this with the others whenever we meet them."

Camilla looked up at him then, and her earlier anger seemed to be dulled, if not forgotten, by the telling of the story and the new conversation. "Were-dragons," she said, and tasted the word on her tongue. "It fits. Speaking of Serrose however, shouldn't you go back to her and your hatchlings now that Nelexi is with us? I think she can fight for us as well as you can."

Alian shook his head. "When you are healed, perhaps, but I don't think Nelexi has my healing arts, however formidable a warrior and protector she is as the Obsidian Guardian. Also, she can't hunt very well."

"That's true," said Nelexi. *"I'm too big. Also, I haven't needed to hunt since I flew into the volcano, thousands of years ago."*

"You're not too big to hunt in the sea," Flameheart reminded her. "You did so for me all the way here."

"True, but it would be a lot harder to hunt enough for dragons."

"Were-dragons it is," said Camilla. "It works."

Flameheart felt her skin flush with satisfaction. She enjoyed contributing things to conversations and being part of them, and even though she loved Nelexi, she had missed human interaction somewhat. These humans were not like her family, but she liked them, and she expected to be with them for a while. She got from Nelexi the distinct impression that their lives were intertwined. This was much different from visiting one Anerian people or village after another. That had been interesting but lonely, whereas Camilla and Lavilor and Sylvara were like brothers and sisters, even if she was still finding it exhausting to understand the language they spoke. She needed Nelexi to help her not only speak but understand without so much effort that she fell far behind the flow of conversation and lost it.

Memories of teasing and being teased swept through Flameheart. "Are you sure you're not a were-dragon, too?" she asked Camilla.

Now Camilla flushed. "Certain. I might be growing dragon traits where I would otherwise be scarred, but I'm hardly about to turn into a dragon myself. It's not even as I were growing wings or a tail."

"Are you sure you can't turn into a dragon? Have you tried?"

"Yes, no, and I'm not going to."

Something in Camilla's tone of voice made Flameheart back off her. The dragon-mage had been about to enjoy it, but then her teasing had made Camilla remember or think something that upset her. It took only a moment for Flameheart to puzzle it out. It had to do with how she and her family had been slaves. Probably, it had occurred to her that Lavilor might tease her like this if they had not been slaves and were now struggling run-aways. Perhaps he did occasionally tease her, but not with the frequency and heart she knew he would if their lives had been different.

Suddenly, Camilla laughed. Something between her and Radiance, or perhaps one of the other dragons since she could speak to and hear them all, Flameheart suspected, since Camilla was no longer paying attention to her.

Yes, that would *be absurd, if I were to turn into a mini-dragon. Especially if I had humanesque features. It would be ridiculous to have a rider who was a dragon.* She shook her head slightly, laughing still harder at the image of herself as a dragon and Radiance flying side by side. Her arms twinged as she bumped the now-exposed skin lightly against something she was not really paying attention to, and she corrected that.

Another image flashed in her mind. Once again, it was impossible to tell what thought was hers and what thought was Radiance's. Their thoughts were one. *It is cool that I'm like this. Once I'm healed, that is. I like it. It is such a visible mark of my bond with you. Not only are our souls one, our bodies are marked. It would not work very well if you were to start acquiring human traits like this, I think.* That did rouse a question. The elven dragons were supposed to be very affected by their riders in an unequal, uneven bond.

Yet almost the reverse appeared to be happening here. It was Camilla who was acquiring dragon abilities and traits and whose whole soul and magic appeared to be permeated by Radiance, not that she did not live in Radiance too. Well, that was a puzzle for later. She did not want to try to figure it out right now. It occurred to her that she could ask Nelexi if she had any ideas, but while the Obsidian Guardian was old and knew much magic, Camilla was not sure if she knew the right magic. Her feelings towards Nelexi were confused for other reasons, too, and so she did not want to have much more to do with her than necessary yet.

By the way, said Camilla, on a subject where her and Radiance's thoughts were not quite one, *I don't think your objection to the word 'were-dragon' is valid. It certainly does not suggest that the were-dragons are true dragons anymore than 'dragonmage' does! If anything, I think less. I think you just want to take the word 'dragon' completely out of there, and that's not really reasonable. Would you prefer if we called them 'elf-human-dragons'?*

Radiance laughed, a rumbling chuckle forming deep in her throat and vibrating in her sides, as did Camilla.

I think that's kind of what 'were-dragon' means. After all, the first 'were-eagle' wasn't an eagle but a human! After that, I don't think 'were-eagles' are either humans or eagles quite. And, in a lot of ways, were-eagles are nothing like the were-dragons. After all, the were-dragons come both genders, and both genders in one, and mate with each other, neither humans nor dragons. As she sensed perfect understanding from Radiance, she commented, *I think you struggle because you use language, but also not as humans use language. Mind-to-mind, like between dragons, is different.*

Sudden fire burned in Camilla's chest as she thought of the cause of this problem. Elves using their magic to twist dragons' natures so that they would and could bond to *them*! Otherwise, dragons would not have so much language, probably language not even as it passed through a human mind but as it passed through an elven mind, a mind even more foreign to a dragon, mixed up in their thoughts. She wanted to kill them all. To burn alive every elf responsible for ever using his or her magic to twist the dragons. And every elf rider who was callous and uncaring towards the dragons more often than not forced to bond to him or her, who did not try to do the best that was possible to correct and not further perpetrate the terrible evil done. She felt like a dragon breathing fire, like a dragon-mage commanding whirlwinds of flame.

Heat blossomed in her hands and along her arms, and Camilla realized what was happening. Shimmering proto-flames were climbing out of her palms and appearing where her new scales were budding – she still could not believe *she* had *scales*. Quickly, she dampened the magic, but she still felt the fire in her blood and bones. Sensing that she had to relieve the gathered magic somehow, she lifted her arm and sent a controlled spurt into the air. At least, it was supposed to be controlled. She did not have very much practice, and so it was only half-controlled, but it mostly went where and how she intended, and posed no great danger to anyone.

Flameheart looked at her with wonder and questions. Alian appeared concerned.

"There's not a problem," said Camilla shortly. She did not have to explain herself to anyone, though she would explain herself to Radiance if it was necessary, though because of the nature of their bond it never was or could be necessary.

Kicking Sand

Camilla watched in ecstasy as Ben lifted off. His wings beat a perfect harmony. His tail slithered behind him, ruddering in effortless synchrony. The wind bore him up almost before he was aware that he was truly, *finally*, flying at last! She laughed for sheer joy as Radiance took to the air several dragon-lengths behind him, and then behind them the rest of the dragons and the were-dragon. She looked over her shoulder and saw Nelexi waited on the beach. If Nelexi took to the air, her huge wing-beats would disturb it for miles around her. Ben did not need that further complication, not now, not yet. He needed this to be as effortless and smooth as possible, to bolster his confidence, to stir his soul, to lift his heart, to make him feel a winged creature once more.

Ben roared in exultation as he caught the column of rising air coming off the beach and let it loft him into the sky. By Alian's direction, the other dragons and riders flew on either side of him, checking the wind currents, making sure that if anything changed drastically he could be prepared and have help orienting himself and landing. Splutters of fires sputtered out of his nostrils and mouth, some of them big enough to count as breathing fire.

Several minutes later, exhaustion settled in, dragging at Ben's wings and pulling his motions out of synchrony. He landed awkwardly and heavily, mentally supported by the other dragons, though it was a lighter landing than he had yet managed. He lifted his head to the sky and roared again. This time a full-blown if weak jet of fire emerged from his mouth.

Camilla started to clap for him, almost without noticing it, as Radiance banked and prepared to land. Somehow, she knew the other humans clapped also, and she was aware of the same sentiment coming from Alian, who was in her dragon form.

A shimmer flowed down Ben's scales as he half-shivered with that peculiar combination of exhaustion and overflowing pleasure.

That night, while she lay drowsing under Radiance's wing, she felt Nelexi's voice of molten fire in her mind. *What is it?* she half-grumbled.

"You will need to learn to speak another language. No, not Sea Elven. We will be able to get by just fine without you knowing a word of Sea Elven, but you will need to speak the Anerian trade tongue. Otherwise, you and the Light Elves will not be able to converse and you will not be able to learn from them, or get anything else done in Aneri."

Why can't I just speak mind-to-mind like dragons? Language won't be a problem, then.

"*Because that is not generally respectful to the ways and minds of other creatures,*" said Nelexi, half-chuckling, half-scolding. "*It is not how they think or communicate best, for the most part. It is why I do not speak to humans or elves casually, but only if I must. You will need to use that ability less than I must, for you can speak to them as they speak to themselves and have for most of their lives. Languages which you do not know you can learn, though you may have need to use your dragon-speech from time to time for other reasons.*"

Camilla growled.

"*Flameheart speaks the language of her people, the Anerian trade tongue, some Ileshian, and some Sea Elven,*" elaborated Nelexi. "*I taught her all but her own language. I can teach you, and you can learn at least Anerian.*"

I suppose. At least then I won't have to speak a cursed elf *tongue!* She smiled and bared her teeth at the thought of speaking a language that was not the language of the people who enslaved and abused and stole from her. She smiled even more at the idea of speaking a *human* language. Surely, human languages were different from elven languages, since even though humans and elves were not as different as the Wood Elves had taught – at least not in the way the Wood Elves had taught – yet they were different, as proven by the fact that humans were far more suitable partners for dragons. In all likelihood, this Anerian language would match her thoughts better and make expressing herself easier. That would be reason enough to learn it, though she begrudged Nelexi for thinking she should not speak mind-to-mind very often with other humans. She certainly was not going to stop doing it with her brother.

"*Flameheart can help you learn Anerian, as well as I. That might make things easier. But I think you will be disappointed. I think Anerian will be difficult and awkward for you at first. It is very different from Ileshian, but not more different from Ileshian than it is from Flameheart's language.*"

So elves and humans are even less different than I *thought?*

"*I did not say that.*" The note of scolding in Nelexi's voice was almost harsh.

Still, I would like to speak a language other than the language of our oppressors, even if that has been the only language we have ever known. She bit down on her lip at the thought of living years on another continent, speaking another language, only to meet her mother again and have to speak to her in the Ileshian tongue. *First she has to be still alive. First I have to learn my powers and defeat the Wizard-King. And then I'm sure we will be too thrilled to see each other again to have other concerns and I doubt she'd mind speaking to me mind-to-mind until she learns the new language, too. My brother doesn't mind.*

"Then we will begin your lessons tonight and you will practice with Flameheart tomorrow."

Camilla growled. So soon? Then she realized it could not be too soon. She had so much to learn, though she was not sure *any*one would be able to help her very much with her magic. To a large degree, she and Radiance would have to figure that out themselves. But she might as well learn the new language while there was nothing else for her to learn. Nor was Nelexi doing *anything* that should be upsetting to her.

"Camilla," Nelexi asked her, *"would you prefer to learn Light Elven? It would be easier, as it is more like Ileshian, but while it would allow you to converse fluently with the Light Elf mages it would not allow you to speak with the Sha'adhri or most other people on Aneri."*

Let's see how hard Anerian is, first. Camilla wanted to believe it would be easy. She wanted to believe the human tongue would feel natural to her, that it would have an almost magical feeling of home-coming.

Several days later, she dropped trying to speak in Anerian to ask Alian a question that had occasionally bothered her for a while but that she had not remembered during any opportune times until now. "Dragons are supposed to bond to humans," she said, "and even the dragons the elves considered lesser can breed and have off-spring though they do not do it very much. Why weren't there *lots* of dragons outside Ilesh? I understand there were some, but why weren't there more? I understand they would mate more often and breed more often with human riders than with elves. And did gold-riders and silver-riders never flee?"

"You're right, and they did, for the most part," said Alian, "but many of their eggs never hatched. The dragons within were stillborn. It was Serrose who told me that wasn't normal, but from our only clutch of six eggs only one dragon hatched."

Camilla could hear the sorrow in his voice. It must have hurt those whose memories he had so much when her eggs and his dragon's eggs had turned out dead. She could not imagine such a thing happening to her and Radiance. It would want to make her kill every Ileshian elf ever – except for those like Sërien, the elf whose form and memories Serrose possessed.

"I'm sorry," she said, trying to tamp down her fury and keep it from afflicting Ben. "Did she tell you why?"

"Sërien and Gloaming did not know, and neither does Serrose. Nelexi has assured us that it does not often happen that way among the unaltered dragons. My only guess is that there is something in the magic of Ilesh on which the altered dragons are somehow dependent."

Camilla felt the beginning of flames licking up from her palm. She had stopped wearing the bandages except when she was asleep the first time it had started smoking. Fortunately, she had noticed, dampened her fire, and gotten the bandage off before it was too ruined. It was not only anger that caused her hands to sprout fire. In the most intense moments of passionate love and intimacy with Radiance it happened just as easily, and sometimes she had to do something about it since while the fire would not burn her, it *would* burn clothes or plant matter or anyone except herself and Radiance – and maybe Ben – if she was not careful. But when it was pleasure, she did not have to worry about the emotional effects it had. It did not harm or upset Ben in any way. When it was anger, she had to be careful about her *feelings,* too.

Yet she really *did* want to blast the Ileshian elves. She *certainly* wanted to blast the Ileshian life-mages. They were as deserving of torture as the Wizard-King himself. Unfortunately, she did not know of any way to go back in time to capture them, torture them as they deserved and kill them, letting off some of her fury in the process. *I don't know if it's* possible *to go back in time.* She thought for a moment that, if she could, then she would change everything and not let the dragons be altered – or, for that matter, let her people be enslaved. Then she realized that, if that were the ways things were, she would not be who she was. Radiance would never have been, and she and Radiance would never have met. *That* was certainly impossible, whether or not it was possible to go back in time to do anything, and the whole question was irrelevant since she, for certain, could not do it ... but if she could, she would burn those life-mages over and over and over again. They deserved it for what they had done to the dragons.

Camilla noticed Alian's concerned look. "It's okay. I – I'm just angry, but it's never gotten out of control. I can manage it."

"Understandably," said Alian. "There are times I and Serrose have felt similarly. There were certainly times when Sërien and Yetra and our dragons felt similarly." He looked like he wanted to say more, but he did not. Nonetheless, Camilla's draconic sensitivity picked some of it up. It had *something* to do with all that stuff about anger being a tool of the Nightmare and fear and something about the Lord of Light and *love.*

It's irrelevant. I don't *want to burn the life-mages in order to make them* afraid. *At least, I don't want to do it in order to dissuade others from doing similar things for fear, though I'm not really sure that would be a bad thing. If love and freedom aren't important to someone, maybe they* should *be controlled by fear! I* do *want those life-mages to be afraid, but not to dissuade them. Because they* deserve *it. I want them to suffer and fear. I want them to be in so much agony they wish they never existed.* "Thanks for answering my questions," Camilla said in stilted Anerian. She needed to close off the conversation and get away from Alian before he got any more involved in her thoughts, and that was as good a way as any. She turned her back, stalked off, and struck her boot into the sand over and over again.

Sand flew up in a spray as she unintentionally dug a hole. For weeks now she had tried not to be angry for Ben's sake, but she could not help it anymore. She tried to keep her thoughts in as much as she could and shield him out – something she could not really do with Radiance, but which she had learned she could do fairly effectively with him – and let her anger seethe after tearing back her sleeves. She intended to keep her fire under control, but in case she forgot she did not want to burn her clothes.

I do! she thought. *I don't know if people who don't care about love or freedom being controlled by fear is consistent with my vision of freedom or not, but I do!* She gritted her teeth and turned the fire between her hands into a tornado of flame and hot air, expressing her anger. It was *so* frustrating not being able to take it out on the objects of her fury. She had *never* gotten to *hurt* an evil dragon- and human- enslaving elf in her life, and she *needed* to. By fire and air, how she wanted to torment those life-mages until they wished they had never lived. Until they forgot who they were. Until the pain the elves had inflicted on her by expecting her to work with burned hands they would not heal was nothing but sheer relief, even pleasure. Instead, she was restricted to kicking sand.

And how, how, *can I ... how can anything* good *come of it? How can I cherish what could not be if these deplorable life-mages had never committed their atrocities?* It all came back to destiny, Camilla thought, as she gathered the energies around her hands together and hurled them in a concentrated blast at the sand.

She was forced to stumble backwards by the wave of heat and wind that struck her in the face and almost burned her exposed skin. She was not sure if she had *intended* to throw that much power, and she had certainly not thought about the result. Where she had hurled the fire, there was now a small crater of half-melted sand.

She felt all the dragons and the were-dragon turn their attention to her. *No,* she thought, projecting her thoughts. *I have this under control. An experiment just didn't go quite as I pleased.* It was a little of a lie, and she knew that everyone would know that. Deliberately lying mind-to-mind was difficult, if possible. But it was partially true, too, and Radiance at least would not bother her about it. Neither would Ben for that matter.

Alian might try to give her a lecture on not experimenting recklessly with her magic, but that was more of a Serrose thing to do than an Alian thing to do, and she did not care. She was not standing for being told what to do or bossed around *any*more. She would tell Alian she had as much right to do as she chose as anyone *including* himself, whether he was made directly by the hand of this Lord of Light or not. Besides, she seemed to be a creature at *least* as unique as any were-dragon as evidenced by her scales. Nelexi would not approve of her anger either, but she thought the Obsidian Guardian would leave her alone and, if she did not, she would tell her the same thing she would tell Alian.

She smiled grimly, wondering if it was worth it to try to blast another sand-crater, this time in a somewhat more controlled fashion. *Destiny.* It seemed *destiny*, or at least fate, was a part of life, whether she or some greater power – but fire and dragon wings, no such thing should exist! – wanted it or not. She and Radiance were fated not only by their own choices and will, but by the choices of thousands of others, including some very evil choices made by some very evil people who had certainly never intended to bring about their bond. She and Radiance were not even responsible for existing. They had not chosen to exist. Much less had they chosen their circumstances, their powers, who they were. Even if some greater power had not chosen it for them, *they* had certainly had no hand in it. No, not no hand in it.

To a great degree, Camilla was who she was because of her choices and intentions, and the same could be said of Radiance. She and Radiance had even met because of her choices, because of who both of them *willed* to be. Yet if any among thousands and thousands of others had chosen differently, not only would their lives be completely differently and possibly even separate – something which now seemed to them no life at all – but they *would not even exist.* If their lives were completely different, would it even be fair to call them their lives? They might as well be different people, in that case, depending on how different their lives were. *Or if we never bonded. I and Radiance would never exist.* And Radiance was even more dependent on the choices of others than Camilla. Radiance had chosen Camilla, had even called to Camilla, but it was Camilla's choice that had permitted that to happen. She could not have even chosen not to bond. That infuriated Camilla more than anything, even though she knew that Radiance had chosen her with complete and utter freedom.

She decided it was worth it to blast another sand-crater. The first was cooling into some sort of dirty bubbly glass mixed with grains of sand. She focused some of her mental energy on controlling and moderating the power while she raged. Nothing made sense. Nothing seemed right. There was *no* denying fate, if not destiny. And her and Radiance's choice of each other … that was hardest of all to think about. She had not had a choice, yet no choice had been more fully her own, nothing had been more perfectly willed by her.

By me, as I was before I and Radiance became almost one person, or by us *as we are now?* Camilla asked no one and nothing as she hurled the power.

Something about the act was not exactly relaxing, but it steadied her. As the fire flowed through her mind, her body, and her soul, it left behind a little of itself, a little of the irrememorable experience of the Heartfire. It washed and burnt away the bitterest and vilest portions of her and Radiance's rage and hatred, leaving behind a fury of passionate love.

"Let us fly and flame together!"

For days after, Camilla experienced moments of dread that Nelexi would berate her – she could not force herself not to care what the Obsidian Guardian thought or said, though no one else affected her that way – but Nelexi did not speak to her apart from her language lessons and did nothing to berate her. Alian, too, never spoke of it, at least not directly, though he had some conversations with her about the basics of magic and reminded her almost casually in the course of these of her own ability to sense magic, something that he said was incredible given her experience and practice, even exceptional, but which she was not alone in. Sensing magic was a skill and an art practiced by many to varying degrees of proficiency. It could be considered magic in and of itself.

She was certain that this direction was intentional and provoked by her display, though she had expressed interest in sensing earlier. Part of her wanted to rebel just for the sake of doing so, but she recognized that he was *not* pushing himself on her as a superior and that he *did* have a point. It was foolish not to acknowledge it simply because she should have thought of it on her own and hated being told *any*thing by anyone except her own soul-half, Radiance.

The cold dreary weather did not put her in a better mood. They had to keep going, but the cold hurt Radiance's wings and sank its claws into her fingers and toes until they burned. Most days it was foggy, and rain and hail alternated with snow. She and Radiance hated the snow, but icy rain was no better.

Ansaifar

Camilla strode beside Flameheart, glaring daggers at any Sea Elf who looked at her. The Sea Elves, in *themselves*, did not bother her as much as she expected. They looked as unlike the Wood Elves as any human did. Their facial features were not much more Wood Elven than her own. They were thicker-built than the average Wood Elf by a significant margin, and they were spectacularly colored. Their hair came in every shade of emerald, turquoise, teal, violet, coral, and salmon, ranging from so dark it was almost black to nearly white. True, green was a common hair color among Wood Elves, but so was brown and black, the only colors Camilla had ever seen in human hair. The Sea Elves' predominant skin colors were coral, salmon, aquamarine, and silver. Their eyes were usually very dark, so dark Camilla had a hard time telling the iris and the pupil apart and so she did not know what colors most of them were. They did not carry themselves like Wood Elves, either. She might not like them, but they were even less reminiscent of the Ileshian Elves than the Fire Elf Aishaena, who was built like a Wood Elf and carried herself like one, and whose skin and hair suggested a burnt tree, one that had survived fire. The Sea Elves had nothing of the forest about them at all, and their city, Ansaifar, was nothing like the Wood Elf hamlets *or* the human city where she and Radiance had been captured.

No, what Camilla minded about the Sea Elves was the way they looked at her – at her arms, in particular. She could not understand their language, but she understood what was going on well enough, though she could not put words to it. She felt like a fool for not having put the bandages back on her arms that morning, when Nelexi told them they would reach Ansaifar that day, but she could not have known. She knew nothing about any society except Ilesh, so of course she had been unable to anticipate this response.

"Where are we going?" she asked Flameheart in Anerian. For some reason, she liked the idea of showing these snooping Sea Elves that the one language she did not speak was their own. That was not exactly true, of course, since she did not speak Ellenesian Trade either among half a dozen other languages including Flameheart's, but it was good enough that she was speaking, in their hearing, two languages which most of them probably did not know very well, though she was not fluent in Anerian – the language that some of them almost certainly knew, since they traded with Aneri, too.

"The only house here where the people speak Ileshian," answered Flameheart. "The family is an elf mage who fled Ilesh with the woman he fell in love with and their three half-elf children."

It took Camilla a moment to process what Flameheart had said. "Wait!" she asked. "That's possible?" *Of course it could be,* she reprimanded herself. *You know not to be surprised anymore when something the Wood Elves said turns out to be a lie. You knew most of it was lies without being told.* Still, she had not thought that Wood Elves and humans were *that* alike, that much the same kind of creature. *How utterly ridiculous every lie they told us was!*

"Yes," said Flameheart. "Nelexi says it happens. Not very often, but sometimes."

Camilla wanted to inquire more, but she doubted Flameheart knew much more than she had told her. She held her arms at her side and tried to ignore the stares of the Sea Elves for a few more minutes until they reached their destination.

Their Sea Elf guide turned off the road and mounted the steps to a dwelling. Camilla was still trying to keep herself from gawking. Wood Elf architecture was mostly made of wood and did not at all resemble these stone buildings. There had been a lot more stone in the city in which she and Radiance had been imprisoned, but she had never gotten a good look at it. The prison was certainly stone, but that was hardly flattering. Still, it was not much less flattering than the Wood Elf dwellings, which were much the same thing as a prison to her and to the dragons. She was *certain* the human city had looked no more like this place than the Wood Elf one. This place was clean and beautiful. Every line could have come out of a painting on the walls of a Wood Elf mage. With a hiccup in her breath, she realized *this* dwelling *was* that of a Wood Elf mage. No matter how different from the others he might be – and she did not *know* what had led him here with a human mate or who he was – he would still be a Wood Elf and would still rouse those memories in her.

The door swung open and, framed in the doorway, stood a woman who looked not unlike Camilla or her mother. She had dark, dark hair, deep brown skin much lighter than Flameheart's, and dark brown eyes. Her face reminded Camilla of her mother, and that brought the tears to Camilla's eyes. Would she and Lavilor ever see her again? Was she dead or a tortured prisoner and slave? How had Camilla relaxed over these days when she needed to do nothing but find the fastest way to free her people that she could? *Could* she not fly straight to Arkane and defeat the Wizard-King in single combat? Perhaps she *could*. She had freed Ben. She had done the unthinkable, the unimaginable.

Her thoughts distracted her from the conversation, and she was only jerked out of them when a man came to stand beside the human woman. He was clearly a Wood Elf, with pale brown skin freckled with lighter spots, deep gold eyes, and emerald hair shot with strands of lighter green. His up-swept eyebrows reminded her of long, narrow leaves caught in the wind. The human leaned against him, and he was speaking to them in Elethrian now, while the Sea Elf who had guided them removed herself. "Welcome. It will be a bit crowded in here, with five of you, but I think we can work something out by nightfall. Come in and refresh yourselves."

Camilla would have balked right then and there, maybe even called Radiance and fled, if not for her draconic sensitivity. She knew the mother was

kind-hearted and honest, a woman not quite like her mother but like enough
that it was unbearably sad and painful. She knew there were children in the
dwelling. One was watching the exchange while hiding under a table. The
other was no longer quite a child and was getting ready to prepare food for the
new-comers while keeping an eye on her mother and father at the door. The elf
she did not sense as easily, but she *knew* he meant no harm even if her whole
body and mind rebelled against his presence. He was far too like her captors
and torturers in appearance and in power. But he was not one, and she knew it.

There must have been a further exchange, but Camilla did not catch it.
She followed Flameheart into the building.

It was dark inside compared to the nearly-blinding brilliance of even
winter sunlight on white stone. While Camilla's eyes adjusted to the lighting,
she heard Alian speaking. "Only four, Lìarz," he said. "I am no human but
something else, and I do not need shelter."

Lìarz? She must have missed the introductions what with her confused
and tumultuous thoughts. That was an Ileshian name, wasn't it? So Lìarz must
be the Wood Elf mage. She wanted to know how he and the human whose
name she still did not know had gotten together.

"You look like a human," said a girl who Camilla could now see fairly
well. She was *clearly* half-elf and she was *clearly* a child. "Or an elf. Are you
an Ice Elf?"

Alian chuckled. "No. I am something stranger, though maybe not by
much, as I do not know of any Ice Elves existing, but I exist and so do several
others as like me as two creatures of the same species. But I can't show you in
here. If we can have a bit of space outside, I probably could."

The child clapped her hands. "Thank you! Thank you!"

The space really was quite small. The Wood Elf, Lìarz, said, "Well,
that at least is something. And there are other possibilities for accommodations
that could be worked out. I understand you were brought here because there
aren't many who are fluent in Ileshian here. I take it you all ran away – except
for you, Flameheart."

Camilla nodded. There was no use in obfuscating that. "Yes, we ran
away. What of you?"

A look passed over his face that told her he was considering her
question, considering *why* she asked it. "I ran away as well. I loved Elamna,
and she loved me, and I would not have her be a slave. We came here and were
accepted here, and we were greatly and pleasantly surprised to discover our
union was fruitful. Did you and Alian meet before or after you escaped?"

Camilla was not going to let Alian get a word in edgewise. "*After,*" she
said. "I can navigate the enchanted border."

She smiled at the expression that passed over Lìarz's face. He had not
expected that, certainly, not expected that a human would ever be able to do
what only proficient mages could do. No one did. No one truly understood how

capable humans were or even admitted the strength of her soul and her magic.

"It's true," Alian said, and she hated him for it. "I and my mate found her after she had escaped the elves but before she had escaped from Ilesh. We thought she would need our protection and guidance to get through the border, but she could do it on her own."

Camilla could not help but remember what had happened when she had wandered off.

She startled briefly as the child touched her scaled arm. "Camilla, right?" she asked. "Did I hurt you? These are *so* cool!"

"Arziel!" called Elamna. "Don't harass them too soon! They just came in. Shall I take her outside?"

"That's not necessary," said Camilla. She did not want to go outside herself. It was *so* good being in here. The stone was warm and blocked the wind, and she could feel the heat from whatever cooking was happening in the unoccupied corner. "Arziel isn't bothering me." That was true. Arziel's interest in her scales was innocent and childlike. Arziel was possibly the most comfortable person in this room, though she was as tall as Camilla despite being such a child. She and Radiance liked Arziel. She held out her arms, crossed over each other, for the child to observe. "I wasn't born like this. It happened when I burned the skin off my arms fighting dark magic to free a dragon. The skin grew back like this. It's only just stopped being tender underneath."

As she spoke a deadly silence descended on the room. Arziel's attention was still rapt in a childlike fashion, but she felt everyone else's attention turn to her, most of all Lìarz's. She wondered if she had made a mistake.

"Hmm." Arziel traced her finger along the scales. "You know a dragon?"

Camilla nodded. "Yes. I know many dragons."

"It's so sad most of the dragons were gone. And I didn't even get to see the black dragon when she came by earlier."

"The black dragon is back," said Flameheart. "You can meet her when you like. Her name is Nelexi."

"Nelexi!" said Arziel, clapping her hands. "I like that name! It sounds kind of like mine! Do you know Nelexi, Camilla?"

Camilla nodded. "Yes, I met Nelexi. I met her a little after I freed the other dragon."

"Can I meet Nelexi and the other dragon now?"

"Not yet, Arziel," said Elamna. "Flameheart can take you to see her after we talk some."

"Why?"

"They came out of the cold. We want to make them comfortable and decide how we're going to keep them warm tonight. Come, Arziel. Would you like to help me roll buns?" Elamna appeared and grabbed Arziel's hand. The child went along with her, even though she was as large as her mother.

Camilla suddenly felt exposed. Lìarz was looking at her scales, now, not with whatever weird interest the Sea Elves had had, but with something keener and possibly more disturbing – or at least more dangerous. He lifted his eyes from her scales and met her eyes. "You're a mage," he stated.

Camilla held his gaze, her own burning, metaphorically if not literally.

"Are you a Dragonrider?"

There was no use denying that either. "Yes. Her name is Radiance." Camilla decided to tell everything. If he had *any* thoughts about the inferiority of humans, let him marvel and gasp. "She's a queen-mother." She bit back her tongue on the impulse to tell him that she could speak to both humans and dragons – and, it seemed, elves – as dragons spoke among themselves. She could tell he wanted to touch her scales. If he did, she would burn him. Nothing would be easier than making her scales burn him on contact. Arziel's touch she did not mind. His she would not allow.

"And you fought dark magic and freed one of the death-bound?"

Camilla had never heard them called death-bound before, but she understood the origin of the name. She also heard the awe in his voice and she treasured it. She did not bask in it, but she enjoyed hearing that awe, that respect, from a Wood Elf. "Yes." She could not hide it anyways.

Sudden confidence infused her and she threw her shoulders back. It was Radiance's pride. She had nothing to fear from this Wood Elf mage. She had nothing to hide, to keep back in fear or shame. *I'll try to see if arrangements can be made for you to be kept warmer,* she promised Radiance. *Otherwise, I'm going down to you, and we'll burn a tree down and let it smolder for warmth for you if we must.*

Lìarz's attention shifted suddenly. "We can discuss magic later," he said, waving his hand. "For now, accommodations are more important I think."

That turned the conversation into a decidedly more comfortable line.

Camilla sat outside on the veranda. Lìarz and Finsaleen, Elamna's older daughter – except that it turned out that she was actually the *younger* daughter, something that apparently was known to happen with elf-human pairings – had gone out into the city to get warm clothing for them. Now, she sat muffled inside a great warm furred cloak with the hood pulled down over her head and the front laced up and, far from being cold, she was warm enough to be sweating lightly. She held a hot mug of something the name of which she could not remember, but Lìarz had told her the Sea Elves traded it from another continent or something like that. She took a small sip of the warm liquid and could not decide whether she liked or not, while Arziel, Lavilor, and Flameheart rolled about, tussling and grappling, in their similarly warm clothing. Camilla could hardly believe how much difference it made.

Radiance was huddled under Nelexi's wing. It was probably warmer than most things, and that was how they had been sleeping on nights when Nelexi did not fly out to scout for possible dangers. They would try to come up with a place for Radiance to cuddle warmly when Nelexi flew out, but for this night Nelexi would shelter her under her wings.

Lìarz shifted his gaze from the playing children to Camilla. "Did I see a magesword on your hip earlier?" he asked.

Camilla still did not *like* him, but being in his proximity for the better part of two hours, watching him interact with his mate and children, and feeling him through her draconic sense had lessened her distaste. Her voice no longer dripped with venom as she said, "Yes. I ran off with it. I figured it might be useful, and I thought it would work for what I needed." She let him wonder about that.

It did not take him long. "Did it?" he asked.

She nodded. "It works for me just like it does for an elf mage."

He tapped his fingers on his chin. "Interesting. Very interesting. If I may ask, just what did you need it for? Getting through the barriers?"

Camilla almost gloated as she said, "No. I could have navigated the barriers without it. I needed it to channel or anchor the magic that was burning my hands."

She watched the flicker of his eyes intently as he spoke and she saw the moment when he realized something else. His eyes turned to her in a new way and she saw him assess something he had not paid attention to before. "Ahh. That explains a lot. Do you have to radiate as much magic as you are right now?"

Camilla answered that by shadow-blending the magic. It was something she had not bothered to do much since fleeing Ilesh, or at least since freeing Ben, but it took her only a few moments to get back into it, not that it was exactly shadow-blending, the magic almost all elves had to some degree of shading themselves into the background, particularly the shadows. It was just that she thought of it like shadow-blending.

She reveled in the look that came over his face. She might not hate him anymore, but she certainly enjoyed it every time he realized that an assumption he had made about the differences between humans and elves was wrong. "Interesting," he said, in a reflective tone, as if he were speaking to himself as much as to her or Alian. "You have the powers of an elf mage, and my son awakens the magic in the mageweapons as no one else I have ever seen, but he lacks any affinity or ability to understand my magery."

"I truly am full human," she said, with a savage smile.

"I did not doubt that," he replied, almost wearily. "But if you two are willing, I would like to discuss magic."

"It would be a welcome discussion," said Alian. He launched into an explanation of what he was.

Part of Camilla enjoyed seeing the surprise and attention on the elf's face. Another part of her wished it was directed towards *her*, though she supposed she would have her turn if she cared to. Still, she wondered if her story was really any more impressive than Alian's, even if she was more unique in the world than he. Evidently, Lìarz had heard about the circle of Dragonrider-mages that had challenged the Wizard-King, even though it had happened while he was still a child in Ilesh.

Over the next several days, there were many discussions of magic between Camilla, Alian, Lìarz, and Lìarz's son, Arilann, discussions which were very occasionally attended by Arilann's friend, another half-elf named Kellan who was the librarian. At some points of discussion, Arilann would often politely excuse himself, but he listened raptly and asked many questions when Camilla described her experiences with the border enchantments and with the Fire Elves. Nothing seemed to fascinate him more than Aglaretë's position as the Grove-born, but there was not much that Camilla knew about that. She might have been able to learn much more from what she sensed of his magic if she *knew* what to look for or how to understand it, but though she could sense a great deal, his magic was more or less unfamiliar to her, and that made it hard or impossible to learn much from it. He had explained why these things fascinated him, too. He felt some call of the forest, but he felt rejected by the forest, but his life felt tied to the trees, or something like that. It made little sense to her.

Meanwhile, to Camilla's pleasure, Sylvara ended up staying at Kellan's library. Camilla no longer saw her often – sometimes she went days without seeing her – and that was very much to her liking. As long as she was no longer in her life, Camilla did not much care what Sylvara found for herself to do, and even if they had liked each other, it would have pleased everyone to have Lìarz's home a little less crowded. Arilann sometimes stayed over at the library for much the same reason. Camilla did not know how to feel about the situation. On the one hand, she felt like Lìarz deserved it for being an elf. On the other hand, he had not asked to be born an elf and he had gone as far as any elf she had ever heard of in rejecting their evils.

Could she really blame the young prodigious mage for fleeing with his beloved and making a life with her when they had children, instead of trying to fight and shed blood and lead a rebellion? Just because that was what *she* would do, what she *wanted* to do? Maybe he had *intended* to do far more for his mate's people than he had, but when they had children, that naturally and rightly became the first priority. She could not despise him for that.

Arziel, however, seemed to enjoy the crowding. She *loved* playing with Lavilor and Flameheart, and with Camilla, when Camilla would play. She was utterly and childishly delighted with Camilla's scales, and she *loved* playing with the dragons and going on rides on them.

Ben was growing stronger, flying with the other dragons and playing in the sea. The Sea Elves were becoming accustomed to seeing the dragons, and comfortable with their presence, according to her sources of information. She fretted over how long it might take him to become strong enough to make the ocean journey.

Belonging

Flameheart perched on Nelexi's paw while the dragon spoke to the young half-elf she had asked Flameheart to bring to her. She had told Flameheart she thought Arilann might be interested to know about the Light Elves. Now, Flameheart did not intrude on Nelexi's conversation, but she wondered why Nelexi had offered to speak to him mind-to-mind, since usually she tried not to speak mind-to-mind to anyone except her riders and other dragons unless necessary. What did Nelexi have to say to him about the Light Elves that she could not have communicated through Flameheart?

After a few minutes, and some spoken responses of his own, Arilann turned to leave. *"I did not share with him anything I could not have shared through you,"* Nelexi answered Flameheart's unasked question. *"I offered that because I do not wish him to think I am offering him advice or trying to influence him. Even though he is half-Wood Elf, you know how easy it is for people to see me as a god whom they should follow, someone greater than they. I wanted to make sure he understood I was only sharing information, as any two strangers, acquaintances, or friends might."*

And that would have been harder to communicate without the mind-touch. Never mind you did start off our relationship by telling me you were a god, more or less. Flameheart got up and slid down Nelexi's paw as the half-elf nearly stumbled away through the sand. "Arilann?" she called. His reaction upon seeing Nelexi reminded her strongly of how she had felt when she first saw the obsidian dragon.

He stopped and turned his head. "Yes?"

"I never told you about the first time I saw Nelexi. I thought she was going to eat me."

"Oh," said Arilann flatly. He waited a moment, then turned away again.

Do you ever mind how terrifying you are? I was just trying to make him more comfortable.

Nelexi chuckled. *"I can't help being imposing. It's in the nature of what I am. And he was not truly afraid I was going to eat him. As for telling you I was a god, I told you, I wonder sometimes if that was a mistake, but you know that what I meant, and what you understood, was never that I owned you or that I was to be your conscience, or that you should do whatever I suggest."*

Flameheart laughed. *I'm bonded to you. We can't help but have that relationship.* She tapped Nelexi's black scales, then started arranging the straps of the new saddle in preparation for putting it on Nelexi. Saddling such a huge dragon was rather a process, but the new saddle that the Sea Elves had made for them was perfect. It was easier to work with than the old one had been even before they had ruined it with sea water, and according to the Sea Elves and Lìarz, this one would hold up to such abuse. Lìarz had spent many days working his spell-craft on the leather and all the buckles. He had even set gems into the saddle to reinforce the spells that would keep the leather always supple and the buckles unrusted. He had promised her that he had also enchanted it to resist being worn away by the motion of Nelexi's scales. It was a perfect saddle, a gift right up there with the gifts from the Light Elves, and nowadays Lìarz spent most of his time working on similar – but much smaller – saddles for the other three Dragonriders and their dragons. *Sha'adhri*. Sometimes, Flameheart felt bad that people were working so hard on something for her and the others, but Nelexi reminded her that they could not do it for themselves and it was not as if Nelexi was taking what she did not pay for. Though it was against Nelexi's nature to even consider whether or not she would get anything out of such actions, or to feel as if she had put someone else in her debt for doing it what it was her nature and being to do, her protection of the Sea Elven fleet was worth far more than a few of these enchanted saddles, in the way of work and profit for the elves.

Why didn't the Light Elves make such a saddle for you? Flameheart asked as she pulled the saddle into place on Nelexi.

"I never asked, and they would never have thought of it. I have not had use for one in longer than you could imagine."

Finally, the saddle was firmly secured, and Flameheart secured herself into it. Nelexi spread her wings and launched herself into the air, to looks of applause and bewilderment by the Sea Elves who had gathered to watch this morning. Flameheart herself was still awed when she saw the huge creature taking off from the ground.

Nelexi gained altitude and entered the cloud layer. Most days, she and Flameheart went out on a patrol of the surrounding regions to make sure there were no nightmare creatures spying on them or causing havoc. They had no routine. Sometimes they went out at midnight, sometimes at noon, sometimes in the morning, and the pattern of their patrol was as unpredictable.

As Nelexi leveled out about the clouds, Flameheart said, *I keep forgetting, you don't have to see to know what's down there.* Their last patrol had been on a relatively clear night, and for some reason it was easier for her to imagine keener eyesight, capable of piercing darkness and distance than Flameheart's vision could – eyesight that Nelexi frequently shared with her – than it was for her to keep in her mind Nelexi's dragon-sense that allowed her to not depend on vision at all for some things, and perhaps for even more than Flameheart was aware of.

Nelexi chuckled in her mind. *"Don't be hard on yourself. We're not bonded quite like others are, and we've only been together for a very short while, but yes. I know what's down there."*

Are you going to talk to Camilla about things?

"No. Maybe sometime, but not now. There are things she has to learn and find on her own. I can't help her with her anger and fear. All I can do is to

keep the nightmare creatures away. For now. A time will come when she must face them, but now is not the time. And I can't help her with her magic, either. There are things I know that none of the others do about it, but now is not the time when I can help her find those things, and telling her what she can and cannot do is the worst way to help her find and acknowledge her limits and capabilities. The best way to help her acknowledge her limits or weaknesses is to say nothing about them at all."

Flameheart leaned out over Nelexi's shoulder to view the clouds from above. It was a view she still had not gotten used to. There were times when the clouds looked from above like she had always expected them to, but there were other times when they looked like something she could never imagine. A sea, but not like the sea. They were otherworldly. *I just wish she would stop fussing and fretting and getting angry. Even when she controls it, I can just feel the waves of anger and bitterness coming off of her. Like* heat.

"Very often there is some real heat involved. And she still does not completely rein in her draconic empathy. I'm not sure she knows how. She's not a dragon and, even if she were, other humans don't have the instincts to handle it the way dragons do. Even if she does as well as most dragons, we might still have these effects. And her anger and fury, which masks a great deal of fear, is a draw for nightmare creatures to gather around, but her anger and fear isn't the only such gathering point. But there are reasons we must keep the nightmare creatures out of this as much as possible for the time being."

Reasons I can't know yet?

"Some of them reasons you can't know yet. Some of them reasons I can't know yet. To a degree, everything runs deeper than you or I can know. Even when I know a great deal more than you do, when it comes to it, I may understand the heart of the matter no better than you do, if as well. The reasons I could give you are not the real reasons, and if you think of them as the real reasons you will be very confused. If we understood them perfectly, then we would know the real reasons and there would be no danger of confusion or misunderstanding, but we never understand anyone or anything to its deepest heart. It is enough to know that for now Ben needs to recover in order to make it across the sea and the peace between the Sha'adhri and the Nations of the Sea is still very fragile and I do not want it to fail. There is more going on in anything than anyone knows. A ladybug, the birth of a child. I would be a thousand times as much a fool as most humans are if I thought I understood the significance of a single one of such things. If I thought I understood the significance of your life, Flameheart, or of the moment when you and I met, or of the seventeenth time you caught a lizard."

Is there a reason you picked the seventeenth time? I don't think I remember that one.

"Not that I know. I just had to pick a time."

They had only been flying for about half an hour, when Flameheart felt it: a lurching, sickening feel that reminded her of what she had felt when they fought the corrupted obsidian dragons. It felt like Nelexi's fire was a shield around her, as the dragon shifted her wings and dove through the clouds. Water droplets condensed on her exposed skin and clothes and make Nelexi's scales and the saddle slick, but she was safely secured.

How many?

"*Not many, but we must destroy them.... You felt the Nightmare's presence a moment before I did.*"

The sickening reek was nearer, now. She knew the instant they came out of the thick clouds into the low-lying fog. She felt them slow as Nelexi pulled out her wings, still falling rapidly but breaking her dive. Then, with a lurch, they actually climbed as Nelexi snapped her wings out the whole way and swung her tail around.

The sick feeling receded. *How did you do that? The trees ...*

"*... are too thick for me to get my fire in. We haven't worked together much yet. I did that with my tail and my wings.*"

Oh! Flameheart gasped as Nelexi showed her. *That is ... amazing.* It had to take a great deal of precision and skill to lace one's tail through the trees like that and smack it around with enough force to kill with a single blow, not to mention knowing exactly where one's target was.

"*It does. It is one of the things I do so expertly because I have been around for a very long time. Such finesse is not the first aptitude of most obsidian dragons. And we make an excellent team.*"

They're still out there, somewhere, right? asked Flameheart.

"*Yes.*" Nelexi was climbing again now. "*We are going to track them down.*"

Flameheart clung to the saddle and wrapped her cloak tighter around them. *I really sense the Nightmare presence before you do?*

"*Yes, now that you're not wallowing in thoughts about usefulness versus uselessness and worrying about the fact that you're not what you don't know and don't want to be. You're my Flameheart, my Kario, and I love you just because you are who you are.*"

Flameheart relaxed, bent low against Nelexi's saddle, as the wind washed over her and rushed in her ears. There was nothing so heart-warming or relaxing as Nelexi's acceptance and love. It burned away all her worries, all her last remaining thoughts about usefulness and abilities. *I love you, too, Nelexi. Just because you are who you are.*

As one, as two, they hunted the gathering nightmare creatures. Nelexi landed on a hill that had been scorched by a fire several decades ago from the look of things – according to the dragon; Flameheart would not have known how forested lands recovered from fire – after obliterating the camp of nightmare creatures that had been settled there. She folded and re-folded her wings, examining the surroundings, then said to Flameheart, "*I don't think I've ever told you this in so many words before, but you know how the nightmare creatures affect people – even me at times, just a little. It's kind of like the opposite, our love, our bond, it not only protects us from the fear and the hate and the self-reproach and all the other things that come of fear, it affects the nightmare creatures a little like they affect us. It disorients them, weakens them, inhibits them from – being nightmare creatures."*

That makes sense. I think you have told me so before, said Flameheart.

I have, in ways, but not like this. You had to understand certain things first. To understand something which you're one of the only people I've met in whom I've seen the potential to understand. Fighting the nightmare creatures need not be fighting at all. It is certainly not to be distinguished from simply being the kind of beings that the nightmare cannot touch. Being people who love and do not fear, who accept and do not hate, who feel and do not despair. Lots of people come to know and understand this in one way or another, but you know it in a way that's very special to me."

Flameheart reached forward and patted Nelexi's scales, then rubbed her fingers along them gently. "I know. When we talked about being Awake, and about what I said about not killing nightmare creatures."

"And so much more. More than I can ever tell you … but I can show you, and you can know – do know."

"Are we going back, or do you think we should still fly?"

"If you are of a mind, let us take to the winds, and see where they bring us. But first…"

Nelexi bent down her neck and carefully breathed out fire – not lava – over the corpses of the orcs and another stranger thing, for which Flameheart knew no name. *Why?* she asked.

"Otherwise, the Nightmare Lord can recover its minions and bring them back to life to wage war upon Areaer anew. Destroying their corpses in fire prevents that."

"Oh," Flameheart said aloud. *What about the others … the ones under the trees, that you couldn't really get to? What will we do about those?*

"What we can do nothing about, we can do nothing about. It is not our concern. But I have asked Alian to take care of that. She can do what we can't."

I know. She can shapeshift, and, anyways, she's much, much smaller as a dragon than you are.

"Right enough," said Nelexi, her voice rippling and shifting with laughter like coruscated light.

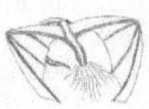

When they returned, several hours later, she walked into a house full of the smells of baking with various pastries and things the names of which she could not remember cluttering every bare surface in various stages of being made. Finsaleen, Arilann, Elamna, and Camilla were in the kitchen doing things she did not understand, while Arziel was carefully decorating some flat cakes or pieces of bread or something. "Flameheart," Camilla said, as she carefully set something freshly out of the oven down on one of the few clear spaces on the stone counters, "Arilann is leaving tomorrow to explore some things."

Flameheart nodded.

"How did you know – guess?" asked Camilla.

Flameheart shrugged. "Nelexi did," she said, and said no more. She would leave it to Arilann to explain, or not, as he wished, the conversation Nelexi had had with him this morning about the Light Elves of Aneri and their history, and his decision-making. She understood nothing that counted of it. She simply went to him between tasks and gave him rather a hurried and uncomfortable hug. He seemed very uncomfortable and awkward, and she wanted to say farewell but knew that any other way would be even more awkward.

Then she fled the house herself. It was not as if she knew anything about the things they were making, or as if more people in that house would be helpful anyways. She had not known Arilann long or well, and would miss him a little, and she did not want to think about how he felt about leaving his family, or about how his mom and dad felt. She had had to part with hers, though some of the reasons were different, and some were similar. His people – if he had any – had no hostility towards what he was or wanted, and hers had, but her family could not have come with her all over the world with Nelexi. Not for long, at any rate. There was still such a sore, empty spot in her heart from leaving them, and she ran out to Nelexi, and cuddled in a curve of the dragon's wing, while Nelexi whispered wordless comfort and belonging into her mind, and she cried softly, whether for grief or for the love and belonging of her bond with Nelexi she did not know.

Fire Dance

Earlier that day, the announcement had been made that Arilann would be leaving. Camilla was not sure it was made like an announcement at all, but she had known and everyone else had known that was why Elamna and Finsaleen were spending all day baking, and why Arziel was helping them so diligently. She had spent a couple hours indoors, getting her hands floury and gooey and helping. It was not hard work, and as long as all she had to do was stir and knead ingredients the others gave her, it was relaxing enough for a time.

The atmosphere depressed her, and kneading dough was not helping her sort her thoughts out, so she left and went to where Radiance waited for her. It was distressing watching Elamna and her children. Arziel was well more than Camilla's age, but she was still a young child, being half-elven, and *she* got all the time she needed to play with her mother. All the time Camilla and Lavilor had never had because of those *cursed* elves who, frankly, no matter what anyone tried to tell her, deserved what they had gotten from the Wizard-King. But she did not want to distress Lavilor, who at the moment was enjoying patting out some kind of preserved goodie with Arziel, and she did not need to distress anyone else there, either. It was Arilann's last day with his family, and though he was not demonstrative with his feelings, she knew that it was hard for everyone.

The fact is, I wouldn't regret the destruction of Ilesh by the Wizard-King of Eltaes, except for two reasons. One of them is what's happened to Mom and all the rest of the human slaves, unless they've somehow managed to survive free in the wilds, which I doubt, since which of us knew anything about that? The elves certainly did not teach us. The other is about those few Wood Elf children who might have turned out like Lìarz or Sërien.

Camilla was still not anywhere near Radiance's, but she could feel the dragon's thoughts form one accord with hers. Radiance spread a comforting mental wing over her, and Camilla leaned into the draconic embrace.

The thing is, there are probably more like them, who just did not have the magic to make anything work. I understand that Lìarz was quite a prodigy, and Sërien at least was a competent mage. There's probably more like them who couldn't get out *of Ilesh. What happened to them? Are they all cowards who will only ever try to do the right thing if they expect it won't cost them anything? Or have the elves killed or imprisoned many of their own? If they're cowards, I don't think I care about them, whether or not they would have had the power to do something. If they're not cowards, I do.*

It was one of those moments when Camilla's and Radiance's minds merged so closely she could not tell where one's thoughts ended and the other's began. *Sërien at least was not a coward, at least not by the end. She and the mages with her might have hoped they would be strong enough to defeat the*

Wizard-King, but they also knew that they were risking the unthinkable, and that even if they won, any of them might be killed. Is it easier not to hate Serrose when she's not around, upsetting me constantly with her elvishness? Or maybe, it's easier to accept her for what she is, and Gloaming's rider for what she was, after living these weeks with Lìarz, getting accustomed to a Wood Elf treating a human as an equal and partner, loving and providing for her and their children? Treating me like a person and an equal, on a daily basis, in his house. And not teaching me. Not trying to get anything out of me at all. Not telling me anything about what I may or may not do, except for when it's clearly his business, like when I'm not to disturb his working or how not to damage his things.

Let's fly!

Camilla knew that she and Radiance mutually thought *that*. She launched herself into an all-out run, not caring what any of the arrogant, scornful Sea Elves might think to see her – she knew that she was exotic and the subject of much talk among them – running headlong through the streets. She wished she had thought to wear gloves before leaving the house. She and Sylvara – though it galled her to think of wanting someone to mistake her for Sylvara, or at least to not know the difference – probably did not look that different to the Sea Elves. With a hood over her face, they probably would not even notice the most distinguishing feature between them, which was that Camilla's eyes were dark brown and Sylvara's were hazel and her skin was a shade lighter and less gold. After all, the Sea Elves were used to a dozen different colors of both eyes and skin, let alone fine shades.

They might even think I could be Elamna – not likely. I don't think Elamna is seen far from the house apart from any of her children, or her husband, very often.

"*Who cares what they think?*" The thought was Radiance's, and half a heartbeat later it was as much Camilla's as if it had been born first in her mind. *They're no part of our lives. They don't matter to us. Who cares if we are exotic to them? Who cares if they do think about us in ways we don't like? They will never get anything out of us. They will never control us, never cow us. We will never be their exotic pet, and we will also never be controlled or have our actions changed by the way they think about us! Never again will anyone but us have any say or influence over our actions – or our thoughts!* As appealing as that idea was, Camilla had a feeling it could stand being thought about more, but now was not the time! Now was the time to put it into action! Now was the time to *fly!*

The next day, Arilann was gone in the morning, before she woke, after everyone had awkwardly said farewell the previous night. No one was worried, convinced he had simply stolen away when there was no one else around, as that would have been easiest for him, but Camilla could feel the grief and longing of Elamna and Finsaleen, and to a lesser extent and in equally different ways, Arziel and Lìarz. Arziel was a child, and Camilla was not sure how long she even expected her playmate – not that Arilann had played with her that much – to be gone, and while Lìarz loved his son and had done what he could for him, and they had both enjoyed each other's company, they had not been close in quite the fashion that Arilann had been close to his mother and, a bit differently, to Finsaleen.

But she did not want to stay around and analyze the way people felt. She wanted to get away from it all. Part of her whispered, *"Why? You must nurture the hate, keep it strong, until it blows into an unstoppable inferno at your command that will consume the Wizard-King himself in a moment."* Another part of her recoiled from the atmosphere of hate that hemmed in and soiled the freshness of love and joy. Hate would not help her and Ben heal. That remembrance was what settled the decision, not that her whole body and soul did not ache to escape the circumstance that made her remember and relive her hatred, so she spent most of the day with Radiance and Ben, alternately riding both of them, since Ben was now easily strong enough to carry her while he flew for short time-periods, and he loved to do so. It made him feel loved, important, accepted, and that was strength and healing.

She blessed the bareback-riding pants Lìarz had given her, with the insides and seat reinforced with leather further reinforced with a few spells to prevent either her skin from being rubbed or the dragons' scales from rubbing through the leather until it no longer protected her legs. As it was, her whole body was deliciously sore from the effort of keeping her balance and seat in dragon flight, but there was not even the suggestion of a blister or a rub-burn to be found on her when she took off her clothes to take her turn soaking in the family's bath-tub.

She seemed to get the tub to herself for most of the evening. It was not as if everyone used it every day, and nothing physical compared to the feeling of soaking slightly sore muscles in warm water. She cursed the Ileshians for never having provided their slaves, who worked to painful soreness as often as not, with even such a thing as this. She also decided to thank Lìarz for it. It was his spell-craft that warmed the water, and while the Ileshians were cursed for having used slaves, she was living in his house and eating food and wearing clothes that he worked for. It was not his job to make up for the atrocities of his people, people from whom he had fled. He deserved her gratitude and thanks no less than if he had been human – or another kind of elf.

Thinking of his spell-craft, Camilla wondered if she should ask him if he would train her. Then she thought better of it. She was not ready to be trained by anyone, let alone someone who looked like a Wood Elf – who *was* a Wood Elf – even if none of the evils of the Wood Elves from which she had suffered were true about him. Besides, she was not sure if her magic had much at all to do with his magic. Remembering what she had done on the beach, it seemed quite a bit different. *Maybe* the Light Elves, being experts in many kinds of magic, would know something about it, or maybe they would not. She would need to have a space to experiment with and teach herself, but it would not hurt to be across an ocean from the Wizard-King to do that in earnest, lest the ripples of spell-craft which she felt betray her presence to him.

That thought caused her to examine the very gentle ripples of Lìarz's spell-craft to warm the water, and she decided she would apply the same eye to her new riding pants. She was sure that her magic was far, far more than his, that there were aspects of her magic that had nothing to do with anything he knew or did, but before long she was certain that she could do learn to do much of what he did. She could not figure out how to do what he had done to heat the water just by examining it, but she was sure that it was something she could learn to do. *So, maybe I will ask him to train me, if he's willing. Not quite yet. I don't think I'm ready yet. But I can't, I must not, put it off too long. I must not get complacent. Every minute that passes, it becomes harder to rescue whatever of my people are still alive. Every minute that passes more may die, or suffer. Every minutes that passes, the Wizard-King may kill and torment others who do not deserve it. Tomorrow, tomorrow I will ask if he is willing.*

The following morning she woke late, to a house filled with excited chatter. When she sat up, rubbing her eyes, Arziel assaulted her. "She can play! She can join us!" the child said, grabbing her hand in a most friendly manner.

"She probably doesn't know anything about the game, and I don't think it's the sort that interests her," said Elamna.

"She can learn!" Arziel cried. "Can't you?" she implored Camilla, completely oblivious to the second part of what her mom had said.

"After she eats breakfast, maybe," Elamna said, giving Camilla a compassionate look as she pulled Arziel gently off of her.

Camilla sat up again, stretching sore muscles that had not been helped by Arziel's playfulness. "Thanks," she mumbled, before getting up and then stretching again. It did not take her long to find the leftovers of breakfast that had been set aside for her, and Arziel did not throw herself upon her again.

"Where's Lìarz?" she asked while she ate, wanting to get the business of asking for his help started sooner rather than later.

"In his work-room, working with Sylvara," said Finsaleen.

"What's he working with her on?" Camilla asked, controlling her voice as carefully as she could.

"Seeing if she has any potential for magecraft. She believes she has at least some potential, since she's a Dragonrider, and from Alian's and Serrose's report, it seems most human Dragonriders have at least a very little. She wants to learn healing magic," explained Finsaleen.

Camilla wanted to scream. She wanted to scream her rage and frustration for all the world to hear, both out loud and with her mind. She did not want to hurt others the way she knew that would do. But Sylvara? *Sylvara?* Sylvara learning magecraft, and probably stealing time and energy that could have – should have – gone to *her?* She was honest and true, had been all her life, had been dedicated, not a sniveling, conniving, treasonous coward. Even *if* Sylvara *had* mended her ways completely, still, Camilla deserved better. And Camilla's magic was far, far greater … maybe Lìarz would listen to that argument. And the idea that *anyone* might think *she* was following *Sylvara's* lead almost made her want to not ask at all. It was disgusting, that. But she had to ask. She had to do everything she could so that she could defeat and destroy the Wizard-King and free the enslaved dragons and whatever other slaves he had who did not deserve it! Those who did deserve it, she would destroy the same as she would destroy him.

Finsaleen took a step away from the anger which Camilla knew she could not keep from leaking through into her expression and eyes even though she did try somewhat. She stalked out to the back porch and decided that she simply had to do some controlled magic practice of her own. Otherwise, the waves of energy her anger was creating might give her away far more easily than an attempt to channel her magic in a very controlled and deliberate way.

She started with a dance. It was a small, simple pattern of steps, and one into which she started to weave a great deal of power, keeping it carefully controlled within the pattern of the steps. Then she added a touch of music in her mind, as Serrose had taught her, matching it to the dance but building it, and keeping it all very, very much under control and very, very restrained. It was like when Radiance readied herself to leap into the sky and froze, poised, for an instant before. It was like – she did not know what it was like, but it took so much of her energy and attention to keep all that power so carefully restrained that she did not have attention for her hatred and that drained away.

As she danced and kept music to the dance in her mind, a pillar or essence of flame sprang up before her on the stone porch, transparent yellow and orange, flickering but keeping shape to her dance and her will. Feeling all that power under such control and so ready was a kind of unbearable ecstasy, but she kept her mind on her dance and her music, knowing that to let go would be to let the energy fly unrestrained, and that would be a disaster.

The flame curved and bowed and straightened, danced forwards and sideways and backwards to her pattern, growing and shrinking, flaring and dimming, pure power harnessed. It fed her its power, which was the only way she had enough energy to keep it under control, and there were times when she felt that ready to slip, like sweaty hands on slick polished wood, but as she danced and formed the music, her control grew more steady, more certain, and more delicate, though no less expensive.

It was utterly exhilarating, and Camilla did not want to stop ever, but there was a time when she knew that she must, for she could not continue to supply the energy for the flame and control it. Perhaps she could, but she could feel the drain on her energy and her mind even now. If she went too much longer, she might not have the control to let go. So, carefully adjusting dance and imaginary music, she let the energy flow of the flame slow, cease, drain away, softly, always under perfect control lest something get away and blow up or burn a hole in the stone. Finally, she let the last steps of the dance falter into nothing and collapsed, sweating, on the porch. It did not hurt yet, but there was a feeling all through her head that told her that she would soon have a terrible headache.

Nonetheless, Camilla – and, by extension, Radiance – were still awash in the ecstasy and exhilaration of the fire-dance. *I could do anything. I could. I could draw more energy, I'm just not sure I want to, and I certainly don't need to right now. I might even be able to defeat the Wizard-King now! Or, after I recover and replenish all that energy, maybe even deliberately build more. I don't think anyone has ever been able to do what I can.* She took a deep, steadying breath, though even her muscles were trembling. *But I want to get all the training and expertise I can. I want to be* certain. *I know I can do it, but I also want to survive. And ... maybe ... just maybe ... this wouldn't be enough, at least if he were to be able to prepare. And I certainly don't know how to make sure of that not happening. As much as we'd like to not need anyone's help, we're not sure ... that we don't.*

Perhaps more than ever, her thoughts and Radiance's were one, in this moment. In the magic, in the fire, there seemed to be no barrier between their souls, and Camilla knew, without being able to say how she knew, that that fire was more than enough to annihilate even the Wizard-King. It had certainly burned through his death-bond on Ben and brought the dragon back to life. And ... even though part of her would not admit it, she knew it was greater than her, and yet that it would fill her and be one with her and never, ever violate who she was, but instead perfect that, just as Radiance perfected her and made her, more truly than ever, who she was, and she was the same to Radiance. It was *their* Heartfire, even if they were also its.

Footsteps and the sound of the door opening behind her roused Camilla and Radiance from their introspection. She turned and half rose from her crouch to see Lìarz standing a few steps from the doorway. Without understanding it, Camilla challenged the look on his face with one on her own.

"Camilla," he said, and she could hear him trying to be gentle, "are you – uh, uh …" He fumbled, not knowing how to say or ask what he meant.

Camilla rose from her knees to her feet and stared him in the eyes. She would not have been at all surprised if there were real flames in hers. "Of course I'm okay. I am perfectly okay. I am in control of my own magic, perfectly so, and it has not and will never harm me. I'm just thinking about things."

"I don't doubt that," Lìarz said, and something in his tone of voice told her that he *did* half-believe her, and she could not expect him to fully believe her, since she was not – *quite* – fully telling the truth. "Your magic is incredibly impressive, and so is your control. However, it is so impressive that, even though I know you were trying to keep it restrained, you were handling so much energy that any mage within leagues of here would have known something was going on, and any trained or intuitive one could have sensed all too easily just how much power you were playing with." He tilted his head. "And that may not be wise."

Camilla hated, *hated, hated, hated* being told what to do. She only hated being given advice a *little* less, even if it was advice she *could* take, which in this case it was not. She had to do something to manage what she felt, and was this such a bad choice? She supposed she could have done other things – somewhat embarrassing, at least from the perspective of others, but had she and Radiance not just decided they did not care about what others thought or felt? And anything was worth it to defeat the Wizard-King.

She stood and stared at Lìarz, unable to think of anything that she *would* say. Finally, she asked, "Would you – *could* you – train me?" That *could* was no plea. It was a question of possibility. Was he enough of a mage, did he know enough about the right things, to help her with her magecraft *at all?*

"Come inside, and we can talk about that – or, if you prefer, we can talk out here, after I get us a couple cloaks."

"I prefer out here," Camilla said. She sat down again, huddling to keep herself warm after all that power had drained away. She did not want to be seen walking alongside him like some apprentice. She was no apprentice. She was no trainee, even. He would be no master or trainer. He would simply help her or guide her, and she would listen, if and when she pleased. After all, she was so different, he might be wrong far more than half the time, but he also might – probably did in fact – have something, or a few things, he could help her with.

Being With

Flameheart lay in a sort of nest she had dug in the sand a few paces from the much, much larger sand-nest Nelexi had dug for herself. It was a bright, sunny winter day, and the breeze that was wafting off the ocean was more to Flameheart's liking than it was most of the time. She longed sorely for the Plains of Zharda, where the sun was never so faint and mist-obscured as it was most of the winter here. She longed for the breezes that blew through uncounted fields of flowering grasses. At the moment, she was soaking what sun she could get into her face – it was refreshingly warm on her dark skin – and imagining the beautiful spectacle of Nelexi, shining black and glowing red, against the wavy green of the plains and the harsh, enrapturous blue of the sky. Or perhaps the layered grays, purples, blues, and greens of the storms rolling across the plains, flashing often with colored lightning, or else pouring rain into the wet, gray twilight even at noon. Nelexi would be just as striking in one of those, her red wings glowing dully of the darkness, her black bulk strikingly beautiful just a few shades darker than anything else.

"What was that?" Flameheart exclaimed, in the language of her people, rolling out of the sand-pit.

The dragon had tensed, mantling her wings and raising her head, even her tail frozen mid-lash. *"Camilla. She is not doing badly. She is managing a great deal of power very, very well, and her control is actually quite excellent, but not so excellent that everything with a lick of certain kinds of magical sense within a days' flight of here, at least, is not going to feel something very, very interesting. And some of those things may know a great deal about it. At least, this is not the kind of energy that draws nightmare creatures like flies to a rotting corpse."*

Should she not be doing this?

"I cannot answer that. She must find the way to practice her magic, and no one can show her that way. There are things I could show her, if she were ready to listen, but even then, most of the way she would have to find herself. And she is not blasting craters in sand with anger-tinted power this time."

Don't mind me. What do I know of magic? You know what I think about magic ...

"You still have not changed your mind at all?"

Do I have to? How I feel has not changed much. And you ... you might not be some of the things that saying you were a goddess led me to feel, but you very much count as a goddess when I said that magic should belong to the gods and be given only when they please and guard. You've told me some things to imply that's not really possible and isn't how the world works, even though that's how it seems to work in the Plains of Zharda. Perhaps the

Nightmare has magic of its own, and the whole argument is irrelevant. Either way, it's not my choice, so it is irrelevant, and I don't know enough to make it anyways, and I have to trust that those – or the One – who does knows and means best, and I do trust that. I can't imagine not trusting that. There's really no reason for me to think about it, and I don't think about it unless the question is asked me. But how I feel hasn't changed, and I can't make it change, and I don't see why I should want to.

"Well enough, and there is wisdom in what you've just said, little Kario."

That made Flameheart laugh. *You? Talking to me about* wisdom? *I would never have suspected.*

"You know what I mean, little rider. And you know what I do not mean." Nelexi swung her neck over and delicately, gently, licked Flameheart once on the forehead.

Flameheart moaned with pleasure.

Suddenly, Flameheart sat up. "Didn't we promise to take Arziel for a ride today?"

"Yes. I suppose I can forget things. Is it about that time?" asked Nelexi.

I think so. Yes, I think they must have had breakfast quite a long time ago from where the sun is ... and from how my stomach feels.

"Well then, go on and get your breakfast, and bring Arziel back out with you, if she stills wants."

"Of course she'll still want," said Flameheart, patting Nelexi's gigantic cheek. "And no one will mind, either. They trust both of us like ... like we were their gods. And you know all of that as well I do." She chuckled.

"I do. But you are fun to tease."

When Flameheart knocked on the door and Arziel let her in, it appeared that everyone else, from Arziel to her parents, had forgotten that this was the day Nelexi had promised. Probably, it had been passed over in all the excitement and melancholy of Arilann leaving a couple days earlier. In fact, it might even have been yesterday and not today at all, that Flameheart and Nelexi had promised. It also appeared that it was an opportune entrance. Arziel had been begging all morning for another person to play a certain six-person game, that could just barely be managed with five people, with her, and Camilla had slept in, not that she would have known how to play the game or been likely to enjoy it, if she even consented to give it a try. Flameheart would have given it a try of course ... in fact, she might have given it a try more than once. The rules were rather different, and she kept getting them mixed up in her head, but the game was a bit like one her people played.

There was not much left over from breakfast, but Flameheart was satisfied with what there was, and just resolved to fill her stomach up well at dinner. She let Elamna know of her intentions, just as she took Arziel, who could not have been more excited or satisfied with the notion of riding Nelexi, out the front door. Arziel was hopping and bouncing around, and quite as big as she was, but she did not do anything more problematic than slip a couple times. Since she had been doing that all her life and was quite used to it, not making much of a bruise or scrape or two, that was not really problematic.

She whooped and hollered with such enthusiasm that Flameheart staggered back and held her hands over her ears when they came out and saw Nelexi standing on the sand, her wings half-lifted, her ears out, her tail lashing, quite putting on a show for Arziel. It was not the first time, either, and Arziel had *no* reservations about trusting Nelexi, no discomfort around her, not even a trace of worry that she might be a human-eating predator. Flameheart rather suspected that Nelexi very much enjoyed that. She also suspected that Arziel was one of a few people who simply enjoyed how huge Nelexi was, without ever having a hard time imagining it.

Arziel threw herself into helping Flameheart saddle Nelexi with a will, and she was quite attentive. She had no difficulty listening patiently while Flameheart quickly and simply explained what she could do, and fumbled over a few words of her language before Nelexi helped her. She even followed the directions quite well, though Flameheart made sure to double-check everything she did. It would not do for the saddle to come off, or even a strap or two to loosen, in mid-flight, especially not with someone Nelexi was not bonded to, like Arziel, on board. Nonetheless, the job took a lot less long with Arziel helping, and in a handful of minutes the three of them were airborne.

Flameheart still had to protect her ears, since Arziel sat in front of her, screaming and hollering with joy when they took off, and when Nelexi banked or rocked on a wind, or when Nelexi did some *very* gentle acrobatics that did not really count as acrobatics at all, or when she looked over Nelexi's shoulder and saw what it looked like to view the terrain currently beneath them from their current elevation. She was utterly thrilled with all of it.

Was I a lot like her? Flameheart asked Nelexi.

"A lot. You still are a lot like her. But you were a little older, and you were riding at first without a saddle which required a lot more of your attention, and things were a lot more frightening and difficult for you, bonding to me and having to leave your family and home behind."

After a while, Flameheart thought she recognized some of what they were doing. *You're not surveying for nightmare intruders are you?* she asked Nelexi.

"I am, a little. It is a part of who I am. I cannot help it. How could I not?"

Flameheart realized she had a point. Unless she was going to fly only over the city, she would be doing so in a way. Even flying out over the sea counted. Nelexi, she and Nelexi, could not be somewhere without being the kind of creatures who – who did not permit the Nightmare. They were not surveying or hunting, so much as soaring and being who they were. The patterns Nelexi flew were often influenced by the winds, and so she was flying some of those same patterns now.

"I'll call Alian if there's a problem, though we could probably take care of most things without doing anything that would frighten, or do otherwise than thrill, Arziel. I think she's ready for a bit more, don't you?"

I think you could pull one of those dives and all she'd do was scream with excitement. I'm not sure it's possible for her to get air-sick. You could roll all the way over and under, and she'd love it.

"Shall I?"

Maybe.

"I think that's a yes," said Nelexi.

She sat on the floor, muffled in many layers of clothes, eating as delicious a concoction as could be made with fish as the primary meat ingredient. It was a lot better than the fish she and Nelexi had tried to cook in their travels, but it was still *fish*. Sylvara paused next to her, and Flameheart half-looked up.

"Want to come to the library with me?" she asked in Anerian. "You could have a second dinner there."

Flameheart was mildly curious to see Sylvara here in the first place. Sylvara and Camilla usually stayed as far apart as possible, and Sylvara spent most of her days in the library with Kellan, learning languages and studying whatever else it was that interested her, except for when she sought out Flameheart and Nelexi to learn Anerian. That was probably what she wanted now, though why she had been with the others Flameheart did not know.

She could feel Camilla's glare on the back of her head, but she did not care. She liked Camilla well enough, and she liked Ben and Radiance just as much, but she did not have to do or not do things because they upset Camilla.

"Sure. Wait for me to finish," she responded to Sylvara.

Sylvara nodded and stood against the wall, her arms crossed in front of her chest in a singularly strange attitude.

In a few minutes, Flameheart was ready. She did not want to spend longer than necessary around this maelstorm of tense and contrary emotions that flew constantly between Sylvara and Camilla, though Camilla seemed the primary source of them. It was not as if Camilla did not radiate them half the time when Sylvara was *not* around.

They hurried through the white streets, which almost glowed in the darkness of fallen night, their strides matched. Before long, they reached the library. Sylvara told Flameheart that the librarian, Kellan, was probably looking over some scrolls or books, or else that he had gone to bed early, while she poured the soup he had made into two bowls, one for herself and one for Flameheart. "Soups and stews and a few other very simple things that take no time or attention to make are the common fare here," she told Flameheart, while they carried their lukewarm bowls outside and sat down on a bench that looked out on the starlit garden while being shaded under the porch. "Kellan almost always burns anything more complicated, though he occasionally orders something more interesting. Now that I live here, I help with the cooking, and he says he likes having a bit more variety from time to time."

"You're speaking Anerian quite well, though you've started to mix it up with Sea Elven from time to time," Flameheart commented.

"Well, I'm learning Sea Elven too. Sometimes it all makes my head hurt," Sylvara commented. There was silence for a few minutes while Sylvara stirred her soup while it cooled and only took occasional sips. Flameheart, even though she was already half-full from having eaten a good meal less than half an hour earlier went through her soup a lot faster.

There's something bothering Sylvara, she told Nelexi. *Otherwise, she wouldn't be cooling her soup while not talking.*

"I know something of what it is," the dragon replied.

Do you ... should you tell me, or should I wait for her to tell me?

"Your choice," said Nelexi, at the same time as Sylvara spoke. "I wanted to talk to someone. Of course, I could talk to Kellan as well...." Sylvara's voice trailed away, and she put her half-eaten bowl of soup to the side and folded her hands in her lap, her head bowed. "I – I've definitely done things very wrong. A lot of them. I can't tell Camilla I'm sorry. I'm not sure you could understand why, but she ... it would not work, and I have. But what does saying even do?"

Flameheart sat still, her own bowl, now empty, put to the side as well. Something was troubling Sylvara, as she had surmised almost from the first, but she did not understand what lay in Camilla and Sylvara's past and the trouble between them very well. Then again, she had never asked, and neither of them had ever volunteered the information.

"I and Shimmer – Shimmer changed me. I don't recognize the Sylvara I used to be. I don't think I'd know her if we met in the street. I don't know what I used to be or want, but I know what I am and want now, and Shimmer is in full agreement with me. We want to know things, everything that we can. Knowledge is and can be so useful, and it's just *delightful.*" Quiet passion silvered Sylvara's voice. "Then we came and thought about how Sërien – that's the elf mage who's body and memories Alian's mate possessed – got together a lot of human Dragonriders, the man who's body and memories Alian has –"

"I know," Flameheart interrupted quietly.

"Okay. Well, we thought that it seemed a lot of human Dragonriders had some potential to learn magecraft, so we thought maybe I could. We really want to be healers. One of the things about which I'm trying to learn everything I can is healing. Herbs, how to find them, how to prepare them, how to use them, when *not* to use them. We want to learn everything we can. There's always a time when you would be glad you knew it, or wish you knew it if you had not. So I approached Lìarz and asked him if he could see if he could train me to be a mage. And he said, yes. We did a lot of tests today, and I won't be any great mage, but I will be able to do some things, and I should be able to heal – I think he said, *mediocrely.*" She switched into Ileshian for the last word, and Flameheart had to ask Nelexi what it meant.

"That makes sense," said Flameheart.

Sylvara nodded, still keeping her eyes in her lap. "It upsets Camilla. She does not trust me. She can't trust me. But it upsets her. I think she feels threatened. Or like I am trying to usurp who she is. Or she just does not want to see me ever, at all, or even remember that I exist, though I know she can't completely ignore Shimmer's presence."

Flameheart tucked her knees up against her chin and swiveled on the bench to face Sylvara. "Why are you telling me this?"

Sylvara brought her gaze out of her lap and turned sideways on the bench to face Flameheart. "Because ... because I wanted someone to listen to me. I wanted to be heard, understood at least a little ... and I don't think this is something Kellan would understand at all."

Flameheart uncurled herself and reached across the space between them to give Sylvara a hug. The older Dragonrider seemed on the verge of sobbing. After several minutes, she pulled away and asked, "What do you think we should do?"

Nelexi had definitely left her imprint on Flameheart, or else Flameheart would never have presumed to give advice. "That's something you and Shimmer have to figure out for yourselves. I'm not you, and I can't figure out what you want for you."

Sylvara almost flinched and folded in on herself, but there was nothing else Flameheart could say or offer. It was true. She *could not* make Sylvara and Shimmer's decisions for them. She could not figure out who they were or what they wanted for them. Even Nelexi could not do that for her. She most certainly could not do it for them. Whether they could do that for each other was something she could not know.

Perhaps what Sylvara was really asking was for Flameheart to talk to Camilla, but that was something Flameheart neither knew how nor desired to do. Whatever was between Sylvara and Camilla, Flameheart had no part in it and no interest in it. Besides, she knew Camilla well enough at this point to know that, even if she felt like it, talking to her would do no good. She did not listen to anyone, except maybe Radiance. All Flameheart could do for her, and whatever problems she had, was to be there – kind and cheerful and carefree, ready to play, ready to listen when *she* wished to talk, and to offer her own thoughts only when Camilla really, persistently asked for them, which was rare indeed.

After Flameheart left her, Sylvara sat silently on the bench. She was cold, and she shivered just a little. She could feel Shimmer's gentle urging to get inside and get warm – or she could come to him and snuggle against his belly – in her mind, like a very soft, gentle whisper, one of which she must always be aware, but which she could put aside and ignore at will. She did not want to move. She did not even want to stir. She missed Arilann. Something about being around him had always put her in a good mood. It had always made her feel *good* in some indefinable way. Valuable was not really the right word, and neither was beautiful. Neither, too, was noble. He did not make her feel like she was a good person. He made her feel good, the way a loaf of fresh bread from Elamna's ovens tasted and felt good in her mouth, or the way a warm bath after playing outside in the snow made her feel good, except it was a different part of her that Arilann made feel good. A part of her that was inside, but not one that being bonded to Shimmer had made her feel. Now that he was gone, that part of her feel empty and cold. It ached. She had never noticed that it ached before, but now that he had awakened sensation there, it hurt.

Shimmer moved through her mind as if to encompass her, like he sometimes did with his wing over her body. She felt his ache, his want to make her feel good, his desperation that he could not do so.

It's okay, she told him. *You've done so much for me. You do make me feel good, even if you've made me hurt, too, but I had to hurt. I had to change. I'm so happy to have met you, to have you with me in the deepest part of me.*

Sylvara did not miss the slight shiver that ran through Shimmer's mental touch. He wanted to be enough for her. He wanted to be everything for her. He was not *jealous*. He had not minded her spending time with Arilann in the least. He had encouraged and enjoyed her friendship with Arilann. But he wanted to be sufficient for her. He wanted her not to crave anything, and if she did crave something and he could not fill that need, he felt unhappy. He felt like he was not good enough.

Or at least as good as you want to be, Sylvara thought, more to herself than to Shimmer though he would not miss it. *And I know trying to tell you that you* are *good enough, and I love you just the way you are, and I wouldn't want you to be different … and that it's not possible for you to fulfill every one of my desires, or for anyone to, won't make you feel any differently.*

Now that she was alone, Sylvara brought her feet up onto the bench, and tucked her knees under her chin, wrapping herself in her arms as far as was possible. It did not do much to make her less cold, but it helped a little. It was kind of awkward, too, in the thick furred skins she was wearing. *And Camilla … I wish Camilla did not react to me this way. I don't know what more I can do. I don't think she will ever understand. I wanted to be able to do more.*

When she and Ben were hurt, I wished I knew what to do. I wished I could actually help. But it won't help to tell her that's what's driving me, even if she'd believe it. It would just make her feel threatened or upset about the fact that she can't always do and be everything she needs for herself.

Sylvara's feelings of despondency and grief turned into anger, as she mulled over this. *It's ridiculous! It's absurd! No one can ever take care of all his needs! It's not possible for anyone to never rely on anyone else! It's just maddeningly insensitive, stubborn, and stupid of her. Doesn't she see that she's more self-reliant than any of the rest of us can ever hope to be, even if she still depends on others far more than she wants to? I might have been insensitive, blind to the suffering of others, and mean in the past, but* how *can she act this way? She's even bonded to a dragon! Skies and fire, she even speaks and hears other humans, like me, the way the dragons talk! She has to know better. She has to know the rest of us deal with far worse, and not because we* like *it. She has to know I don't mean any harm. How can she be so angry and mean all the time? I'm not the one hurting others now. She is! How can she be angry at* me *for wanting to be less dependent on others, if that was even what I'm doing?! How can she be angry that I want to be helpful?*

She can make her own choices. If she feels pressured into learning from someone she doesn't want to work with because I'm doing so, and there can't be anything I do, or do better, than her, then that's her problem, not mine. It's not fair to be angry with me about it. It's cruel!

Shimmer moved like a silver wind through Sylvara's thoughts. Why was she angry? Why was her mind so cluttered with bitternesses and hates? Was life not good? She had not been denied what she wanted – what they both agreed was a worthy goal they desired to pursue. Right now, she was the one spoiling her life with useless hatreds and hurts, when if she stopped dragging them behind her, they would not harass her tail either. They came from within her right now, not from Camilla. Camilla was not around. Sylvara probably needed to come and sleep with him tonight. But he could not keep her safe from the anger and hurts if she insisted on brewing them in her craw and breathing them all over the place. She would have to be willing. Was she? He wanted her to be.

Flameheart sat against Nelexi's hard, warm side, with the dragon's red wing a glowing presence on the upper edges of her vision. Nelexi lay on a hill that rose above most of the surrounding territory and most of the low fog, and the dragon and rider enjoyed the vista of rolling fog, broken here and there by the green suggestion of a tree, and occasionally by a hill that rose above the fog. It looked like a white-blue-gray plains of a more gently-moving sea, spreading out over the sea itself, veiling it from view and fading in indiscernible increments into the sky. The sky was almost as wondrous. Great fluffy, tattered clouds, white and gray, sailed through it, here and there opening to reveal a vision of blue, or letting through a ray of sunshine, then closing together and opening a new window into the higher skies.

She plucked a blade of grass and twirled it between her fingers over and over in an endless loop.

Nelexi swung her long neck around to look at her chosen, causing the dragon's shoulders to move, and Flameheart felt the echoing vibrations of the movements in the scales against her back. *"You wanted to say something?"*

Flameheart's mouth stretched into a wide smile. *I wish I could hug you!* she thought, and felt Nelexi's answering mental embrace, as solid and heart-warming as any physical one, especially with the dragon's scales all around her. "I did. Sylvara … sometimes she bothers me. Camilla, I like her company, when she is not radiating that hatred and … whatever else it is. It makes me want to run away from her. It sort of hurts."

"I know exactly what you mean. And I know what you mean about enjoying being around her, otherwise. It is sometimes so fun to watch you play together. Remember that day in the sand?"

I do. "Does she bother you, too?"

"Not like she bothers you. I am a dragon, and we are made to communicate in that way and to handle it. I have been around for a very long time and have a great deal of experience with it. But she could be a challenge to a young dragon, and you are not a dragon. She tries, but she cannot fully succeed until she deals with it within herself."

It's been very bad recently, since she and Sylvara both started taking lessons with Lìarz. Whenever she sees Sylvara … and most of the time when she is working with Lìarz or thinking about it. And she does not spend as much time playing. I think it was much better when she played, or after she played with her magic her way.

"I don't disagree, my little Flameheart. I am not even sure Lìarz is the right person to teach her, but Alian is part of that, too, and it is not right for me to step in all the time. It is not as if I were even always right, and being right can be so much more than that."

"I know. You've explained it to me often enough. You can't give other people, even me, your experience and your knowledge, and even if you could, it would not be right, because who I am and what I am is not you. It would be like trying to make a spear by taking many branches and cutting them and tying them together, instead of waiting and searching for a strong one of the right size."

"Exactly, and I don't think we should talk more about Camilla and her

problems. We do enough of that, maybe even too much, already. So tell me what you wanted to say."

Just that I like Camilla and I wish … I wish she'd be likable more. I want to play with her and Lavilor and Arziel. And Finsaleen. And both Sylvara and Camilla have this tendency to want me to belong with her and … I'm not sure what they want me to feel or think about the other. But I don't want to be part of any of it. It's not as if they say anything either.

"I understand.… Just be with me."

Flameheart gasped as Nelexi shared her vision of the scape before them, with all its highlights and detail, and all the richness of Nelexi's experience and thoughts. She saw things in it that Flameheart did not. Some of that was because her eyes saw differently than the human's. Some of that was because of thousands of years of experience that allowed her to infer what others could not, as one could make guesses based off the weather as to what herbs would grow best in the year. And some of it was also experience, but it was not physical vision, not exactly. It was thought and understanding in its most primeval form, the thing which is to poetry as poetry is to other language, fresh-sprung and raw, not yet constrained, confined, or diluted by the transfer into one form of language or another, verbal or not.

Nelexi had never shared this much with her before.

What seemed like hours later, when Flameheart had nearly forgotten the thought, though it still slept in the cocoon of her marvel, Nelexi said, *"That's not true. I've never shared this with you before, but I've shared not unlike this with you a great deal. Much of it was early in our relationship and is part of our bond, as this is now. It was so much and our relationship was so new, you did not notice it in this way."*

I … see … breathed Flameheart. She skipped across the hillside to Nelexi's nose. "Fly now?"

Nelexi snorted, half-nodding – she could not really nod with her head rested on the ground – and letting out a puff of smoke with just a flicker of fire in it. Flameheart dodged it and slid to her.

"Shall I mount by your head or by your tail?"

"Let's try the head today."

Flameheart nodded. She backed up, half-skipping, and then broke into a run straight towards Nelexi's head. She took a running leap at the last moment, caught her fingers carefully on the edges of Nelexi's scales, found slippery grips with her feet and knees, and half-climbed, half-slithered her way on. As soon as she was half-way secure, on a remotely level surface, she broke into a run again. Her feet slid gracefully on Nelexi's scales and she never lost her footing, until she reached the saddle and dropped lightly into it, turning as she did so to face forward.

Nelexi's wings rose, fanning the wind into forceful gusts and eddies. The dragon lurched to her feet, broke into a half-run of her own – except there was hardly space on the hilltop for a half-stride, and launched herself into the air. Her grace was a *far* more impressive feat than Flameheart's, though her take-off left deep gouges in the earth.

When Flameheart looked behind them, it looked like fog was collecting in them, though they could not have been that deep. Half her height, perhaps?

Nelexi banked once she gained enough altitude, and Flameheart asked, *"We hunt the Nightmare?"*

She knew the answer already. Only she did not hunt the Nightmare. It was not like when she hunted a lizard to eat. Though Nelexi had not hunted to eat in such a very long time. Flameheart did not know how long, though the dragon had implied she had hunted to eat once.

Flameheart. Their name was Flameheart. The flame with which the Nightmare burned before them was no weapon born of hate, scarcely even a response to the Nightmare's sickening attempt to challenge, but their hearts. They lived. They loved. They were one.

Camilla leaned close to Radiance's neck as the dragon caught a draft of warm air. The ache in Radiance's wings was nearly omnipresent, but the weather these last couple of days had blown in a warm, southern squall off the sea. There was so much fog and cloud the temperature did not even change much with the passing of day and night. It made Radiance more comfortable than she had been in a long time. Ben was getting more comfortable, too, and he was now flying with confidence and ease, even if he had no endurance and could not handle erratic winds. Camilla had ridden with him the previous day.

Now she tried to meld her mind with Radiance's and forget the frustration of magery practice. She refused to let someone like Sylvara be her better. She refused to let anything deter her. But she found the things Lìarz had her do frustrating and useless. Some of it was nothing but a boring waste of time. Why did she have to listen to him play two pipes at once, accenting the melody of one with harmony on the other? Why did she have to learn to play either? Sometimes, Lìarz told her, singing would do, but Camilla could not bring herself to sing like *that* in front of *him*. Not that she could not have. She could certainly sing and dance another column of flame from midair, and maybe she could put a little more effort into shadow-blending the magic than she had last time. In fact, she *had* done it again once, outside the city walls, with Radiance and Ben. But why should she do it in front of him? She was sure he would not – could not – appreciate it.

She hated him. She hated his Ileshian mannerisms. She hated his Ileshian magic. She hated all of it.

So why had she asked for him to teach her magecraft? Was it only that she could not let Sylvara be better at *any*thing than she was? Then again, Camilla had always been certain that she could be a mage, that the elves were not better than she was. And she could. She was a mage. The mageweapons responded to her. Was that not enough? No, it was not enough. The mageweapons responded to Arilann, too. She missed him a little, but not enough to think about it often.

This was not the time to think about her problems with magecraft and Lìarz. This was the time to enjoy the skies with Radiance.

Only when her mind and Radiance's were most one, were their minds their own. Only when her thoughts could not be distinguished from Radiance's, were they truly her thoughts. She could not have imagined how wonderful it was to be a Dragonrider, though she recognized in her heart she had always known. In her heart, she and Radiance had always been made for one another. When she Recognized Radiance, she had become everything she was meant to be.

There was nothing like this, soaring through the skies among the clouds, the clouds and the earth floating past below them, on their wings.

A winged horror rose out of the clouds, poison dripping from its fangs. There was only the moment, the oneness, the love, the wonder, the joy. There was only Radiance-Camilla. They did not enjoy the presence of that blight of fear and hatred that had no place in the joy of their oneness. They swerved towards it and breathed a long, burning blast of fire that washed it from the sky. Its ugliness had no place in that wide, wide beauty of burning joy, where all was one in endless space to fly.

Serpents

Camilla sat on the floor, watching Lìarz put the final touches on the enchantment to send a scroll to his son, detailing that they would be leaving Ansaifar, due to the encroaching mass of nightmare creatures and slaves of the Wizard-King that had nearly become a siege, and some sort of plan Lìarz had for Arilann to be able to come back to his family. The Wood Elf mage had invited both her and Sylvara to watch while he enchanted the scroll to find his son, since he did not do this thing regularly and it was their only chance to learn what they could from observing it. Camilla tried to ignore Sylvara's presence on the other side of Lìarz, and she did not know whether this was one of the only moments she was not grateful for the ability to hear the thoughts of humans as dragons did, and even speak into the minds of humans as dragons could speak among each other, or not. It certainly made it impossible to be completely ignorant of Sylvara's presence, since she felt her mind and could not do anything about it. At the same time, Camilla did not trust Sylvara, and did not want to have Sylvara be anywhere around her and not know precisely where Sylvara was – and be able to know far more in an instant if she wished. Sylvara had certainly changed, but Camilla was still not certain of the extent of the change and how far she could trust it, and she most definitely did not *like* Sylvara and never would.

She tried to bend her mind back to watching Lìarz's spell-craft, trusting Radiance's presence in her mind and thought to keep an eye on Sylvara, too. *No. Don't think about Sylvara. Thinking about what you think about her and how much you hate her will not help you learn the magic, and it's not necessary to protect you either.*

There were times when Camilla thought that Lìarz's magic was a great deal more complicated than it needed to be, but she could not really know. She could not do some of the things he could that she had tried, though she could certainly do things he never could. *Pay attention,* she reminded herself, but it was getting harder and harder. There was something about the way Lìarz did his magic that did not sit right with her. She could not mesh it with the way she and Radiance thought. She could not ride it as they rode the wind. Camilla was beginning to consider the possibility that there was not really anything she could learn from Lìarz. Maybe a spell or a technique here or there, but not how to be a mage. She and Radiance would have to discover that on their own. There was no one else like them, and maybe some things always had to be discovered, not learned with a teacher.

Lìarz finished, and Camilla felt all the pieces of the spell slip together into a perfect, vibrant harmony. She reached out the gentlest mental finger – lest she disrupt and undo Lìarz's hard work – and felt the magic. Something in her said she could do this, too. Lìarz held the tiny scroll for a moment in his hand, then tossed it lightly into the air. Camilla felt him add more magic, more energy, more of himself. The rolled scroll took to the wind like the wings of a butterfly.

Just like that, she and everyone she knew – except for those who were lost – were going to leave Ellenesia in a few weeks. Ansaifar bustled with as much activity as the human city she had briefly glimpsed with the elves' hurry to get themselves and their things together in time for the first fleet to leave before the new week. There was a hum made of the voices and movements of the Sea Elves that she had rarely heard in Ansaifar before, but now it was constant.

"We're not fleeing," Radiance whispered in her mind. *"We're going to a place where we can become stronger so that we can better do what we shall."*

We fled before, Camilla replied. *We fled before, the night the Wizard-King destroyed everything.* Camilla's blood boiled. Her plan to escape and then come back to free her people had gone awry. Her mother *must* be alive, *must* have survived somehow. She would reunite her with Lavilor. None of it was fair.

She needed to get to some place far away from other people who could be hurt, so that she could practice her magic alone and learn how to use it. Or maybe she should fly right now to the castle of the Wizard-King in Eltaes and blast the whole thing into a burning crater. No, that would not free or rescue any slaves or prisoners. The Wizard-King would surely know long before she and Radiance got there. She might burn herself to ashes simply fighting his forces, and not even get to him. Besides, she fully intended to survive, and she did not want to leave Lavilor without a sister, too.

There are two things I need to be able to do. I need to practice shadow-blending so that I can get to the Wizard-King before he knows I'm there. So I can get to his prisoners and free them. And I need to find some way to channel all that power and live through it. Killing the Wizard-King cannot possibly take less power than freeing Ben did, and neither can freeing the rest of his prisoners.

It was a shame that she had to let them be tortured for longer, but there was not much that she could do about it. She could not get to where they were to free them. The idea that she needed anyone else to teach her was intolerable, but as intolerable as it was, if she could learn faster by having someone teach her, it was worth it. So, who might be able to teach her? Lìarz's magic did not work for her, but … as much as Camilla hated it, she remembered that she had not felt about Serrose's or Alian's magic the way she felt about Lìarz's, but Alian refused to teach her, and Serrose was not here, and Camilla was not even sure how much she trusted Serrose. There was something wrong about the were-dragons, too, but it was not their spell-craft precisely. But since it was not their magic that she had a problem with, would it be possible for her to find another one to train her? Alian would not, and Serrose was taking care of their young, never mind that Camilla did not like Serrose, but might she be able to find another one who would teach her? From what she understood, there were a number of them. Maybe there was one who came from a human-dragon pairing who would be willing to teach her what she *could* be taught, what she *could* learn that way. And perhaps someone whose powers were more unique than most, though still not nearly as unique and exceptional as her own, would be better suited to helping her.

Though the matter of her uniquely exceptional powers was something else to be considered altogether.

The gentle songs of birds in spring floated through her wakening mind. She stared up at the dim, golden light filtered through Radiance's wing. She had slept outside with the dragon last night.

"Camilla, I realized something," Radiance said, suddenly waking her rider fully.

Almost before Camilla formed her query, in confusion over what Radiance was talking about, the golden dragon was explaining it. *"I figured out why the way Lìarz is teaching you is not right. I think you will be able to do the complicated things that you cannot do now but he can, but thinking of them as complicated is not the right way to learn. The way Lìarz practices magic and teaches it is like if I tried to teach a youngling to fly by describing exactly how and when to turn the joints of the wings, just how and when every joint and muscle of the tail should flex, and so forth. I do not know all those things, and no youngling would learn to fly by being lectured in that, no matter how well she learned the pieces. But the way you dance and sing the column of flame is how you should approach all magic. You just need to learn more, play more, practice more."*

In a moment, it made so much sense to Camilla. It was what she had felt all along. It fit perfectly.

But magic is dangerous, playing with it doubly so, Camilla protested weakly. It was not really a protest. She did not care what the others said or what they cautioned. Even if they were not malicious and cruel like the Wood Elves of Ilesh, it did not follow that their intentions were always the best *or* that they were right about anything about her. At the same time, she knew the power she played with could be dangerous. She could not forget what had happened the first time she played with it, when she navigated the border wards of Ilesh, sang her magic to the skies, and then was brought down from the skies with Radiance by dark magic and captured.

"So is flying. Whether one is more so than the other, it does not matter."

Thank you, Radiance, my heart, my wings, thought Camilla. She pulled her hands out of the furs and touched the membrane of Radiance's wing. She ran her fingers along the smooth surface, slightly wrinkled in its folded state. *Maybe soon I can learn to make a wall of fire around us, so that we are safe, and keep you warm so our injuries do not ache.*

Radiance's gratitude, her relief at the thought, flooded through Camilla with such intimacy that it was her own. The human stood, bumping her head against the dragon's wing, and leaned against the dragon's shoulder for a moment, then stooped under the dragon's raised wing and stepped out.

Anger flooded through her with such force it felt like molten fire in her veins. And it might have been. It was all the elves' fault, all the fault of so many, and the Northern Horror. They kept her from her birthright, her magic, herself, they would have if they could! So much suffering was their fault! The dragon's injuries were their fault, injuries that would never leave her as long as she lived! She knew they would only grow worse as the dragon aged. She knew of other slaves who had that happen to them. And she was still so young, not nearly full-grown, not yet two years old! It was unfair, unfair, cruel!

The human gestured. The dragon threw up her head. Fire rose from around the human's feet, sparked and trickled from her dragon-touched hand, flamed into a writhing column, a glowing, burning serpent. Fire flowed from the dragon's mouth, breathed into the sky, a flood of molten glory, flickering, ragged, setting the air glowing and burning.

Beauty flowed in the air, burning, scorching, living and destruction, a destruction that was life and joy, reckless life, total abandon. Freedom such as even Camilla had never dreamed. It tugged at her, joy now, not anger and misery, that flowed through her veins, the life of the magic, whether she wanted it or not – and how could she not want it? It was the fire that bound her and Radiance, the fire that was their oneness, their united self that could never be separated again.

Anger, distrust, unhappiness rose in response. She was not bound to another! Her power was hers and her alone! There was no greater power, no one who held her power or her destiny – or even her life – in his power!

Out, beyond the shimmer of power and heat from the fire, up from the earth, out from nowhere and within and without, a form took shape, gray and rough like stone, humanoid and without definite height but conveying the impression of something supremely tall. The tail of an amber-scaled snake rested over the feet, and the body of the snake wound up the body. Its two heads rested, tongues flickering in and out, amid a nest of wildly flying hair, like the tails of a thousand snakes. Amber eyes, more dead than the glassy sightless eyes of the dead, stared out of the stony humanoid face. The monster held out a hand.

Time paused, unraveled, and flipped about, like food that would not stay still in the stomachs of the living, like if her heart were another living creature, moving inside her.

Camilla and Radiance did not need to know to hear. The draw, the appeal, had always flowed through Camilla's veins, always haunted her thoughts. It tugged against the essence of fire, yet was her own drive. She acknowledged no power over her, nothing that was not herself that gave her life, that made her destiny, that gave her power. There was no power outside her that was greater than her or could fight her power over herself. Her power and life came from herself alone. It must be! It must!

But it is not so nothing can hurt me!

It is not? Is not that no horror of undeath can ever touch you?

No slavery. My will is mine *alone. And no one should be able to hurt another, someone innocent, ever! I should* not *have been hurt! But it is different from that.*

Incoherent desires that, in some way, always tormented her rose like twin serpents in fierce, realized combat, but serpents still, moving too swiftly, too sinuously, sometimes too hidden, to be seen or understood or named, or for their battle to be recounted. She wanted nothing more than to run into the fire that was the heart of the earth and their bond and embrace it with all her – their – heart. She wanted nothing more than to flee forever, to be apart, herself, with no need of another, no connection to anything greater! She wanted there to *be* nothing greater, ever! Her very life seemed to hang on it, necessitate it. Both serpents strangled each other, both serpents golden-hued. Life was wrong, reality was wrong, it must be a lie, all of it, for what was right was inherently impossible, intrinsically contradictory.

The fire wavered, then surged. Every flicker of its energy, every shimmer of its glow, twanged through her and Radiance's heart, reminding them that they were one yet two. They were one as much as Camilla herself was one and as Radiance herself was one, yet two. They were each other, yet not each other. Their unity was *right*.

The fire leapt out, and Camilla and Radiance came as one to their senses.

Camilla could not control it, could not decide if she wanted to control it or to let it rage, anymore than a moment before she had been able to decide – or could decide now – if she wanted to embrace it or to cut it out of herself forever because it did not come from her and her alone. She could not now decide if she wanted it to be something other than her – or, yet more horrible, greater than her - or not, something that was hers alone, nothing more than her, without any potential to be better than her or provide her anything outside herself.

But another presence was near, and time was ... not time.

Camilla and Radiance felt the power flowing through her, the incredible magnificence and uncontainable force of it. It was too much for her, yet all she wanted was it. It sated and hurt and … and … and … and ….

Odaza watched the fires and watched their power flow through Camilla and Radiance. She knew, though Camilla did not, that Camilla would not be able to hurt herself again with the power, not unless she called much, *much* more of it, for she saw what to Camilla was still the future. Most Ellenari struggled to comprehend how Time flowed for the time-born, but it was easier for Odaza than most. She watched and waited, and reached out with her affinity for time. This was a moment that must be contained, yet must be. It must not be cut short but must remain to the fullness of what it was for the time-born dragon and Dragonrider, yet it could not be allowed to go on, to ravage the world. It must be kept and contained until the time was right for the time-born for her to pass on.

Even now, with all she was and saw and experienced and knew, there was so much Odaza did not understand about the mistakes and misunderstandings of the time-born.

Magic on the Sea

Camilla hated being on the ship so much. She could not get space alone, and she did not want to play with her magic, her fire, on the ship in front of or around the Sea Elves. That alone would have been enough, but it was fire, and ships were vulnerable to fire, and she knew the Sea Elves knew that and feared it. Even if they trusted her control, which was unlikely, they would still be uncomfortable.

That was a big reason she was uncomfortable, but it was not the only one. She could not sleep with Radiance, and her poor dragon's injuries ached constantly after a few days. Radiance could not rest properly when they were between islands, and it was hard on her being in the air so much, even though she and Ben both followed in the wake of Nelexi's wings so it was much easier for them. Radiance was still rather small, small enough that sometimes, when the seas were very calm, she would swim up to the ship and put her neck over it, or even rest a little of her weight on the stern, and let it carry her to a while.

Then Camilla could sit next to her and stroke her scales, and sometimes Camilla could climb onto her neck and go for a ride or a swim with her. She was tired and sore, but not so tired and sore she did not want to take Camilla for a calm flight now and then. Camilla did not know how to swim, and ordinarily she would not have chosen to learn in the ocean, but with Radiance and Ben's attention focused on her – and the Sea Elves, who belonged to the sea as much as dragons belonged to wind and fire – she was not too worried about it. Mostly, her confidence was in her two dragon friends. They always knew exactly where she was, and exactly how she felt and how she was doing, and they were so strong that, at least as long as the seas were calm, they would never have any trouble rescuing her.

Right now, she leaned against the rail, wet from spray off the sea, and watched Radiance wind rather lazily through the waves between the ships. Her gold scales and wings shone so beautifully in the green of the waves, and the colors the two made as they both reflected off each other were truly magical. As a mage, Camilla did not think that was an exaggeration, and what Radiance had said helped her to realize it. Magic was reality. Magic was who and what they were. So the reflected colors and kaleidoscopes of color were magic, too. It was so surreal and calming. The motions of swimming were different from those of flying, and sometimes the sea offered Radiance some relief, too, especially as she got better at riding the currents that the ships caused by their motion through the water.

Songs drifting through the air pulled Camilla out of her serene contemplation. The fleet was even worse than the city. Most of the time in Ansaifar, one could ignore the fact that there were others not too far away if one wanted to, and getting completely out of the city altogether was an option.

That was not the case here. The closest she could get was going for a short flight with Radiance or Ben, short and infrequent because of how severely taxed their frail strength was by the journey alone. There were other people on this ship with her, at least one of them always awake, and there were so many ships, similarly occupied, all around her.

Were she and the dragons making a mistake by going to Aneri at all? This voyage felt like such an irritating waste of time that she could not do anything with. Would she be better off having gone with Radiance to bring down the Wizard-King of Eltaes? Maybe if she had just done it and tried, she would have known how. Radiance's realization may have been the key. If she tried, if all she thought about was the magic and knowing it, perhaps she could do whatever she needed to. She could not stand the thought of letting the Wizard-King ravage a minute longer than was necessary, or letting anyone who might be her friend or innocent suffer a moment longer when she could, maybe, do something about it.

Then again, she could not – yet – do whatever she wanted and chose, simply by the wanting and choosing. Not to mention what had happened other times, but she had freed only Ben from the Wizard-King and had not been able to free the other dragons, and she had been injured and unconscious from that. Even though she was stronger now, she might not be strong enough.

Perhaps that was it. She and Radiance needed to learn who they were better. They needed to know who they were, understand not just who they were as individuals – since they hardly were distinct individuals anymore, though that mattered too – but who and what they were as *one*. Then, when they knew perfectly – or at least well enough – who and what they were, they would be able to defeat the Wizard-King and free all whom they loved. They would be able to change the world and make it *right* or at least as right as it could be. *Their* unity was right, so there might be a right, after all, though Camilla was not sure what she thought about that.

At last, she had gotten to take a different ship from Sylvara. It was *such* a relief not to have to deal with Sylvara anymore, especially after she decided she did not need or want any more lessons from Lìarz. It had been a last minute arrangement, since she had only decided that on the last day before they sailed, but given how few belongings they had and how adaptable some of the Sea Elves were, it was negotiated easily enough. Simply realizing she would not have to deal with Sylvara's existence for the entire length of the voyage was enough to convince Camilla she was right, even if she *did* want Lìarz's lessons, which she most certainly did not, after what Radiance had pointed out.

She only wished she got a chance to practice again, but that was impractical at best on ship. Camilla was convinced that having Sylvara's presence around, in addition to all the problems inherent in the voyage, would have been too much. Despite her determination to give Sylvara a chance, *knowing* there was more to the other woman that she wanted to accept or admit, she was not sure she would not have killed her. It would be easy enough, the action of a moment. And, if she was being particularly gracious, it was not so bad for Sylvara to have Lìarz's lessons entirely to herself, though not of course his attention. Camilla did not have much of an idea what the voyage was like for that family, and though she could have found out if she wanted to, she did not care enough.

She did know that her brother was already quite bored with the journey, even though he got to play with Arziel and Arziel's family *and* his sister – and Flameheart, sometimes Flameheart and Camilla, sometimes Flameheart and the elf-human family. It was not much trouble for little Sleet, who did not have any injuries that pained him constantly, to pick Lavilor up from one ship and take him to another. Lavilor was adept at climbing up and down the ships, and he was learning to swim quite well and a great deal faster than Camilla. That was part of why she practiced as much as she did, because he did and he liked to, though she would have practiced anyways in order to be with the dragons more. Besides, no skill or knowledge was ever wasted, at least not if one gave up nothing to learn it, which was the case here!

Despite his boredom, or at least his professed boredom, Lavilor seemed very cheerful, and Camilla *knew* that he appreciated the fact that she and Sylvara were no longer fighting and hating each other all the time, if only with looks, concealed tone of voice, and thoughts. Not that he *liked* Sylvara, but he tolerated her, and Camilla had contented herself with the certainty that Sleet would and could look after his rider.

Camilla looked up as the air shuddered under passing wing-beats. Alian! She was shearing awfully close to the boat, and Camilla felt the song of the sailing Sea Elf and the boat shift as she dropped down, skimming her wing right by the sail, as if preparing to land on the boat, and then – mid-wing beat – blurring into red mist and then appearing in human form on the deck a pace or so from Camilla.

The sailing Sea Elf broke off her song and scolded angrily. Camilla could not understand all the words, but the tone would have made it clear enough alone and she *had* picked up quite a handful of Sea Elven words over the past months and weeks, never mind that she did not even have to try to pick up the emotional content seething over the surface of the elf's mind. It was something about how Alian better not scare her again and that was downright spooky, and Camilla was pretty sure some of the words were curses.

Alian responded more graciously and smoothly than Camilla imagined possible and promised that he would make sure to let her know if he did that again – or something like that. Finally he turned to Camilla, who all the time had been waiting a little impatiently, certain that he had come to talk to her and not to pass on some message to the Sea Elves.

"You want to learn magic, don't you?" he asked.

Camilla stalled. "Not the way Lìarz understands or teaches magic."

"I know that," said the were-dragon, "and I'm glad you discovered that. But you asked me a long time ago about wind-reading, and I would not teach you for reasons that aren't entirely unrelated to what you have discovered yourself, but I can point a few things out to you now. It won't really be magic you will be learning, but it might help you."

Camilla huffed. "Sure. Sure."

Alian shifted in a way that reminded her uncomfortably of a dragon. "Watching you, I'm not sure your magic isn't more like the way the Sea Elves sing to the sea than the way the Wood Elves practice their magic. I think I may have suspected that almost from the first time I met you."

Camilla stomped. The wood of the deck made an odd, hollow thump and thwack. "My magic is not like that of *any elf,*" she growled, making the words as insulting and curse-like as she could.

Alian seemed amused, and Camilla wondered why. He was not usually like this, and it was irritating her, though she had not seen him in a long time, so maybe he was like this most of the time these days, though why she could not imagine. "I did not mean to suggest that it was. But you have seen only the Wood Elf magic, the Sea Elf magic, and what I and Serrose do, which is very like the Wood Elf magic. Your magic *is* very unlike the Sea Elf magic. I just think their approach is, in some ways, a little more suitable to yours than the Wood Elf approach. Not like, but not as unlike, either. Is that okay?"

"I guess."

"Until you know something other than elven magic, it will be hard to make other comparisons or point things out to you in other ways. And I don't think you are much like any human mages I know of, either. You and your magic are very, very unique, in very, very many ways." Alian bit something else off, and Camilla did not miss it.

"I hope you mean that. All of it," she said, after a brief moment of consideration. "And I hope you are not trying to … pacify me. For your sake." She did not care how preposterous that sounded, and it was not. She had no doubt she *could* kill this were-dragon if she wanted to, untrained as she was and trained as he was. The only question was whether whatever it was that created – no, better not to think about that. Not right now at least.

"I am not," said Alian. "At least, not by telling falsehoods. By clarifying what I mean, yes. I don't want you to be angry at me, certainly, and if you are upset about a misunderstanding, I will certainly try to make myself as clear as possible."

Alian was jesting. Camilla was sure of it, and she did not like it. "To the point. What else did you have to point out to me?"

"To watch the weather and the sea. Let yourself feel the little things as much as the big ones, and ignore neither. You probably know most of this already, and are doing some of it unconsciously, but I don't think it will hurt to say it. Pay attention to how the song of the Sea Elves and the magic of their voices and the ships interacts with the sea and the wind, the air and the weather. Just get a feel for it. Nothing in particular, and yet everything and anything in specific. Don't try to force it into a pattern, but when a pattern fits don't disregard it out of hand either."

"That goes without saying," said Camilla. It made sense, and she was not going to admit any more learning than she had to. "Is there anything else?"

"If I think of anything, or discover anything in particular I think you might want to direct your attention towards, I will be sure to let you know. And take or leave my advice as it falls. I know you will, but I just want to make sure you know that I understand that. I know you don't care about my approval, but you do want me to respect you."

Alian smiled at her, and Camilla wondered if and how she should ask him about his mood. She did not get a chance. Before she or Radiance could figure anything out, Alian turned, looked out over the ships and judged the best way to take off, taking into account the wind and the spacing of the ships. Mid-jump, his form blurred into red mist.

Camilla understood the Sea Elf's fright at Alian's maneuvers, as the were-dragon's tail flicked right past the rail with easily enough force to shatter the wood, and her claws broke the surface of the rolling seas. Camilla wondered if this was responsible for Alian's mood, or if it was something else. Maybe just being over the ocean reminded her of something. Or it could have something to do with Serrose and their hatchlings. But there could be so many things she would not know about in Alian's life, or the lives that were not Alian's but that affected the were-dragon much as if they were, that she could not know about.

But how was it at all reasonable or acceptable for Alian to consent to watch over and guard and take care of her and these other dragons, when she had a mate and hatchlings who might be in at least some danger? Even if they were not in danger, how could she consent to spend so much of her time away from them, and during such a formative time of their lives? It made no sense to Camilla, knowing how much she longed to have had her Dad, to have had real play-time with her Mom and brother, knowing how much she had missed! How could Alian be so casual about that, even if slavery was not the cause for it in her case?

She decided that she would confront the were-dragon on that the next time they met. In the meantime, Alian did have a point. This boredom need not be wasted, and the were-dragon was absolutely right. If she watched the magic of the weather and the sea and the elves, she might learn a great deal. The way dragons learned to fly.

Hours later, Camilla lay curled in the nook that was her sleeping place on the ship. *"Camilla."*

Ben's mind-voice gently woke her out of half-sleep.

What is it, Ben?

"You don't need to be antagonistic towards Alian." Camilla could not miss the implied undertones. She made certain assumptions about everyone, as easily and naturally as breathing, but Ben thought she did not need to make them about Alian. She knew the were-dragon well enough by now to offer a little more tolerance, if not trust.

There was not anything Camilla had to say to that, and Ben was inclined to leave it be. He only wanted to share his thought, once he had figured things out. Now that he had done so, he was inclined to conserve his energy as well as he could, and let Camilla sleep.

Camilla curled up tighter and closed her eyes as tight as she could. Ben was handling this journey quite well, better than expected, but it was not doing him any good. She wished she could relieve him, trade places with him sometimes, but that was impossible. They could not trade bodies or rest and energy like the were-dragons could change forms.

Discordant Fires

"Let Esdeshë know that I am going to be landing."

Camilla got up and growled under her breath. So this was how Alian meant to let the Sea Elf sailing the ship know when she was going to pull her landing-and-shapeshifting-onto-the-deck stunt! Alian had given her the words she needed to use, to make this simpler, even though by now she probably could have figured it out on her own. Her grammar and pronunciation would probably be atrocious, but she would be understandable. That was not the problem. Camilla realized that she should have guessed that this would be how Alian would let the Sea Elf know when he was coming, since it was so convenient and would work so perfectly, but she did not like it. Nonetheless, it would be terribly rude to Esdeshë not to, and Camilla had no reason to think the Sea Elf deserved the fright over her ship, besides the fact that it was probably safer if Esdeshë knew what was coming and was not frightened.

Trying not to seem upset however was more than Camilla thought it was reasonable for her to attempt.

"Thank you," Esdeshë replied, when relaid what Alian had said. Esdeshë was miffed. Camilla knew it.

She also had no reply to the thanks, so she got out of the way and clung to the rail while Alian pulled her stunt. It was fantastically beautiful, she had to admit. At the same time, she did not particularly want to see Alian at all, even if Ben was right and she should be a little more gracious. It was not as if Alian had ever been or seemed to be an elf. Yetra had been a human. Alian was just asking her to do something because it was convenient for her and did not cost her any effort. Because it was the obvious way to do it. Because she was as special as the Wood Elves had told her that humans were not, and she could do things no one else could. Not because Alian thought she was her slave or servant, to be ordered around at her pleasure.

Lavilor, who had been playing a game he had learned from Lìarz's family with her a moment before, tugged on Camilla's sleeve as Alian came in and neatly transformed and landed on the rocking deck. Camilla could sense his excitement.

Is this the first time you've seen Alian do this? Camilla asked him mind-to-mind. It was hard to talk – and be heard – with the wind from Alian's wings and the rocking of the ship and the fact that, while the sea had not made her sick yet, she was not quite comfortable with everything about the ships. Besides, she liked talking mind-to-mind with Lavilor and he did not seem to mind.

"No. Many times before. Alian does this often on the ship with Lìarz's family."

Camilla did not know why, but for some reason as Lavilor responded, she suddenly realized something. She strode – or at least, strode as well as she could manage – across the deck and stopped in front of Alian with her hands on her hips. "You know something?" she asked, and then did not bother to wait for a response to her question. "You could transform over the ocean and then *climb* onto the ship. Getting a little wet in your humanoid form should not bother you when you spend most of the time in your draconic form." Camilla was proud of her wording. Alian was neither human nor dragon, and she had called neither form either human or dragon, only like the form of a human or a dragon.

Alian smiled at her. "I could. I did not think of that. Thank you for telling me."

"You. Didn't. Think. Of that?" Camilla enunciated each word for effect. "No, I didn't."

"Now!" said Radiance, reminding Camilla, and the Dragonrider did not give Alian a chance to say more. "Well, there's something else you did not think of. Something even more important. You are no longer healing Ben. None of us need you to hunt for us, heal us, or protect us. You should have left us a *long* time ago to be back with your mate and your hatchlings! *If* you should have ever left them!"

Camilla paused, and Alian did not respond. Fury fanned into a flame. "Or is this because you think that I am chosen by some grand destiny and that you were chosen by some grand destiny – I think you called it the Lord of the Light – to guard and watch over me, and that this is more important than the hatchlings you and Serrose have and having time with them? I tell you, *no!* I was a slave! I did not get to know my dad. I did not get the time with my mom I should have! *Don't* do that to yourself and your hatchlings. And, by the fire of all the dragons in the world, there is *no* destiny but what we make ourselves, and I do *not* need you to take care of or watch over me! But your hatchlings might!"

Camilla was so caught up in her passion she hardly noticed Alian take a step back. He held up his hands and said, when she took a breath, "You may have a point."

"I *may* have a point?" Camilla half-growled, half-hissed.

"You may have a point," Alian repeated. "My reasons and thoughts are not what you imagine them to be, but you may have a point. I am not here for the reasons you think I am, but you may have a point that I am not needed here and that I should be elsewhere. In part, I had not thought about how things have changed. In part, I thought it would be good for me to be around when you arrive, but that may be simply an imaginary scenario of mine that may not come to pass. I will think about this."

"Now!" insisted Camilla. She pulled back as she realized that she was about to shout her thoughts and feelings to everyone around, and instead directed what she did not pull back from her draconic shout straight at Alian.

The were-dragon was more sensitive to her speech than the Sea Elves or even most humans, anyways.

Alian flinched, then straightened with an air that made Camilla think of a dragon raising her wings in and stretching her neck up. She could almost feel the mist-like wings enfolded the human-shaped were-dragon. "Camilla," he said, and his voice was no longer soft, listening response, perhaps slightly exasperated, but never defensive nor aggressive. Now it was firm and harsh and certainly not pleased.

"We are were-dragons. If you feel that you must communicate as dragons do and that other speech will not meet your needs, there is no reason that you should not speak to us as dragons do. In fact, if that suits you, you may do so simply because you prefer it. But do not use it to try to enforce your will and understanding on other people." His voice grew softer now, almost understanding, and Camilla *hated* it for that all the more. Who was he to think he was above her? Who was he to feel like he was better than her? "You do not use it to try to make other people live or think as you think best – let alone when they have already understood what you are saying and told you they will consider it because you may be right!"

Camilla stood straighter and threw her shoulders out with a gesture that echoed and re-echoed across her body with Radiance. She felt like a dragon throwing her wings out. She was more dragon, *far* more dragon than these were-dragons. "You will still think about it right? Or do you only listen to those you think are being reasonable and because I have done something that you do not like, you will now decide not to think about what I have told you, or even that you will do otherwise, because you do not like me and it is not truth you care about?"

Ben's voice hissed and slithered in the back of her mind, and Camilla felt a part of her – a part of her that was so interwoven with Radiance it was impossible to tell where one ended and the other began – listen. Was she *trying* to provoke Alian into fighting with her? Because that was what it looked like – she was being as antagonistic as she could and she was interpreting what Alian said, and what he did not say, in the most antagonistic way possible.

"I do not know what you want, Camilla," said Alian, with the breeze of a sigh. "Is it that you care about whether I want to listen to you, or is it that you care about whether I will listen to what you've said, what you believe is right?"

Alian's question arrested Camilla mid-heartbeat. Which was it? "Both!" she screamed in his face. Then she embraced Ben and brought him as close in to who she was and how she thought as she always should have, as she had when she freed him from the Wizard-King.

"Then I do not know what answer to give you. I will think about what you have said. Am I right that you are uninterested in any other conversation?"

Camilla brought her hands together in front of her chest and a flame breathed up out of them. It flickered and danced along the under-curves of her chin. "Just go," she said, her voice a breath of calm compared to what it had been.

Alian turned and, like he had previously, took a running leap from the ship's deck, sailing over the stern. The ruby mist formed as his body skimmed the tops of the waves, and as a dragon she rose up, her wings stirring through the waters, but her tail flicking a comfortable distance from the ship. Lavilor touched Camilla's sleeve again as Alian rose.

"The twins who sail with Lìarz," Lavilor said, "like watching how close Alian can get. It is so fun! It is a game!"

"I don't want to talk about Alian," said Camilla, staring into her flame. Like almost all of her fire, it did not smoke.

"Okay, then," said Lavilor, "but what was that fight about?"

"The obvious. But I said I don't want to talk about Alian."

"Okay. You have gotten a lot better with your fire since the last time I saw. It looks like it dances."

"It does," said Camilla. She sat down gracefully without disturbing the flames and held out her hands to show them to Lavilor. They increased in size and continued to lick at the undersides of her face.

"It really does," her little brother said, admiringly, but keeping a comfortable distance. "Can you make it – anything?"

Camilla nodded. Even when she spoke, it was as if she lived in silence, but silence that was not disturbing or dead, silence that was huge and full with music and harmonies no sound could express, silence that allowed the music to live when any sound would have stifled or drowned it.

"Then I want – a dragon!" said Lavilor.

She said nothing, but the flames took the shape of a fiery dragon, with wide-spread wings and flickering tail of flame, the whole shape outlined and formed in fire. It moved, lived, danced. The small part of her that was not consumed in the silence of the hot-burning flames remarked that it was not really a surprise, but she worked with Lavilor like with no other – except those whose souls were welded into hers. It was easy for her to let his desire and his thoughts become a part of the shaping of the fire, for her to channel them into the fire as it breathed. The fire hissed and sizzled, almost but not quite quiet, yet even its soft, hot voice had the feel of a silence as great as the sky.

Then she moved her hand and two dragons rose in the fire. Their wings and necks caressed her shoulders. Lavilor oohed and ahhed.

She did not look up from her creation, the extension of herself. "It won't burn you, Lavilor," she said quietly.

He edged closer and put out his hand. "It feels hot. Very hot."

"Does it hurt? Put your hand as far in as you can as long as it doesn't hurt. I won't let it hurt you."

Lavilor obliged, and Camilla felt it. At the same time, all she felt was the fire. It was not hard to keep it from burning her brother. It did not want to burn him, it only needed a slight nudge, a reminder of how not to burn him.

After a while, he pulled back. "It feels … strange."

"It do-does," said Camilla. Her voice shuddered as she finished. Her fire shuddered. Her soul shuddered. Something pulled at the fire in a way it never had before, inserted itself into the fire. It blunted the inner flame that had lit in her magic when she freed Ben, cutting her off from the Heartfire. As soon as it started to blanket the inner fire, indecision reached into Camilla with it. The Heartfire was greater than herself, and she had never decided how she really felt about that. Part of her longed for it, ached for it, with a pain that was like the pain she would feel if she were cut off from Radiance in the same way. Part of her wanted forever away from anything that might be greater than her, anything that might be destiny or a greater being, anything that might have a right to tell her – as Ben had tried to tell her – how she should do things and what she should and should not do.

"What happened?" asked Lavilor, instantly sensitive to something going wrong. His fear felt slick and cold against Camilla's mind.

Radiance and Ben brushed closer in against her, warming her. With them, they brought a bit more of the Heartfire, and indecision wavered and slithered through Camilla. Reach out, reach through the blanketing, and reconnect with the Heartfire, pulling it further into herself, or accept and embrace this separation from it? She needed *nothing* outside herself – and Radiance was not truly outside herself, Radiance *was* herself – to live!

The fire in her hands sizzled and went out.

A voice of fire that was like the Heartfire yet had nothing of the Heartfire in it, a dragon's voice, spoke to her.

"Come with us. Come to us. Learn from us. Immortality and power that is within you alone shall be yours. You have only to learn it, for you have it already. You must only capture it, isolate it, and claim it for yourself. Then no other will make your destiny, no other will claim your magic, no other will have its influence in your soul."

As the dragon spoke, waves of fear and consternation from all around her broke over Camilla. She stood, Lavilor clinging to her, to see for herself what spoke and what provoked fear and worry from everyone around her, more people than she could count or name, even with her draconic sensitivity. Then she felt a wave of pride, of confidence and courage and encouragement, riding underneath the worry and fear.

Black dragons circled against the sky. They were much smaller than Nelexi and had brown wings and spinal stripe instead of the glowing red, but there were many of them. Nelexi hovered between them and the fleet, and Camilla knew they feared the Obsidian Guardian dreadfully.

Then *she* feared the Obsidian Guardian. Nelexi would take the choice out of Camilla's hands if she could. She was the embodiment of the Heartfire, and she would bind Camilla to the Heartfire and never let Camilla choose or escape. Everything wanted to make Camilla its slave. It was not just the Wood Elves, it was the were-dragons, Alian and Serrose, it was Nelexi, it was everyone and everything whose path she had ever crossed!

"I know you think that you and the dragon are one self, but we are the ones who are immortal and powerful, we who have no riders and have escaped the bonds of what you call the Heartfire. You, and you alone, must claim your destiny, your magic, your fire, your soul. Even your dragon, had she not bonded to you, would be a slave of the Wood Elves, like her mother and her mother's mother and all her relations? She is not special. She has not chosen to be free. You have. You alone have chosen freedom! Be free!"

The voice flickered and burned its way into Camilla's bitterness, her rages and discontents.

"You will have your true power, forever outside the power of any other, only when you claim your power from the Heartfire and take it for yourself alone."

Camilla clenched and unclenched her fists. She was barely aware of Lavilor clinging to her arm, of Sleet's voice at the back of her awareness. She could not think straight, yet it seemed everything ought to be so clear. The Heartfire had not been part of her before she freed Ben. Yet, for some reason, she could not call the fire with a whisper of dancing thought now. The dancing thought would not form, or else the fire would not respond. Not as it had come to her recently, when she danced the fire on the porch, or many other times, most recently a few minutes ago when she called the fire and merged herself into it to escape from her confrontation with Alian.

Insensate fear and rage crawled into her being with a fire of its own. Was she even on this fleet of her own choice? Did she know where she was going or why? Could she leave whenever she wanted to? No, not like Alian. She was trapped, a captive, a slave. The Sea Elves were no different than the Wood Elves. The black dragons were right. Nelexi was using her as a tool for her own ends. What else would a creature so ancient and so powerful want with her? She had always been uncomfortable about Nelexi's interest in her, about the black dragon's attempt to guide her path or at least suggest paths to her, her insistence that Camilla learn certain things, and those first, unguarded intrusions into how Camilla chose to live and think. Obviously, Alian wanted to use her. Otherwise, the were-dragon would have left long ago to be with her young. Alian had nearly admitted as much with his explanation of why he had stayed with Camilla so long.

This was wrong! It *had* to go! No one would use or control her or think they had *any* power over her ever again!

A whisper ghosted through her mind. *But don't they? Don't they have power over you? Don't Radiance and Ben have power over you? Doesn't everyone you love have power over you? Doesn't it open you up to the power of others every time you love someone?*

All coherence fled thought. *No!* Camilla screamed, soundlessly but with every power she had. *No* one had power over her! *NO ONE!* At least, no one would have power over her as soon as she learned who she really was! All she had to do was insist upon it.

Fire cut across the sky-scape of her mind. Fire flowed across the skies above her. The Heartfire pulled at her and her fire pulled at her, and she knew – though she hated it – that the Heartfire had always burned in her fire and always would, however much it was dampened. It was part of her bond with Radiance, the heart of fire that welded them into one.

Above her, Nelexi dove, wrapped around and around in fire that shimmered at the edges of her scales. The other black dragons split, trying to attack the ships. Camilla saw Alian trying to guard another flank, smaller and slightly more nimble than Nelexi, but unable to bear the full brunt of a diving black dragon. Nelexi took one, right into her flank, and the other dragon's fire swirled harmlessly around her scales. The Obsidian Guardian only staggered in flight, while the dragon whose dive she had intercepted seemed stunned. A moment later, it was done for, as Nelexi's back tails racked across one wing.

Fear! Fear! Fear!

Watching Alian play tag with two of the obsidian dragons, protected now and then by Nelexi who stayed just involved enough to keep more from ganging up on the more vulnerable were-dragon, reminded Camilla of who she was and what she believed. Shimmer and Sleet worked behind Alian, small wings of shining silver, essaying forth and nipping, sometimes breathing fire, helping to keep the black dragons from flanking them, but too small and vulnerable to really get involved in the fight. Ben and Radiance were not yet there, and Camilla did not want them there.

She reached out and spoke to Alian. *You have hatchlings. Do not endanger yourself so that your hatchlings will never know you. That is how I never knew my father. Do not do this.*

Alian did not respond, and Camilla realized she should not distract her. She wondered if she could help, but –

The thought never had to be finished. Now that Camilla looked closer, she could see that the obsidian dragons were clearly disengaging. One of them, then a pair, got themselves clear and turned tail, fleeing into the winds. In a few moments, they were all clearly following.

Immortal

Flameheart sat astride Nelexi as the two soared high on the winds. They were the first to see the flight of obsidian dragons winging in. *Why are they coming again?* asked Flameheart. *Don't they remember what happened last time?* The last time they had fought the nightmare obsidian dragons, Nelexi had killed three of them. The obsidian dragons usually did not fight Nelexi at all, but scattered and fled as soon as they saw her. Attacking her was unthinkable.

"It is almost unprecedented, but it is not unprecedented. Nightmare dragons have attacked the Obsidian Guardian before, though more often it is what the Obsidian Guardian is protecting that they attack."

Flameheart leaned over Nelexi's neck as if that would give her a better view. The dragon was already sharing her view with her rider. *Then why are they attacking? What do they want? What do they gain? The sinking of a single ship?*

"They are the Old Gods, Flameheart. They are the Nightmare."

And we love, thought Flameheart. She felt Nelexi descend. She was not afraid, not this time. She did not panic. She did not worry that she was useless or worse, a liability.

Then the obsidian dragons spoke.

Flameheart doubled over Nelexi's shoulder, laughing. *Immortality? Immortality! It is* you *who are immortal! They* can *be killed.*

"You, too, heart of my fire. We are *immortal. The Heart of Fire will welcome us both to immortality."*

And they are not. Not as they are. It *was* ironic. But there was no way they could tell Camilla that. She understood it. She *had* to understand it, or at least know it, if she chose to. There was no way they could tell her. If she would not believe her own knowledge, she could not believe what they told her either, and she would certainly think they were interfering with her life and trying to control her.

We would be, wouldn't we? Not perhaps by intent or the way she would understand it, but we would be.

"Like breaking a dragon out of her egg instead of letting her hatch on her own. Sometimes she can't hatch on her own and it is necessary to break her out, but if it can be helped, it is better not to."

Flameheart and Nelexi watched as the renegade obsidian dragons flapped nearer and nearer, and terror broke out among the Sea Elves. Even up in the sky, Flameheart thought she could feel it. *We have to protect them!* she nearly screamed at Nelexi, clutching the leather of the saddle.

"I know. We will." Nelexi's voice was ineffable calm, as steady as a rock lodged in the sea floor, unmoved by any current or storm or tide, as steady as the earth itself that remains, washed and scoured forever by wind and rain

and ocean.

Flameheart felt like no one could hear that voice and fear again, or at least fret while that voice spoke. There seemed to be nothing steadier than Nelexi's wings. She knew, the next moment, when Nelexi spoke to the Sea Elves. *"I am here."* It was short and simple, but it reminded them. And more than a few of them had been there when she protected their fleet a half year or so ago against these same obsidian dragons, killing three of them.

The obsidian dragons drew nearer, and Nelexi rose to engage them. *"Flameheart, your voice and presence are to me much what I am to you,"* she said.

Flameheart put her hands on Nelexi's obsidian scales and yelled into the wind in her own language, heedless that no one would hear her voice or be able to understand her if they did. "Do you want to be immortal? Find the love that guards you!"

That day marked a drastic change in Flameheart's interactions with Camilla. Nothing she could say, and no way she could respond to Camilla's accusations would alleviate the older girl's concerns on the few occasions that the Dragonrider spoke them – or more often, yelled or growled, though she also had the capacity to share her problems or perceived problems in a voice so cold and calm yet foreboding the wrath within like thunderheads about to burst. Flameheart thought, "We did not do anything except protect the fleet from the obsidian dragons, and what else could we have done?" ought to have been more than enough, but Camilla would not believe her and insisted that Flameheart and Nelexi were trying to control her for their own ends and bind her to their secret magic so that she would perceive that her power came from them, and so would be controlled by them. She would not go into any more detail than that and, in fact, she did not even precisely *insist* on anything. She simply declared it and told Flameheart and Nelexi to go away and leave her alone.

Then, one day, she reached out to Flameheart in the same way Nelexi often spoke to her. Her voice was so different from Nelexi's, yet there *was* something in it that was deeply akin to Nelexi's, and like Nelexi's, it was dominated by fire. An undertone of fire that was profoundly comforting, enfolding and embracing, ran through its highlights, though it was scorching and fierce in a fundamentally different way, and that scorching fierceness was directed at *her. "You don't belong here, and you certainly don't belong trying to influence me through Ben."*

Flameheart felt Nelexi support her in a way that was so fundamental it was as if the Obsidian Guardian were the air she breathed and yet all around her like supporting rock, yet leaving her free to move however she saw fit. There for her the moment Flameheart sought her, and even if Flameheart did not seek her, but also not imposing herself. It was the best relationship in the world.

Ben isn't yours, Flameheart replied. *I'm not trying to influence you through Ben at all, and he can make his own decisions. He's not mine either.*

Flameheart thought Camilla stumbled a bit at that, but she raged on. *"Keep yourself away from me and mine. Don't you have enough already?"*

Flameheart clutched for Nelexi physically and mentally. Without the black dragon's support, she did not think she would have been able to hold her own against Camilla. Her thoughts would have been completely overwhelmed, incinerated. Even so, Camilla's fury raged against her mind, singeing her within. It was a bit like how she always felt around Camilla when she was angry, but immeasurably worse. Could this dragon-mage not see that she was the one trying to force her influence on others? Flameheart could not even talk properly to Ben – at least, she could not hear anything he said except as relayed by Nelexi. Mostly, she did not even try to talk to Ben. She and Nelexi just played with him in the ocean sometimes, often with Lavilor and Sleet, and sometimes with Sylvara and Shimmer, or just with the dragons.

"That's enough," said Nelexi. Flameheart felt the black dragon raise a barrier of her own between her rider and Camilla, incomplete but definitely there. A few moments later, the contact vanished altogether.

For the rest of the voyage, she tried not to interact with Camilla. Nelexi would not talk to her much about Camilla, and she was poised between a pity and sympathy she knew Camilla would not accept from her anymore, if she ever accepted it from anyone, and something harder, harsher. Whenever she thought too much about Camilla, Nelexi would usually distract her, and Camilla did not mind-touch her again, though she somehow knew that Camilla was mad at her for poisoning Lavilor with her influence and, at times, considered her and Nelexi to be 'of Sylvara's ilk'.

She was not about to stop playing with Lavilor and Sleet however, or with Ben when the red dragon wanted to participate. Nor would she refuse to offer Lavilor comfort, sometimes holding him but more often simply sitting next to him, when he was overcome with grief and wept for the life he had lost – in a way that was so much worse than the way she had lost her family. Even though Ben was so exhausted that his play was usually of the lackadaisical sort, Flameheart could tell that he was getting stronger.

It was her favorite voyage so far, because she could ride Nelexi most of the time and she was rarely sea-sick, but she also got to eat the food the Sea Elves made. None of it was her favorite food, but the Sea Elves were extremely accommodating and gave her the best they had. Sometimes, they were almost uncomfortably accommodating, but when Flameheart felt that way, Nelexi would point out that she was doing a service for them, providing them protection that they could never get for themselves, and it did not cost them very much to keep her rider healthy while she was protecting them.

Several times, they stopped by islands for the other dragons to recover and regain their strength. Then, she got to walk on firm ground and find the ever-in-season tropical fruits. She could not gorge on them without having them come out the other end far too quickly, but she could still enjoy many of them. Funnily enough, Nelexi assured her that some of the ones she did not like at all were the favorite foods of other people. But her enjoyment of the islands was sullied because Camilla tried to make sure that she and Lavilor did not have fun playing together on the beaches or in the trees. They liked to play games like hide-and-seek once the dragons made sure that an area was free of dangerous snakes and other animals, or build sand volcanoes and run in the surf.

But though Camilla did not try to force her brother not to play with Flameheart, whenever Lavilor and Flameheart wanted to play, she either invited Lavilor to play with her somewhere else, or stood there, watching them and making herself quietly – loudly – intrusive, radiating disapproval, anger and superiority or whatever it was that was going on with her. Flameheart tried to ignore her, but she longed for a return of the comforting fire that had so often hovered around Camilla even when she was most angry or embittered. There were still faint echoes of it, but they were stifled by something else now. It made her heart ache, even though she had Nelexi. Maybe it was just the promise of what could be, the memory of what was, and the hope of what ought to be that made her sad. Camilla's fire had all the tragedy of a thing marred now.

So, sometimes it was Flameheart who cut short the play with Lavilor, too heavy of heart to continue under Camilla's presence, even though she dearly enjoyed playing with Lavilor and in someways he had become for her the home that she missed so dearly. He and Nelexi, both. Then she would go to Nelexi, who would enfold her in her presence and in the fire of her heart, the fire that rose from a deeper heart, that promised and whispered so enticingly and convincingly of all things made right, healed and made whole in a flood of molten flame. Sometimes, Nelexi would cover her with her wings, but more often she would take her into the sky, where Flameheart often felt as if a song was being born in her throat and heart, but one she could not yet give voice to or which would be ruined if she tried. It had to be born in its own perfect time.

The Nightmare creatures seemed to follow them in a straggling convoy across the ocean, and now and then one or maybe a cohort caught up with them. They were ugly and deformed and often dripping with poison and gore, and sometimes Flameheart felt as if it infested her too, especially after she thought about Camilla or had to interact with her. It was hard, then, for her to simply be herself, free and full of the fire of promise. Occasionally Lavilor and

Sleet fought with them, occasionally Sylvara and Shimmer.

Oftentimes, Flameheart felt as if Lavilor were the bonded twin of her soul. Just being around him usually refreshed her, brought the flames in her heart to roaring delight again, soothed and comforted her. They did not have to speak and usually did not, but she loved him like no one else. His Sleet was so beautiful, too. The silver dragon was growing into a length as sinuous and fluid as a serpent and always shining silver. Never, thought Flameheart, had she seen a winged creature so graceful. The movements of his wings, the liquid grace of his form, were so much like the whispering tongues of fire that licked at air or fresh fuel, so much like fire that sometimes he seemed to be a silver flame himself, yet almost a sea serpent too.

Do you see Sleet like I do? Flameheart asked Nelexi one day.

"No creature sees any other quite the same," said Nelexi.

Flameheart said nothing in return, simply took the reply to ponder. Right now, Sleet was sporting below them with Lavilor clinging to his neck, and in a few minutes Flameheart asked another question. *Does it sometimes seem to you that Sleet is the wrong name? That it does not fit the dragon as my name, Flameheart, does?*

"It is possible," said Nelexi reflectively. *"Ben's name was not always Ben. It used to mean to waver, to be unsteady and unsure, but Camilla called him Ben, changed his name to that. Or it might be that we are missing some-thing or not seeing clearly, either the dragon or that for which he is named."*

They flew on, banking and gliding while Lavilor and Sleet frolicked below like a creature born of river and fire. They were so beautiful in their play, and Flameheart's heart constricted thinking of her old home, her old family. Dragons were so beautiful, so wonderful. Was it really a decree of Zharda that they not be allowed upon her Plains and that their riders were never to visit again, or was that a misunderstanding, something that's true meaning was lost to the winds of time?

Suddenly, Sleet reared up, banked, and climbed suddenly. A strange, rancid odor that smelled like what Flameheart always imagined when she thought of the River of Death – though she had been told it did not smell like anything more sinister than any other wetland – reached her and Nelexi as they suddenly dropped altitude and the wind from the ocean met their nostrils.

Flameheart saw it then, sliding between the ocean waves like a marring, towards the fleet whose leading edge broke the water a furlong or two behind the dragons. *This one comes from in front!*

"The Nightmare does not come from *Ellenesia only or precisely, Flameheart,"* Nelexi chided gently.

Can you fight it? urged Flameheart, almost panicking. Despite her proximity to Nelexi, despite everything, foreboding and fear, something like despair, seemed to strangle her with the smell of the monstrosity. She could not have said what she felt, never could. It was a pit of nothingness that had no name. It was a marring, a ruinousness thing, or ruinousness itself.

"I can drive it under, perhaps chase it away for a moment. I cannot defeat it once for all. I may not even be able to keep it far." Nelexi's voice was as warm as lava, as solid as bedrock, dark as comfort and support, bright as hope.

Can you keep it from me? Flameheart asked, struggling in the grips of rising hysteria. Any moment now and she would drown, and who knew what would happen to her then. *No, no, NO!* She was trying to remind herself of all she was, all she loved and enjoyed, and it was not working. She could not remember.

"Hush, Flameheart. Be still, heart of my fire. There's nothing to fear, nothing to fear. I love you. I will always protect you with my very self. You're safe, flame of my flame. Safe, always. Nothing can harm you now. The Heart of Fire awaits us, is within us. Safe, Flameheart. You won't drown, not in this. In the Heart of Fire – one day you will. That's a promise."

Flameheart clung to Nelexi's voice, as gentle and earnest and fierce, but all with softness, as that of a mother. Past the words, past the thought, there was the meaning, and past the meaning there was union and love. She clung to the voice, and let the voice wrap itself around her, enfolding her. As Nelexi spoke, she flamed, and her flame cleared the air. The wind rushing past Flameheart now bore the essence of the Volcano the dragon had once shown her. She clung to its promise, and even the stench of despair could not resist it.

Nelexi twisted through the air, like a sea serpent herself, and the ocean boiled into steam around them. Flameheart's hair fell lank across her face. Nelexi's scales and the leather of the saddle both turned slick. Terrible cries of anguish past despair tore at the very edges of her hearing, then Nelexi's voice cut through it all with immeasurable softness. It was surprising how firm softness could be, how tender ferocity was. One just had to get into the heart to realize it. The heart of gentleness was the firmer the gentler it was, and tenderness was the spring and volcano of ferocity. Rage was a poor, infantile imitation, weak and brittle by comparison.

And that was when the song was born. It rose up in Flameheart's throat, clear as water, thick as lava, bright as fire, impenetrable as volcanic rock.

> Heart of the deeper heart
> Take me away, take me deeper
> Fire in the deepest part
> Sing me the promise, sing me nearer
>
> Earth flows forth from a sea of flame
> Ever renewed from a heart of fire
> That never grows feeble from ages that pass
> Renewed from within, a living heart of fire

Heart of fire, tempest so still
Womb of fire, that to the earth gave birth

Souls long born from the living flame
Flames re-issued from the soul of fire
A conflagration long due as time rolls by
To enfold earths and souls in arms of heart's fire

So, heart of the deeper heart
Return me home, return me steadfast
Oh, fire in the deepest part
Draw me to haven, draw me at last

Fire so deep, the flame-well of life
Bright as the sun, molten and melting
Form re-forming in the blackness all life enfolding
Earth is submerged in her heart of fire overflowing

Shallim-Araldor
Heart that beats within our hearts
Fire that fans our flames to life

Fire that whispers and enchants, light
All to fire and vision entrances
And flame will cover the world again, once born
From fire reborn again, and wings of fire soar!

So, heart of the deeper heart
Take me within, take me your kin
Fire in the deepest part
Wrap me all around, enfold again

Camilla stood on the prow of the ship, watching the land rise out of the sea between the sails ahead of her. She was soon able to discern actual detail on the headlands, which seemed to be a mixture of rocky cliffs and shallow, open bays, all gleaming in the light. She thought white towers sparkled on the promontory directly ahead of them, where a cliff-dominated shoreline dropped down into a gentle bay.

Camilla could not wait any longer. Radiance swam alongside the ship, and Camilla grabbed the rail and swung herself over and around. She landed, as they had intended, on Radiance's shoulder and struggled to keep balance, as the dragon's scales rolled over her muscles and she swerved away from the ship, unfolding her wings. Sea-spray from the mounting waves half-soaked Camilla.

If she had not been so close to Radiance they were almost one mind, she would have fallen. As it is, they worked together in as much synchrony as the arms and legs of a coordinated acrobat. Radiance reared up out of the water as they rose to the wave-crest, and Camilla slipped onto her shoulders, her legs resting against Radiance's muscles as if the two of them had been molded specifically for each other.

Then they were climbing, Radiance's wings driving her through the winds with smooth, sure stokes, alternating with the gliding down-sweeps. The wind was rising and it blew from the west. The dragon pulled even with the leading edge of the fleet, then ahead. Camilla's heart sang with the joy of the sky. They passed briefly under the wheeling shadow of Nelexi, and Camilla rejoiced that now she could part ways from the huge black and red dragon.

Then the city on the shore came into glorious focus. Veins of rock of other colors, greens, blues, reds, and grays wove through the towers and buildings of the city. Subtle shades of gray, here and there darkening to a true black, had been woven through the stone-work to create an entrancing effect that was amazingly more like the effect of flowing water and light than anything else. She had not seen any cities other than Ansaifar and, now, this one, Eskeliae she thought, but there were both similarities and differences.

Themes relating to the ocean dominated Eskeliae, as they had Ansaifar, and white stone was also predominant, but for all that, they were very, very different. Both were pieces of art and Camilla briefly wondered how they had been planned and designed by Sea Elves who did not ride dragons and could not view their cities from above. She wondered what the effect would be on the ground. And, she thought, she liked Eskeliae more than Ansaifar, not that there was anything wrong with Ansaifar, other than certain attitudes of the Sea Elves which were probably as much of a problem here as there.

Recalling that, she remembered that the Sea Elves had, until recently, been at war with the Sha'adhri, the Dragonriders of this new continent. They might not exactly welcome the sight of her and Radiance, even if peace had been made. Then again, they had to know that she came with the fleet from Ansaifar, so she decided not to worry about it too much.

Just at that point, she noticed Lavilor and Sleet flying up beside them. Gently, she touched her brother's thoughts with joy. *Lavilor.*

She felt his bright, happy response. This was good. Solid land again was good. Many things were good. Then the deep sorrow that would mar every moment and never really go away: Mom was not here. Mom was gone.

This time, Camilla did not assure him that she would rescue Mom. How could she really know that their mother had not been killed? She could not. She could hope, but she did not know, even if she would not doubt either. And, regardless, she was not with them *now*, even if Camilla did find her and bring them back together.

The city grew larger, spread out beneath them, revealing ever subtler patterns and new pictures in the shapes and gradients they formed. Camilla marveled at it, but she could not let it distract her. She and Lavilor could finally part ways with both Sylvara and Nelexi. The first thing she was going to do was find the Sha'adhri. She did not need them to show her and Radiance what it meant to be dragon and Dragonrider, but it might be helpful to them to know dragons who had not been twisted and deformed by the elven magic. It might even help her with her magic more than anything else, since what she really needed was to know herself. After that, she would decide whether she really thought it was a good idea to go to the Light Elves as Nelexi had suggested, or whether that was just the black dragon trying to control her. But the first order of business was to find and meet the Dragonriders. She could not imagine how wonderful that was going to be.

Camilla did not really own anything, but Lìarz had bought her more of a wardrobe than she had ever owned before. There were outfits for both warm and cold weather, and clothes made to be beautiful as well as ones made to be functional. She also had a packet of basic tools and some of the most basic herbs. So, when the fleet came into the bay below Eskeliae, Camilla and Radiance were waiting with Lavilor and Sleet. Radiance and Sleet rolled in the sand nearby, satisfying their curiosity about what the sand on a different beach across the sea would be like. Ben had dug himself a sort of den in the warm, thick sand further down the beach, and was drowsing, overtaken by exhaustion. His tight, sore muscles relaxed in the warm sand. Lavilor hopped, skipped, and ran back and forth between his friends.

It was not hard for Camilla to keep an eye for the ship that had carried her and her things, not after living every day for months on it, or having to find it again and again whenever she went flying. In so large a fleet, some of the designs that the Sea Elves had painted on their ships were similar, but not one was quite like any other, whether in shape or color.

Hours passed, while the sun dropped low over the sea dazzling her watching eyes, before that part of the fleet came into the unloading docks. Meanwhile, more people than Camilla believed possible hustled back and forth, moving and organizing and unloading, sometimes with calm, exact order, as if everything were in order, sometimes with excited voices, earnest and discovering, and occasionally with a bit of dismay. Camilla guessed that some things had been mis-placed, either left behind or somehow put on someone else's ship. Either way, it was none of her concern.

Camilla took her things, including a fine saddle for Radiance, from Esdeshë, one of the two Sea Elves who sailed the ship she had ridden in. She carried them to where Radiance and Sleet frolicked and asked Radiance to keep an eye on the bags and make sure they did not get sand into them. Then she ran back with Lavilor, as the ship that had borne Lìarz and his family, as well as Sylvara, was finishing unloading. Straightening her spine and getting her breathing under control as quickly as she could, she approached Lìarz and asked – politely demanded, rather – for Lavilor and Sleet's things.

Lìarz had them handed to her and Lavilor, and her sore muscles trembled under the weight of Sleet's saddle.

Lavilor tugged on her arm again and demanded her attention. "What is going on, Camilla? Are we leaving without the others?" he asked. His eyes demanded an answer.

"Don't you want to? I want to find the Sha'adhri, the Dragonriders here, as soon as possible."

"Wouldn't the best way to do that be to go with Flameheart? She knows." He looked worried, unsure, in a way that hurt Camilla more than anything else could.

"Flameheart's dragon, Nelexi, wants to make me what she thinks I should be. Lots of people react that way to my powers, you know. I want to spend some time away from her."

"I don't think Flameheart is like that. I like playing with her."

"I know, and she might not be. She was just chosen by Nelexi a few years ago. She might be being used, too." She did not believe Flameheart was innocent, though. She was too quiet – unwilling to get involved in certain kinds of things. Camilla just knew Flameheart was a part of it, and knew it too. She was certainly not too young to get involved in intrigue and manipulation. Sylvara had been a deceiving, venomous shanxthar from when she was much younger than Flameheart was now, not that Camilla knew Flameheart's age precisely.

"I will go with you," said Lavilor in a way that hurt Camilla even more. She knew exactly what it meant. He would go with her, since she made him have to choose, but this was not his choice and he did not approve. She hated doing this to him, but for both their sakes they had to get away from people like Nelexi and people like Sylvara. Maybe not permanently – probably not permanently – for Nelexi probably would not let her escape and *would* go back to the Sha'adhri she manipulated too, but at least for a little while.

"You'll see them again," said Camilla. "I just don't think they'll make meeting other Dragonriders as much of a priority as I want to. But we'll certainly see them again." She was not sure why she spoke. Lavilor understood her well enough, not to mention the time they spent in empathic contact, to know how she felt, what she did and did not mean and *how* she meant it.

Lavilor changed the conversation for her. "How will we find these – Sha'adhri?"

Camilla strode back towards the dragons. "I will ask. I speak enough Anerian trade tongue I should be able to make my need understood. I'll get a map perhaps. If the Sea Elves can't or won't help me, I'll find some humans. It won't be hard for me and Radiance to do that." The one down-side of her decision to refuse all interaction with Nelexi and Flameheart was that her lessons in Anerian had ceased with them.

Lavilor nodded, almost bouncing. After all, she was carrying the dragon saddle, which was most of the weight. He was only carrying several changes of clothing, possibly some toys, and probably a tools kit including a knife or two. "I speak Anerian quite well, I am told! And I speak Sea Elven, too! We won't have any problem being understood."

Camilla wished she could reach over to tousle his hair, but that was not possible with the saddle trying to slip out of her aching arms. "I'm glad of that," she said. "And if I have to, I will do things another way."

This time, Camilla and her brother dragged their things all the way to where Ben dozed. The red dragon raised his head from the sea to look them and the bags and equipment over, then stretched out again in the sand. It felt good between his scales. The humans put their things just far enough away from him he would not shower them with sand when they got up, but close enough *no* one could possibly think they might be able to get them with even a sleeping dragon guarding. *Though why I'm concerned about thieves out here, I don't know. It's highly doubtful any of the Sea Elves would want to steal our things.*

Since there was still an hour of daylight left, maybe two before full dark, Camilla and Lavilor mounted Radiance and Sleet bareback for the short ride back to Eskeliae. The dragons landed, and Camilla finally took an eye to the city up close, even though the light was falling. The gates stood open, carved like mounting waves, with facing of different stones to create an effect like the texture and shading of a wave. Over their heads, the arches loomed, no less impressive, carved to resemble foam. Staring at it, she was so taken aback she actually took a step back.

"What?" asked Lavilor.

"The city. The dragons," Camilla whispered. "Look at the city. Whatever the war between the Sea Elves and the Dragonriders was, it left this intact. It permitted the Sea Elves to *maintain* this. Does this look like a city ravaged by war to you?"

Lavilor shook his head, but Camilla knew he did not have an idea in his mind of what a city ravaged by battle *would* look like. After all, dragon fire probably would not do much to this city.

"Well, whatever it is, let's get those directions," said Camilla. She took his hand in hers again and walked into the city. She hoped they would not come across Sylvara or Flameheart, but this city was easily big enough that was unlikely to happen in an hour or so, unless Sylvara or Flameheart were actively trying to find her, which would be as suspicious as anything.

Camilla swallowed her distaste of the Sea Elves and the way they looked at her – she had forgotten to wear gloves – and approached one. In fact, the way they looked at her sort of made it easy to speak to them. In short order, she and Lavilor were directed to the Library of Eskeliae, which a rather pompous Sea Elf told them was "sadly, quite a poor thing, but a much improved, glorious thing it is quickly becoming, now that the dragons are no longer a threat and our people must flee Ansaifar on Ellenesia, bringing with them all that glory that is portable, though doubtless a new city will rise upon the shores of Areaer somewhere." There was a bit more to it that Camilla did not understand about *why* or how this new city would rise, but she did not care about it. Walking away, in the direction she had been told the Library would be found and keeping the landmarks in the front of her mind – she had taken the liberty of touching the Sea Elf's mind to see them directly so there was no doubt she would mistake them – she commented to Lavilor how pompous and absurd the Sea Elf's flowery speech was.

Lavilor giggled – almost sadly – in response.

The Library was unmistakable. The wall around it was carved everywhere with the usual waves and sea imagery, of course, but scrolls and books had been woven into it with an artistry that made Camilla wish the world were other than it was and she had the opportunity to make beautiful, artistic designs. The waves flowed into scrolls; the curl of a breaking wave was the curl of a scroll. A wave flowed out of a book. Another scroll was the tail of a fish. Even in the diminishing light, it was distracting enough to make Camilla have to fight the impulse to stop and stare at the walls, examining them inch by inch. She could feel in Lavilor's grip in her hand that he was interested, too. Radiance's glow in her mind told her the dragon was savoring every inch of this through her eyes.

A minute later, Lavilor was hurrying alongside her, pointing out every animal he saw in the artwork. Camilla smiled. At least he was happy right now. She was almost tempted to leave him to examine the wall, but decided against it. There was no way she was leaving him alone in a city among people she did not know. It would be too hard for Sleet to rescue him out of here if something went wrong.

The wall opened in an arch that was just as wonderfully carved so that it seemed as if it had to be there, not for the sake of utility, but because the wholeness of the art demanded it. Camilla and Lavilor stepped into the shadowed garden, and there too she could see patterns and pictures emerging – or, rather, she felt them teasing on the edges of her awareness and knew that if only she could stop to consider them, she would start to appreciate them. Instead, she pressed on over the path towards the main building, a main building just as artistically crafted. Even inside it, everything had a pattern, an art to it.

Anger uncurled inside Camilla's stomach. She could understand the Sea Elves' pride in their cities and libraries, though this was no poor thing! But it was utterly unconscionable that they lived in luxury and peace, to be able to build all these wonders, and yet would spare no thought for those who were not given the opportunity to have an art of their own! They had not enslaved her people, but Camilla got the distinct impression the Sea Elves did not care about anyone other than themselves. Even if they could do something about the unfortunate situations of others, even if doing something cost them so little it was not worth considering, they would not bother. Meanwhile, her people had no space or allowance to make art of their own. The closest to such a thing she had from them was the constellations. They were not even allowed to choose or pattern their own clothing! They were not permitted to do *any* art, or left much time for it either.

It was dark fully dark outside when they left the library, and Camilla was even angrier, far too angry to appreciate the designs now. First, it had taken her a long time to explain what she wanted and needed, even with a bit of help from Lavilor – who was mostly enamored with the animals in the designs on book shelves and pillars and walls and even the flooring – but that was not why she was more than frustrated. It was not anyone's fault that her grasp of the languages was poor and that what she wanted was not something they had to deal with. How many people came to Eskeliae wanting to know how to find the Sha'adhri? It was no one's fault they weren't prepared for the request.

No, what made her angry was the demand for payment once they had decided what she needed. It was such a simple matter to make a rough map for her with all the information they knew – which was not that much, being a people of the seas and not the inland regions – to help her. It was not even a few hours taken out of a human's life span! It had probably taken less than two hours in all, and that could not have been more than a minute to these creatures who lived for hundreds of years! And they wanted payment for it and a little scrap! In the end she *had* paid them, since they were not impressed by her arguments and finding the Dragonriders was more important to her at the moment than picking a fight with elven pride and indifference. Of course, it was not *her* who had reminded her of the importance of things. Ben played a huge role in that, with Sleet, and Radiance helped, too. Ben was starting to become more than a little bit of a nuisance, but she was thankful to him for this even if she was mad about it too, and he had not complained – like her brother – about parting with Flameheart, so she forgave that, too.

In the end, Lavilor payed with a shell he had been given by Lìarz – at least, Camilla thought it was Lìarz. As she led the way back, cursing the darkness, her map tucked into the breast pouch of her tunic, Camilla said, "You did not have to do that. I'm sure I could have found another way, and I wouldn't want to make you part with such a beautiful, unique gift!"

Camilla felt the shrug of Lavilor's hand in hers. He did not seem bothered by more than her unhappiness. "It was meant to be used like that," he said. "That's the Sea Elf currency." He seemed proud of the big word and rolled it around importantly on his tongue. "I have some more, umm, what humans use as currency, to use with humans if I have to, since Sea Elves are traders so they know and have all the currencies. But mostly I have Sea Elf currency, and Lìarz told me that Sea Elf currency should work most places! People prize unique and shiny things!"

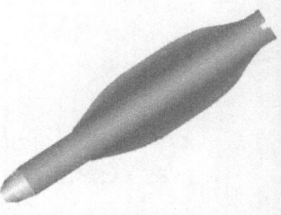

Rolling hills, broken here and there by a mountain, spread out as far as the eye could see. She had never seen land so dry. Here and there groves of trees grew in depressions or along shallow runs, but even those looked dry compared to the trees Camilla was used to. Everywhere else was brown and yellow, countless leagues of brown and yellow in every direction, broken here and there by a bit of dry green. Something about it disturbed her deeply. Another part of her was glad to see something so different from anything she was used to.

A road, a mostly straight and narrow patch of pale brown, almost white, cut by ruts and ditches, ran at a slight angle to their flight path. *So people come here,* thought Camilla. *Is this just a route used for trade with the Sea Elves, or does anyone live here? Have we just missed the signs of them so far?*

They landed when the wind shifted, became harder for Radiance to fly through. Beads of blood formed on Camilla's lips when she moved them, and every bit of exposed skin was dry and cracked. Her eyes were dry to the point of pain, too, even though she had kept them closed more often than not, though the dragons reported only slight dryness. *It feels strange,* was how Radiance put it. *It doesn't hurt, not yet at least. It just feels different. Weird.*

Their second day of flight – if calling it a day made sense, since they flew with the wind patterns, not with the rise and setting of the sun – saw the road fall away behind them and to their right, southwards. If anything, the land grew drier.

When they landed, a timid, shy Lavilor approached Camilla while she sipped from her water. "Camilla?" he said in a quiet, almost broken voice.

Camilla did not think Lavilor had ever addressed her like that before, except perhaps for when she had been very angry.

She closed up the water-skin and looked at him. "What is it, brother?"

He looked away again, as if he were afraid of something, then back towards her. "Our water runs low. What will we do if we cannot find water?"

"Find water," said Camilla with a defiant shrug. "Or make it."

Lavilor's eyes widened, but his tone was as subdued as ever. "You can do that?"

"I can do whatever I must. I freed Ben."

Lavilor voiced then what Camilla had been thinking for a long time, though she did not know quite how long. "If you can do anything, why do we not ride to free Mom?"

Camilla snarled. That was *such* an unfair question to ask. She was still thirsty, but she tucked the water-skin away, and lay down in the shade of Radiance's bulk. She was tired, but the dry heat kept her half-awake, mulling over what felt suspiciously like guilt. Could she make water? Honestly, she did not know. Lavilor could not. Could she find water? If she knew *how*, Camilla was certain she could find water. It fit right in with the rest of what mages could learn how to do, but even though Camilla was an exceptional mage who could do things no one else in the history of Areaer had ever done, that did not mean that her instinct could teach her everything. Alian had shared with her a little of the art of understanding weather and what that meant, but it was only a beginning. Finding water might be another art that she could not learn in a few days by instinct alone. If she had years, she was certain that she could, but days were another matter.

The guilt nagged at her, pulling her farther out of that half-sleep. Radiance slept, and her mind mingled with Camilla's only as a golden nimbus, much like how her scaled bulk shaded Camilla. She was not treating Lavilor well. She was not treating Lavilor like she loved and respected him. She was not treating Lavilor the way she wanted to.

I will never, ever be conquered by the Wizard-King. But that does not mean I can't die, or that those I love can't die. It must not mean that.

Camilla had to learn how to not take out her justifiable anger and frustration at the world for being so *wrong* on her brother. It was not his fault, any of it. It was not his fault that she did not understand, either. It was not his fault – or Mom's fault – that they did not have the power that she did. So that power could not be the *only* answer. But she really had to learn to stop hurting Lavilor just because she was upset.

Camilla was almost afraid to think the next thought that came knocking. What if someone was right? What if anger *was* the influence of the Northern Horror? It did not help her love Lavilor, who was right here with her, that was for certain, and it had *not* yet freed her Mom or anyone else. She was not even sure it had anything to do with how she had saved Ben. Maybe there was another way.

Yet anger *could not* be wholly wrong. There had to be a balance. Anger was so much of who she was, so much of the natural, fundamentally *right* response to evil things hurting those she loved.

The wind was shifting. She got up and walked to where Lavilor lay next to Sleet. The sun had gone down, and it was now for warmth more than for shade that they stayed close to their dragons.

Lavilor stirred at her approach, even though she kept her footfalls soft.

Camilla spun in place. She felt it *now*, a mind – *minds* – that were trying to stay hidden, to not be noticed, that wanted to kill. Fire sprang up like a fountain out of the ground around her feet and danced over her whole body; more fire sprang into life around her hands.

A thunk and snap; a whistling flight, a thud. Ben screamed; Camilla felt an explosion of pain over her chest and ribs, felt as if she had been knocked. She staggered a moment even though she was not the one who had been hit. The fire *roared,* streamed out, as if it had a will of its own; *her* will for its own.

Men *burst* into flames. Their screams made a horrible, cacophonous harmonic to Ben's. Firelight washed the whole world with flurries of ruddy light. Radiance and Sleet reared up, Sleet sheltering Lavilor, Radiance pushing off, taking half to the air, powering herself forward with her wings but skimming the ground with her legs, and another burst of fire put an instantaneous end to the human screams. The grass started to catch fire. Ben's cries mingled with the roar of flame.

Lavilor's hand gripped Camilla's sleeve, unconcerned at the fire that licked over her body. "The fire!" he said.

She *felt* what he meant, heard him as dragons hear. The fire was out of control, devouring the grass now, and it would burn until it had no more fuel.

It would *not*. It was her fire, born of her will, sprung from her heart. It would *not* threaten those she loved. It had done its purpose, if too late.

Blisters and rashes streaked over Camilla's skin in an instant. *She* fought not to scream at the pain. *The magesword.* She drew it. Holding it did not hurt. Her scales were not affected. Just the rest of her body. Energy flowed into her and then out. She collapsed, the magesword underneath her.

Pain. Tearing. Something torn inside her, torn away from her. Camilla felt every minuscule tearing that comprised the whole. It was torment unlike any she had experienced before. Something – some*one* – she was losing, leaving behind. A part of her was being torn away. Someone who was part of her was being torn out of her, and with him the part of her that was joined to him was being torn and shredded.

The tearing was far, far worse than the pain of her burned skin, but Camilla's overwhelmed mind could not cope with any of it. Pain and loss and grief in mute, uncomprehending darkness.

Something reached out to her through the darkness, fire that burned, that hurt and healed, fire that was strength. She recognized it, even though she could not know what she recognized. Something that was not acceptance, that was certainly not acquiescence, that *was* purpose, determined, unrelenting purpose, bloomed with the fire that burned. It was *will*.

> Depth of fire, heart of earth
> Brightest, heaviest stone, crushing
> All around, place of birth
> Never ending, deeper burning

Purging fire, depth deepest
Under the weight of rising fire
Breathing skies, from our rest
Molten burning, seas swimming e'er

Fire that burns, seeks no respite
Fuel subsumed in glory of flame
Fire that wills, knows no despite
Heart of fire, that makes every claim!

Then there was darkness, and the unsoothed pain of something torn, and blind mourning.

She sat upright and screamed before she knew it. Her burned skin sent flashes of pain through her at the movement that only complemented the deeper pain. Ben was gone!

Camilla quieted her wails, but sobbed in misery, her tears stinging the burns on her face. Ben was gone – dead – and as she mourned, she realized she had not treated him as he deserved. She had not respected him, his knowledge or his wisdom, or his right to make his own decisions. She had not respected the fact that she did not *own* him.

And she had let him be killed. And she had not even been able to be there for him while he was dying.

He meant so much to her. He had been so much to her. He had been the only balance to keep her anger from hurting those she loved. And she had not appreciated him, had not loved him as much as she should have or shown him how much she ought to love him, and *now he was gone!*

Radiance paid silent vigil to her rider's grief, and her mourning twined itself with Camilla's, now and again given voice in a keen that was, strangely, beautiful.

Lavilor touched her – gently. "Cam," he said, as if he hesitated to speak to her at all, "I'm … I'm sorry."

She looked up. "It's … not your fault."

He sat down and put his hands over her scaled ones, the only part of her where there were more than a few contiguous inches of undamaged skin – or, in this case, scales. "I know. But I'm sorry. Even though I couldn't know … Ben, like you do."

"No," said Camilla. "I'm sorry."

He looked at her questioningly. The rising moon glimmered in his eyes. "For what? It's not your fault either."

He could not know that, Camilla thought, but she focused on what she wanted to say before all this – happened. It was as relevant now as then. "Maybe, but I'm sorry to you. I haven't been kind to you. I've been rude to you, taken out my anger at other things that aren't your fault on you, ignored your thoughts and advice. I'm sorry."

Lavilor looked like he did not know how to respond. He moved towards her, opening his arms as if to hug her, then shrank back. Finally, he settled for, "Cam, you're my sis. I love you."

Camilla did not say anything, and Lavilor did not ask her to.

Radiance reared up, and Sleet followed. Camilla turned her head to watch the gold and silver dragons, though even that small motion chaffed and hurt.

Radiance turned her head towards Camilla, her jewel-like eyes burning. *"Ben is free. Forever,"* she said, to Camilla, but also not to Camilla.

Majestic under the moonlight, she approached Ben's glittery corpse. Sleet followed. They stood on either side of the dragon who would never fly these skies again, and the sight of their homage struck fresh grief, poignant almost to despair, into Camilla. It was held back only by the fact that Radiance seemed to feel no such emotion and her pose was not born of such an emotion.

> Fire that burns, seeks no respite
> Fuel subsumed in glory of flame
> Fire that wills, knows no despite
> Heart of fire, that makes every claim!

The words burned like fire through her mind, recalled from unremembered depths. In unison, Radiance and Sleet reared up and breathed fire over Ben's corpse. His red scales glowed red and orange in the firelight as they were not able to glitter in the moonlight.

Camilla opened her mouth to speak, but Radiance said only, *"Hush,"* and Lavilor spoke softly behind her ear. "They tore down and trampled the grass around him already, so it won't catch fire. If it does, we'll put it out."

Camilla reached to him mind-to-mind. *You knew they would do this?*

"I felt it."

Slowly, Ben's body caught fire. When the wind blew their way, it brought the stench of burning flesh. Camilla shivered, even though she was sweating. She felt numb, now.

Lavilor sidled closer. "Are we all going to die here?" he asked in a low whisper, almost startling Camilla in her numb state.

"Not if I can help it," she answered when the meaning of his words had penetrated.

"Can you help it?" His question was piercing.

Camilla fought the impulse to lash out. "I don't know," she answered with painful honesty. Even the motion of talking stretched and hurt the damaged skin on her face.

"Do you think you can?"

"I ... think it's possible," Camilla answered, thinking carefully.

"Clearly, other people can do it. As evidenced by the road and by the ... ambushers." She wondered if there might have been a different way to deal with them. Then again, when they hurt Ben, that had not put her in a state where she could have figured out how to capture them alive. "It's a shame they're all dead, because otherwise I'd ask them how."

Otherwise, she would dive into their thoughts and memories and discover how.

Camilla could feel the tension from Lavilor as he debated whether or not to ask her something. She still felt like she was on fire, even though fire itself had never burned her.

It was like the air pressure shifted before Lavilor asked, "Do you think we could ask Nelexi? Would she know?"

"Probably." Even in this much pain, Camilla still could not stand the thought of Nelexi. "But I don't want Nelexi around. I won't ask. But if you can convince Sleet to ask, I couldn't stop you if I wanted to."

I'm not going to die. I'm not going to die. I can survive this. My own magic is not going to kill me, Camilla forced herself to think through the pain, idly tapping the blade of the magesword. The green-gold light flared with every tap.

The thought of the pain she would have to endure made her almost *want* to die. Riding Radiance in this state would be torture. Nothing the Wood Elves had done to her had ever hurt quite like this, quite as much as this did. But Radiance had endured when her bones were broken and she endured the constant pain that wounds that had not healed quite right caused her, especially when it was cold. For Radiance, and for Lavilor and Sleet, Camilla would not give up.

And for all those captured by the Wizard-King, especially Mom, if she was still alive.

The skin was not burned off of her, like it had been burned off her arms when she rescued Ben. It was just burned. It would heal without magic she did not know.

Camilla cursed in her mind at the thought that *Sylvara*, with her determination to learn healing magic, might actually be helpful here. Goodness, she *might* even have been able to heal Ben, since Camilla did not know exactly what had happened to him or what could and could not be healed.

That was when the guilt crashed over Camilla with such potency it almost completely submerged the pain of her burns. If she had stayed with Nelexi and Sylvara – like *Lavilor* wanted, like even Ben wanted – then this would not have happened. Ben would not have been killed.

Maybe she ought to ask Nelexi, or at least ask Lavilor and Sleet to ask Nelexi, if she could not bring herself to do it herself. Otherwise, she might be the reason more people she cared about died.

Pain and grief submerged thought, as Camilla tried to endure.

"Humans come."

It was Sleet's voice, and Camilla jerked upright, pain ripping across her skin. *I ought to be watching. Listening.*

These humans were not a threat but, all the same, they could be. She had failed again.

Radiance's fire and wings enfolded her. *"You are injured, my Camilla. You protected us as well as you could, and you are hurting now."*

Radiance's love warmed Camilla within and without. *We are one.*

Nonetheless, Camilla got to her feet, biting her lip at the pain. "You don't need to, sister," said Lavilor, but there was no way that Camilla was facing people from a position of weakness, whether that weakness was real or apparent, whether she even knew which it was. Radiance and Sleet were exhausted from burning Ben; Camilla could not show weakness.

Just because these humans were not here to kill them that did not mean they were safe or friends. Just because these humans did not have any immediate ill intentions did not mean they could be trusted.

Camilla did not trust anyone except for those she knew.

Grief

Camilla stood with one hand on Radiance's shoulder and the magesword drawn in the other hand. She thought it helped a little with the pain, but she was not going to test it. Eight people walked towards them through the dry grass, carrying no lights of their own under the moonlight. They were led by a bent old woman who leaned on a gnarled staff and whose long white hair was still thick and flowed around her shoulders like moonlight made flesh.

They stopped some twenty paces in front of the two dragons and riders, and the old woman straightened as much as she could, using the staff for support, and made some motions with her free hand, while speaking in a language which Camilla had never heard before.

"We have seen the bonfire and come," she said. "What happens here?"

Haltingly, Camilla spoke in the Anerian trade tongue. If none of them understood, Camilla would speak to them mind-to-mind, but for the first time she understood Nelexi's caution. People might react very poorly to such communication. They might fear evil spirits, or feel violated or – other things that Camilla did not have any understanding of. Not now, fighting through pain and trying to speak in a foreign language she only half-knew. "A dragon died here. The dragons burned him. Someone killed him. Someone died."

The old woman raised her hand and began to say that she did not understand. A man stepped forward from the back, sliding between the others. "It sounds like Trade," he said, "though different from the Trader's I know. May I?"

The old woman leaned on her staff and took his hands in both of hers. She whispered something over him, a blessing, and then he stood beside her and faced the Dragonriders. "Say that again, if you will," he said.

Camilla repeated her words. She did not know what she was doing wrong, so she did not know what she should change or correct.

He frowned in concentration. Camilla could feel the intensity of his concentration. Then he turned to the old woman and translated.

They had not realized that Camilla could understand them well enough, so he translated for the old woman as well.

"We are glad of your presence here, Sha'adhri. But we grieve for what befell you here. We fear that we may not ask for your blessing after what befell you in our lands, but if there is anything we can offer you, you have only to ask."

Camilla closed her eyes, struggling to concentrate. This was getting well past her limited grasp of the language. She struggled even to stand upright, let alone grasp the niceties of a language she did not speak past the pain and exhaustion. She shivered.

Without Radiance's support, mental and physical, she would have collapsed. She hated showing weakness, but this was an opportunity she could not turn down. "Lavilor," she said, "talk to them. You speak the language better than I do."

Grief crashed down upon her like a physical presence, as shining silver Sleet carried Lavilor a few paces forward. She did not hear what Lavilor said. She could not focus on or feel anything but a grief that felt more substantial than her body. It was just her and Radiance, and Lavilor and Sleet now. Ben was gone.

Radiance carefully snaked her head around and blew affectionately, and very, very gently, in Camilla's face. The slight breeze pressed her thick, unruly hair back and stung the burns on her face.

The magesword dropped from limp fingers, its light fading, and Camilla slid down Radiance's side.

She was weak. So weak.

But Radiance was strong. *They* were strong. Camilla-in-Radiance was strong.

Sometime later, hands touched her and lifted her. Camilla's limbs burned with the need to stand, to fight, to struggle.

"Relax. It's all right." It was Radiance's voice and awareness shared with her rider. *"I watch. I guard. I am here."*

Camilla gave herself up to that reassurance. Trusting Radiance was like trusting herself. If Radiance watched and guarded, it was if she herself did. She let herself be moved, not as if she had enough strength left in her own human body to have resisted. Burned everything to ash, perhaps, but that would include herself. She lost herself in Radiance's presence.

The pain was dull, removed. She was aware of it, but she did not feel it. Her eyes opened, but she did not resolve what she saw. Coarse, brownish light. Shades and wrinkles. A vague sense of something moving. Something tilted.

"It's a tent." With Radiance's voice, an understanding both of what she saw and of what it looked from outside blossomed in Camilla's mind. Canvas pitched up and held together to make a shelter.

That led to more understanding. Lavilor had negotiated with the people of the steppes. She now knew how to look for water in these plains. They had made something for her burns, and the bandages that wrapped her skin and kept these poultices against her wounded skin were what made Camilla's body feel strangely bulky.

The flap that served as a door to the tent rustled and she mind-felt

Lavilor's presence and exuberance before he came into view. She tried to raise herself up, but her whole body twinged with pain, and she decided it was not necessary.

"Hi!" her brother said, sounding brighter and more excited than she remembered hearing him sound in a while. "I heard you were awake! Radiance told Sleet, and Sleet told me!"

"Of course," she half-groaned, half-scolded.

Lavilor sat down on the bedding, for all his exuberance careful not to do anything that might cause her pain. "Are you feeling unwell?"

"Is that even a question?" she retorted, looking up at him. "But it's good to see you feeling well."

Lavilor nodded, then suddenly quieted down. She felt the pressure in the shift, but she resisted the urge to dig into what he was thinking.

"Cam, do you know," he asked, "these people and the Dragonriders, these Sha'adhri, they have an interesting relationship."

"Tell me about it," said Camilla. Her interest might have been keener if he had not just overwhelmed her with excitement, but at the moment her energy was drained. She felt Radiance move closer, supporting her, and supplementing what Lavilor told her with her own knowledge, more direct and immediate, and easier for her rider to process.

"The Dragonriders, they revere them. And it's really, really interesting. Because, apparently, the Dragonriders will look into and judge disputes for them. If someone gets murdered, people are encouraged to wait for a dragon, or they might even go on a journey to find one, so the dragon and rider can help them figure out who's responsible and why, and who didn't have anything to do with it. I was listening to a story, one of the only ones they'll share with other people. According to them, before they made this arrangement with the Dragonriders, families or hamlets would go to war and feud for generations over things. Now, the Dragonriders get involved if they do that for long enough, and they help them resolve things so it doesn't turn into war." He cocked his head. "Don't you find that interesting?"

"Uh, not really?" asked Camilla. "Dragons *can* sense motivation and feeling, even thoughts. So it makes a lot of sense. Even if you can't find *who* murdered someone, a dragon might be able to tell who didn't fairly well."

"That makes perfect sense, but still, I think it's interesting." Lavilor sounded at once strangely exuberant and thoughtful.

"No," Radiance responded to Camilla's unspoken worry. *"We sense nothing of that here. They aren't helping us because they expect us to help them resolve a dispute or figure out a problem. But in return for what the Sha'adhri do for them, they offer shelter and aid to the Sha'adhri, and especially to new dragons and riders who are, or might be, looking for the Sha'adhri, to join them."*

So that was not what Lavilor was thinking about. It had not really *felt* like it, but it was still a concern to Camilla. From what she had picked up, resolving these situations could sometimes take a very long time, far longer than she wanted to spend seeking anything but her goal, besides the fact it had to be harder if one spoke even the Trade language so clumsily.

No, the source of Lavilor's consternation was probably something else. Riding a wave of emotion, she did move a little, despite the screaming pain that tore across her skin, raising herself on one elbow a little to look at her brother. "Lavilor," she said, "this *ought* not to be strange." She cursed herself for her choice of words and what they must sound like. "I don't mean it ought not to be strange to you. But I mean it seems strange only because the elves so completely disrespected and disregarded the dragons. They never even thought about what dragons are, what they want, what they can do."

Radiance humming in her mind shocked Camilla, it was so very at odds with the rage she felt.

But Ben, anger had not helped Ben heal ... the hole inside of Camilla where Ben had been seemed to be larger than the world, and she felt all her anger, *everything*, collapse into it. Radiance filled all of her, and Camilla did not think she would be breathing if not for the dragon, but even Radiance could not fill the hole that had been torn out of her when Ben died.

"Are you okay?" Lavilor's insistent voice reached through the shroud of emptiness blanketing Camilla, and she realized he had been speaking – maybe asking that one question – for some time now.

Camilla opened her eyes to stare up at the top of the tent, or maybe her vision just returned to her. She had fallen back on the pillow, and she had not even felt the pain even that small motion must have sent across the burns that laced her body. It was hard to make sense of Lavilor's question, even with Radiance helping her, thinking with her.

"I don't know. I miss Ben ... so much." Her throat closed up over a sob.

Lavilor reached over her, and she felt his fingers stop and hover less than an inch from her skin. He drew back his hand, and leaned further forward, then back, at a loss for what to do.

She reached out to speak to him mind-to-mind. *It's okay. You don't need to comfort me.*

His face crumpled, and Camilla wondered if she had mis-stepped. "I didn't –" she started to say, but Lavilor just crumpled further, his shoulders folding in, the picture of dejection.

What can I do? Camilla stopped her cry just short of possibly screaming in the minds of everyone in the encampment. She could feel them, dozens of them, going about their business. It was hard to hold in her despair. Her loss. Ben gone. Just a few minutes ago Lavilor was happy beyond all expectations. Now he looked – not as crushed as she felt, but that was only because that would be impossible.

She did not stop her cry short of being felt. She felt the backlash, dozens and dozens of people arrested mid-task, mid-thought, by a cry of grief and pain that had nothing to do with them. She wanted to turn her face into the pillow and hide. Cry until – she could not give up. She could not despair. Yet, oh how she did. She was not enough. Whether it was her choices or her power that were insufficient, she had let Ben die. Could she really do what she said she would? Yet she had to. There was no one else.

I will *be enough.* The thought echoed hollowly in the space carved out of her by Ben's loss.

Not just Ben's loss. The loss of her Mom. The loss of Lavilor's joy.

Lavilor spoke, so softly she would not have heard him if she did not hear as dragons hear. His words were an echo of her thoughts. "Mom." He said. "She could be ... like Ben. Not coming back."

"I don't know." Camilla's voice felt raw, her throat as if it had been scraped by sandpaper. She wished she could promise him more. But she had to be honest. It was not as if dishonesty were any use. He knew. So did she.

Radiance folded mental wings around her. *"Don't give up. I'm here. You have me. You have all of me."* A rush of golden mist and flame swirled around Camilla. *"We can do this together."*

You have all of me, Camilla echoed.

"That's right," said Lavilor suddenly, his voice echoing painfully in her skull. These rapid mood changes were not natural. Was she imagining something? Were they imagining something? No, Radiance did not think so. "I was supposed to make sure you get something solid to eat as soon as you properly woke up."

With that, he was gone before Camilla could ask any questions. But Radiance answered them, bringing Camilla's semi-conscious memories back to her. Lavilor had spoon fed her gruel and water, when she had been just conscious enough to respond. The healer had wanted to do it, but her little brother had insisted, as Camilla would have known he would, remembering when he had fed her like a bird and made a game of it, when she had burned the skin off her hands – rescuing Ben. Suddenly, what could have been a pleasant memory of laughter turned into an abyss of grief. Blindly, Camilla reached out to Radiance and clung to the gold dragon with everything she had, like a panicked creature falling down a cliff grasps and holds out of instinct and terror more than strength.

One finger gently caressed a small patch of undamaged skin on her face. "Cam, sis," said Lavilor, and the worry and love in his voice instantly recalled her attention.

"Lav?" she asked, her voice choked with unwept tears, her mind pulled into a maelstrom of despair where she could not remember what he had gone for or why.

"I brought you a meal. Are you w-well ... enough to eat?"

In the midst of the grief, the grief that her little brother was the one looking out for her, while she was hurt and could not look out for him, pierced Camilla's heart. "Th-think so," she said, her voice slurred. "Hands work."

If she was careful, it did not hurt too much to get herself on her elbow. After all, her elbow was not burned, being scaled, though the scaling ended around there.

He put a bowl of some sort of stew or soup down next to her with a spoon in it. Getting the food from the bowl to her mouth without spilling it or hurting herself became a slow, carefully calculated process that did not leave much room for anything else. The despairing grief was like an immense pressure at the back of her mind, waiting to enter, but not able to flood through her for the moment, while her mind was so devoted to the intricate task at hand.

When Camilla swallowed the last chunk, she eased herself back down and exhaustion from grief and the toll of healing took over from there. She slept.

She was only vaguely aware of chanting, of the smell of incense, of a ceremony conducted outside and all around of cleansing and warding. Radiance whispered again and again that *she* watched over Lavilor and Sleet, that she guarded them with her and Camilla's united will, that if she were needed Camilla would wake, but otherwise she should rest and recover. That they were not alone. Not ever. They were *together.* Two and one.

The days that followed were torture. She could only sleep so much, and once she had slept that time, she was left to the mercy of remorse and loss. She was too weak to continue, and she knew it. Her oath to do better constrained her and she *was* mortal. Using all the power that legends and myths attributed to immortals only drove home the weakness of her mortal flesh. She had to let her body heal.

There was, of course, the possibility that if she killed herself with the power attributed to immortality, she would be reborn immortal. There were times when she was sorely tempted to follow that through and see what would happen, but something held her back. Part of it was Radiance. Part of it might have been the fact that she did not *know,* and she was not about to make another rash mistake so soon. If it were necessary, she would do so, but it was not necessary now, so she would not.

So instead she languished in grief and remorse. That Ben was gone. That she had not respected and honored and loved him as she should have.

That much of Lavilor's joy seemed gone, and she was in part responsible. Not that she knew just how much she was and was not responsible for. If dying in the throes of her power would make her an immortal, then she was responsible for so much. She should have fought the Wizard-King when he attacked Ilesh and saved her family and so many more. As an immortal, she would certainly have a fighting chance, maybe not to destroy him, but at least to protect what she loved.

That only raised the problem of freedom and power that she did not have the strength to deal with right now. Was everyone immortal inside, and they only had to find the will to freedom to tap it, and if they desired freedom enough they would become immortals forever free? Something about the world seemed so desperately wrong, and if she had not found the solution yet, she would not find it now.

Lavilor kept her company sometimes, but Camilla would not ask him for more. The dragons assuaged and healed a little of her grief regarding him, telling her – showing her sometimes – the new friends he had found, in particular one boy named Laoirn, with whom he spent most of his days playing and learning to speak, since Laoirn did not know any Trader's. There certainly appeared to be a deep bond between the two, and that brought a flicker of joy to Camilla.

She wondered if Lavilor would want to stay here with Laoirn when they went on. The thought saddened her, yet it was also a touch of relief. He would be as safe here as anywhere, she thought. Especially since apparently she could not protect her friends even when she was with them.

How, with all her power, was she so impotent?

Radiance moved in with all the blinding of the sun transformed into love and Camilla's thoughts faded as stars when the sun rises.

Flameheart sat on Nelexi, watching the sunset fade over the ocean. The Obsidian Guardian might as well as have been a small hill, at least as far as the view was concerned.

She wondered absently if Lavilor and Camilla had found a different beach from which to observe the same view. It was beautiful in a soft, quiet kind of way, but also a glorious one. Tatters of cloud that were hardly visible during the day turned to colors of dreadful glory as the sunlight glanced on them from the other side of the world. The ocean streamed with their life. Every minute, the colors darkened, shifted from golds and reds towards purples. The sky reminded her of certain sunsets over the Plains of Zharda, but the smell was wholly different.

The sea was fine to look at, but she hated being on it.

"No," Nelexi's voice whispered through her reverie, in answer to the question she had almost forgotten having. *"Camilla and Lavilor are not staying. Camilla wants to part from us and to get to the Sha'adhri in Dragonsong Forest as quickly as possible, and Lavilor and Sleet are going with her."*

You're concerned about them? asked Flameheart as the colors in the sky turned another shade of mauve and purple-gray.

"Yes. In a way. Camilla has no idea of the dangers she could face out there. Her experience is more limited than she has had the opportunity to realize."

Flameheart leaned back against the ridges of Nelexi's back. She wished the wind would blow from the plains, not the sea. She did not care for the smell of the sea. She had had too much of it for too long. *In that way, not unlike me. But I have you.*

"And you are learning to understand that my experience does not mean that I know everything, or even very much, but only that I have a better grasp on what I do and not know, and what I cannot know."

... Yes. But ... You do know a lot about some things. Like poisons and what can be eaten and dangers of the wilderness to avoid.

Nelexi chuckled quietly. Flameheart felt the vibration in her scales more than she heard it.

Are we going to go after them? She would miss Ben.

"No. We will meet again soon enough, since we also are going to Dragonsong Forest, but it will do Camilla good to be on her own. To perceive that she has her own space and is making her own decisions. What good I cannot know, but I do know that it is not my place to force myself where I am not wanted."

Not always. I may not know much of the history of the Sha'adhri and the role you have played among them, but I know that sometimes you have forced yourself where you were not wanted at all.

"Depending on the perspective."

Flameheart stopped at Nelexi's words. Suddenly, the dragon sounded tired, very, very tired. Nelexi had never sounded tired before, not like this. She had been a little tired, sometimes, when they were flying to save the Sea Elf fleet from the obsidian dragons and to meet with Camilla and Lavilor and Sylvara, with Radiance and Sleet and Shimmer and Ben, though they had not known it, but not like this. This was not the ordinary physical need for rest that even a god was subject to, though not to the degree that mortals were. This was something else. The weight of the ages Nelexi had known. Perhaps the weight of the lives she had seen gone astray, the unnecessary suffering caused by the choices of others that she either could not or did not have the right to intervene in.

"There's not much of a difference, Flameheart, if there is any at all. There are things I can and things I can not do, and there is very much that I can do if it is wanted, if I am wanted, or otherwise not at all. No, it is the call of the Heart of Fire. It has been so long for me, but it is just a little while longer before I return and take you with me. The Heart of Fire lives in me, but it is time for me to return. With you. When it is our time."

Soon? Energy lit Flameheart's mental voice. She tightened her hand on Nelexi's scales.

"Soon. But I do not know how soon. Your whole life is soon to me."

The wind blew, dry and fierce and beautiful.

She paced out from Nelexi through the drying grass and weeds. Gently rolling hills swept away forever, their ripples fading into smaller and subtler patterns until they mated the infinite blue. Golden-green, deeper greens, drier golds, speckled the nearer rises and falls, before the variety faded into one, and then the color grew blue and grayer with distance.

Her heart was free. Free as the infinite plains and the wind that washed over them forever, whispered in the grasses, howled on the rises in its heights, rushed through the depressions.

This was life.

It was more like home than anywhere she had been in a long time, far more like home than the Plains of Orosië on the other side of the mountains. Even the scent of drying grass and the pollen of the weeds was like the Plains of Zharda.

Like. But not the same.

Even after years away, she could never confuse the smell. So much was like, but also just that tiny bit different. And the likeness made the difference cut even deeper. Homesickness rushed over her like a flash flood, so strong it made her want to cry.

She rushed back to Nelexi and flung herself against the dragon's warm scales. She let her tears dampen the black scales, while Nelexi wrapped her comforting presence around a girl who was for a moment not Flameheart but a bereft, lonely, homesick Kario.

As they traveled north, the hills grew smaller, and the land spread away, flatter than the ocean, for as far as the eye could see, ending in a very faint haze. It did not dull the ache in Kario's heart, and she sensed a similar desire, but with less pain, in Nelexi. Flying was easier than landing, since Flameheart had not seen the Plains of Zharda from above except in the last few days, after Nelexi had bonded to her.

One night, the light of the moonlight shifting on the grasses, as they were blown gently by the breeze, would not let Flameheart sleep. She sat, cross-legged, on a very small hillock, Nelexi's huge head to one side of her, the moon a little to the other side and in front, though it was high in the sky, watching and waiting, her mind as silent as the earth under her left.

Flameheart shifted and rested her chin on her hand. *Nelexi,* she asked, finally, *you desire – yearn – too.*

"I do." Nelexi's voice had the bare, smooth honesty it always did. Not unflinching, for unflinching implied that it did not shy in the presence of pain, whereas Nelexi's voice indicated no pain from which she might shy. No, it was unveiled.

For this? asked Flameheart, motioning slightly with her chin. *Something this reminds you of?*

Nelexi took a moment to consider. *"No. Or not like you mean it. For me, it is the Volcano. It has been so long. I did not feel the yearning much until I met you. But every moment I am with you, it grows. You are a little heart of fire."* Nelexi's voice was heart-stoppingly affectionate.

There are times I think it is your name.

"It is. It is yours."

Flameheart did not reply, just sat, watching the moonlight ripple on the grasses and glitter on Nelexi's scales. It looked like blood on her wings and stripe, but that was not what stilled Flameheart's heart with something that was almost joy, and almost grief, and perhaps neither.

She knew it the same moment Nelexi did. The earth shook as the

Obsidian Guardian flung herself to her feet and keened or sang. Flameheart had not known Nelexi *could* make that sound.

Ben was – *home*. Ben had flown Home.

The grief that blew through Flameheart was not without hope. It did not hurt any less than that. Ben had flown Home. And she was homesick. More homesick, that he had gone. He would not be a little bit of Home to her in her homesickness. And Nelexi was truly, honestly, *Homesick*. As much as she was. It was the same.

There was as much as joy as grief in Nelexi's keening, and the joy made the grief sharper. *Soon. Soon. Soon.* The thought was a minor rhythm in the Obsidian Guardian's song.

But *Soon* was not *Now*.

The Fire was in her, she was Wings of the Flame of the Earth, yet she yearned to swim through the Flame once more, to have the Fire flow fresh and molten in her veins, close over her head, cascade off her wings.

But the joy sang past the grief. Ben had flown Home. Ben flew through the Flame now. Forever free of the dark cold, the horror and the stain. Healed, as only Home could heal. Cleansed, as only the Fire could cleanse. Wait he might, in longing for his rider, his second rider, and perhaps in some suffering for her sake and any others for whom he must wait, but there would be no despair. Nelexi – Flameheart knew that deeper than her bones. That Fire would burn away all despair, any temptation to despair, with the unspeakable conviction of its Flames. That nothing would be able to forever outrun the Flood of Fire that would one day renew the earth from whose Flames first it issued forth. That Flame was the primal thing. Sorrow there might be, and pain, but the torture of despair was no more.

That was peace. Ben was freed, and ever since Flameheart had seen the dragon, she had wanted that for him more than anything. But she missed him, even though she could never speak to him like Camilla could.

Flameheart half-started as she became aware of Sylvara's footsteps behind her. She turned on her rump.

"What happened?" asked Sylvara.

"Ben is Home," answered Flameheart.

Sylvara screwed up her face, and Flameheart realized she used the word for 'Home' that her people used. Sylvara would not know it.

"I mean, *how?* That's what Shimmer won't tell me."

Somehow, Sylvara had known what Flameheart meant. Flameheart shook her head. "I don't know. Nelexi hasn't told me."

In that moment, Nelexi's emotions shifted. Her keen ended in a roar, and primal rage blew overhead. *"Dragon-slayers. Those who hunt dragons for prestige, for what they call honor and glory, for their scale-armor. They are dead. Burned alive in the dragon-mage's fire."*

Underneath the announcement, where only Flameheart heard it, Nelexi responded to her rider's half-cringing question before her wrath. *"I am Guardian of the dragons. Those who slay them, I slay."*

I do not understand. If that is what you are, why was it not your place to protect the dragons from the Wood Elf life-mages? Surely, that is no less an offense against the dragons.

Nelexi's response was as tender as ever. *"You are right. It is no lesser offense. But I cannot yet explain to you all the reasons why I could not do so."* Even quieter, if such a mental voice could be quieter, Nelexi said, *"I cannot right all wrongs done against the dragons."*

Over Flameheart's head, Sylvara asked, "Should we have been there? Do they need our help?"

Nelexi towered over both of them, and the earth quivered with a low rumble that originated in her chest. *"Not now,"* she answered and said no more.

Flameheart stood, but that did not shake the images. It was as if she had double vision, as if she saw two worlds, yet the two visions were almost overlaid over each other. In one, the moonlight shivered on countless miles of grassland. In the other, rivers of fire flowed down a black mountain glowing red; fountains of fire leapt in the sky. All was flame, red and sun-bright white and dark.

"Do you mind?" asked Nelexi, a curious quality in her voice.

Flameheart shook her head slightly ... *No. I don't think so. ... I'll get used to it. Why?*

"Because it is, in part, my ... fault. I think. I do not know how it happened." Nelexi's voice sounded as confused as Flameheart had ever heard it. *"But it is as if I have drawn your mind and experience closer to mine than I knew was possible. I do not want to have hurt you."*

I am not hurt. But I thought you kept distance between us, kept much separate from me, lest I not have the ... choice to be me. Lest I be smothered in what you are, and instead of knowing things, be confused by what you know.

Nelexi's voice was very distant. *"Is this that, what I warned of?"*

It does not feel like it.

"It does not feel like it to me either. And it is what is." A sense of acquiescence, more, of rightness. The matter settled.

Flameheart was quiet for a while. *I love you, Nelexi. I've always wanted to be close to you.*

"This is the beginning."

Flameheart turned, and suddenly remembered that Sylvara and Shimmer were somewhere around. This felt wrong to be witnessed by any others.

"Do not worry. Sylvara and Shimmer concern themselves and do not intrude."

Reassured, Flameheart paced through the trampled grasses and put her hand on a scale of Nelexi's nose, near the dragon's nostril. "You're mine," she whispered, kissing Nelexi's scale.

"And you are mine."

"I'll never be lonely again." The words barely left Flameheart's lips.

"Nor I." The tone of Nelexi's voice was a mental caress, a kiss as real as any physical touch. Flameheart's heart burst.

When the sunlight woke her in the mid-morning, it was hard for her to believe that Ben was gone. The night before was but a memory. Yet she had only to close her eyes to see the springs of fire, and sometimes they flashed across her waking vision. The song of fire was in her, now. And while her thoughts and what she knew were distinct from Nelexi, she knew her mind for her own and Nelexi's mind for Nelexi's, there was an abiding sense that they were one on some primal level. That some knowledge or experience which was fundamentally the same had made them absolutely one. Even their names were no longer separate. It was hard for Flameheart to remember which name belonged to whom. Sometimes, for a moment, she thought her name was Nelexi and that the black dragon's name was Flameheart.

Her yearning was not less either, yet it was without the loneliness. Instead of lacking something, the yearning itself felt more complete. She desired and longed, but without the pangs of misery.

She was Flameheart.

Human Is Enough

Camilla could feel Lavilor's approach. She sat up, then placed her feet on the dirt ground and stood, as he stooped and entered the tent that had been relegated to her.

He stopped. "Are you ready for that?" he asked, adopting an affectionate pose she had never quite seen in him before. She wondered if it was learned from that friend of his, Laoirn.

Camilla nodded. "I have to be. I can't sit here, waiting on their goodwill and depending on their resources any more. And I'm well enough to ride." She softened her voice. "But that does not mean you have to go with me."

"That – you can't," Lavilor told her. "The healer told me she wasn't sure you'd make it. So much of your skin had been burned. I know you're stronger, you heal better than most. But you can't be ready for that. It's only been a few days."

"What I'm not ready for is lying in bed, depending on other people's goodwill and not doing anything except having the same thoughts flying around in my head over and over again, and –" her voice choked "– missing Ben."

Lavilor nodded, as if he understood, but he did not, and paced into the tent. He draped himself bonelessly over Camilla's bedding.

I'm really not good at thinking about loving people, thought Camilla. *Even though I ought to be good at it.* She sat down, her half-healed skin protesting with pain that made her want to scream. She felt Radiance support her, but for once Radiance's thoughts were inscrutable to her.

"Lavilor," said Camilla, though he did not look towards her, "you can stay here if you like. I'm not asking you to come with me. I won't be sad or hurt if you don't." She stopped, trying to get her words together. "I think maybe – I'm not sure you shouldn't stay here with your friend. I'm not a good sister. I'm not good at understanding what hurts you and how to love you." She swallowed, her voice breaking on a sob. "And I'm definitely not good at taking care of people. At protecting people. I think you and Sleet might be safer here – with these people – than with me. Especially since I'm going to –"

Lavilor stirred, and Camilla stopped.

"If I stay here," he asked, and Camilla thought he was almost crying, "if I stay here, will you go?"

Camilla nodded. "Soon. I want to meet the Sha'adhri first. I think knowing them might help me to understand what I am and use my power. I apparently – I want to do this right. I want to *succeed.* But if you stay here, that will become my absolutely first priority."

Sleet's presence loomed into Camilla's mind. She was amazed at how large his presence felt. It had grown so much in the last few days, either that or she had not noticed it until now. Something like approval, but not, dropped down from his mind into hers.

Lavilor looked at her, then, and held out his arms. Camilla returned the gesture, though she winced with agony when he scrambled out of his boneless sprawl to hug her. She bit her lip until the blood ran.

When Lavilor let her go, he paled. "You – I – I thought you were better."

"I didn't say it doesn't *hurt.*"

"You're not ready to go. You'll kill yourself if you go now. But I'll stay here." He got to his feet and dashed out of the tent.

His words struck Camilla like daggers. Would she? She could not trust her own confidence now. Or was it all a trick of the Nightmare? To make her believe that her will and her heart were not enough, in and of themselves?

For the Northern Horror was a real enemy and the Nightmare was real – or not. It had to be fought, at any rate. It threatened all she loved, including herself, herself and Radiance.

Perhaps they would fly straight for Ellenesia and confront the Wizard-King. All they needed was the courage of their hearts, their confidence, their flame, and above all their love. They would have to find some way to get back across the sea, but they would manage. With Lavilor as safe as they could ever ensure him, they would manage. They would do what they should have done a year ago, what they might have done a year ago if not for … lots of things, some of them being those cursed were-dragons' attempts to undermine her confidence. But if she did not let the weapons of the Northern Horror find a foothold in her soul and her feelings, if she confronted the Wizard-King instead of running and putting off what she knew she ought to do, then they would be victorious.

They were only weak because they did not believe in their own strength. They would not let that continue.

Camilla slumped against the bedding. Her head swam from the pain and exertion, and she did not want to spend another night, another hour, like this, like a captive. Even though she was not locked in a stone cell with iron bars, but rested in a tent that would move aside with a touch of her fingers or ignite with the barest wish. Even though Radiance would often slip her way between the tents, careful not to knock them over with her wings or a flick of her tail, and stick her neck through the flap, so that her head rested inches from Camilla.

If only she had been watching. If only she had been waiting, aware, careful. Ben would not have died.

Lavilor and Sleet would be safer here. These people would have no patience for dragon-slayers and Sleet would be safe sleeping among their tents. Lavilor would be safe with them, too. It was not perfect, but it was the best

Camilla thought she could find. Certainly better than *she* could do, however much that hurt. Whether or not it was that she *could not* do better, or whether it was her fault for lack of care, she could not trust herself to never fail. But, here, Lavilor and Sleet would be safe and happy, and she and Radiance would be free to rescue Mom – or at least avenge themselves and everyone else on the Wizard-King. She would think about what came next after that.

The sense of recovered purpose and determination comforted Camilla immensely and built into a bulwark that held back the raging madness of her grief at Ben's loss. When she slept, her scaled hand on Radiance's scaled snout, it was more peaceful and restful than any sleep she had had since Ben died.

Camilla started to wake. *It's okay. It's just Lavilor come to speak with you, and there's no emergency. Rest.* It was Radiance's knowledge, Radiance's voice, and also her own.

She slipped back into the much-needed *real* sleep, but when she woke it was with the vague knowledge that her plan would not quite work. Radiance's snout was not under her hand anymore. The other part of herself soared over the grasslands under the burning blue sky, hungry and hunting. Only half Radiance's mind was on her rider.

Camilla sat up, and knew immediately that she was stronger than she had been the previous evening. Every morning and evening, she was stronger now, more healed. The pain was still torture, yet she was aware, somehow, that it was receding, but also that it did not help that she kept tearing the newly-healing skin by moving. Yet, even so, it was healing, and she could not wait to be gone, caught between torture and torment.

It was not long before the healer-woman came. She chided Camilla relentlessly for not being more careful with her healing burns while she changed the bandages. Camilla could not say anything to her, but the healer had figured out days earlier that the Dragonrider understood whatever *she* said. Camilla ignored her, her eyes and face as inexpressive as she could manage. She did not like the healer-woman, but there was no reason to be angry with her, since Camilla had no more reason to think her evil than she had to think her good.

When the healer-woman was done with the bandages, she sat down across from Camilla, her hand holding Camilla's scaled ones. Camilla debated pulling her hand away. She sensed where this was going, and she did not like this person. "What are you?" she asked. "Never mind. I know I can't understand anything you say, but you are something different. You are human, a Dragonrider, yet not. I should not be so surprised when you heal what seem to be mortal injuries, when your hands are scaled and clawed like a dragon's, though the shape of mine. But dragons, too, can die of wounds, and of burns, though they be creatures of fire, and today it is obvious what I suspected before. The healing scars are not natural human scars. I wish you could tell me what you are. Are you a messenger from a god? The child of the dragon-god?"

Camilla had had enough. She pulled her hand back, a small but sharp motion, and glared at the healer-woman. She did not have the mental energy to learn her accursed language, and she did not care to satisfy her idiotic curiosity, and talking about gods and god-children was just too much. *If* she had known the language well enough, she would have told the woman, "Absolutely not. My parents are human. My father died in an accident as a slave. My mother is dead or captured. Do not taunt me. And I am *human*. Never, *ever* question that." But it was not worth it to learn the language and she was not sure if she should give into the impulse to tell the woman mind-to-mind or what reactions that might cause. Nonetheless, she would not have anyone implying that she was anything less or more than *human*. To be human was enough, and she was as proud of her humanity as anyone could be.

The healer-woman left, not a moment too soon.

Camilla waited in utter boredom, though she was not putting up with more than another day of this, especially if the scars were as far along as the healer's reaction suggested. *"Lavilor is coming to you,"* Sleet told her, and Camilla thanked him.

It was only a few minutes before Lavilor arrived, carrying Camilla's breakfast and a small breakfast for himself. Camilla had learned a day or so ago that he ate two small breakfasts now that she was well enough: one with Laoirn and his friends, and one with her.

"Saorl bothering you?" Lavilor asked, sitting down and placing the bowls between them.

Saorl was the healer's name. "Yeah."

"I suspected as much. She's been talking about how you're a half-god or something and she wishes she knew more for some time. And I –" He shrugged. "I can't do much to tell her anything. I tried to tell her you'd get mad."

Lavilor's voice chased the last of Camilla's anger away. She would deal with that later, but he certainly seemed to be a great deal *happier* than she had seen him in a long time. Confident. She picked at the soup.

Lavilor did not go after his any faster. Camilla could sense he had something on his mind and waited. Finally, he said, "It won't work."

"What won't work?"

"Me staying here, while you go –" He did not finish the sentence again. "I tried to explain what I wanted, that I lost my family and I wanted to stay with Laoirn, while you would go to the Sha'adhri." The smile he gave her – or her dragon-sense – told Camilla more. He thought she would not want him to tell them more about her or what she was really about. He was right. "They told me that won't work because I'm a Dragonrider. Dragonriders can't live with a clan, because they solve disputes, and if a Dragonrider is with a clan, even though dragons sense only the truth, that could make the dragon and rider biased. In disputes between clans, they could be biased towards their clan. In disputes between people in the same clan, they could be biased for their friends or against people they don't like. So they are honored, and they can visit their families, but they can't live with a clan. Even then, they're not supposed to judge disputes involving their clan. Either way, it doesn't matter. I and Sleet can't live with the clan." He seemed downcast, and Camilla sensed the reason why.

Her heart ached with it. At last, he had a little of what the elves had stolen from them as children, and he could not keep it. "What does this mean for your friendship with Laoirn?"

Lavilor straightened and spooned another mouthful of soup. After swallowing, he said, "I'm allowed to visit for days or so. And Laoirn can come with me, in a couple years, if he chooses. But Laoirn isn't ready to leave his mom and dad yet." Lavilor balled his hand into a fist, but Camilla sensed nothing of the rage she so often experienced. "It's wrong, though," he said.

"It is," said Camilla. "I guess we'll have to go to the Sha'adhri together. You should be safe in the valley where all the Dragonriders live, and where only Dragonriders are welcome. And maybe you can make new friends there."

"I'm not leaving Laoirn. I'm visiting as often as I can," Lavilor said, with all the certitude of someone explaining that the sun rose on one side of the sky and set on the other to someone who had somehow remained ignorant of that fact.

Camilla held back a sigh. Maybe when Lavilor made other friends, he would forget this obsession, though a part of her told her not to think that. She had seen Lavilor's friendship with Laorin through the dragons' eyes. She had felt what it meant. Still, what did she know of free friendships, of what they could be? Regardless, now was not the time to challenge Lavilor and explain the dangers of the journey, even though that ought to be obvious, but she *would* do it later. Maybe it would not be necessary, however. Maybe when he went to visit Laoirn, other dragons and riders would come with him, dragons and riders who were taught to watch and would not make the mistake she had made, and more than just one or two of them. That might be safe enough.

And as long as Lavilor understood, and as long as he was as safe as Camilla could get him, as long as, if he was in danger, it was not because she had not made it possible for him to be safe, then that was enough. She was content with that, and the rest was his choice. It was not as if she would not be going into danger with Radiance.

Nonetheless, her heart wrung. She just wanted him to be safe. She did not want to be worrying about him, wondering if he would be safe if she stayed to protect him, while she went to rescue her Mom if she lived, and avenge them all if she did not. Not that she was not going to take her vengeance whether her Mom lived or not. Only, if Mom was dead, it would be only vengeance.

"When do we leave?" asked Lavilor.

The note in his voice stopped Camilla short. He wanted to spend more time with Laoirn. Would it hurt? Who was she to think about things this way? Ignoring his and Ben's desires had gotten Ben killed. And it was only her desire to hurry that made her want to go forward, no real knowledge that that was best. Besides, had she not decided she was going to listen to people better? Though she was going to have to figure out how to get that Saorl away from her.

"Half a moon. Unless they want us gone before then," Camilla said.

Lavilor jumped into the air, almost knocking the half-empty bowls of soup over.

As Camilla anticipated, dealing with Saorl was something of a trial. She had spread her notion of Camilla being the half-human child of the dragon-god (or whatever it was) among everyone, or maybe the notion spread of its own once a handful of people saw or heard about her scaled arms and hands. As Camilla's health improved, it became impossible for her dragons' hearing not to pick up on what people said, even though she did not intrude on their minds. At least it was better than having someone suggest her powers might be due to being part elven, Camilla thought, since they were attributing it to the dragon-god, but then she reconsidered that and decided that it was just as bad. But she did not want to cause trouble for Lavilor by riling them up by speaking inside their minds.

Nor did she want to spend the time and effort to learn their language. However, she did acquire a few words without trying. It was not enough to explain herself or drive her point home, but she was able to growl, "I'm human. *Human,*" every time Saorl (or anyone else she had to interact with) suggested otherwise. And eventually, "Human is enough." It was very stilted communication, but she was not sure it mattered. She was communicating her feelings and desires, and they probably did not even care what she had to say.

When a week had gone by, Camilla managed to convince Saorl (in part through the medium of the man who spoke Trader's) that she did not need her services anymore. She slept under Radiance's wing, on the softest bedding they had, and wore the clothes she had from the Sea Elves, washed frequently to keep them soft, but other than that wore no bandages except on the worst wounds. She was frustrated, nearly to the point of pain, by the wait. She was unable to do anything. The dragons shared what knowledge she could learn (such as how to look for wells) with her, but there was nothing she could do to contribute towards any of her goals, except to do nothing and heal. She did not even look for food or help to prepare it. As for washing her clothing, she was glad not to do that. When she had to do it, she would, but it was slaves' work and she disliked the reminder.

Nothing healed the wound Ben had left behind in her soul. Radiance's love kept her living, and her purpose kept her sane, but the wound ached, day and night, as inexorable as the pain of her burns had ever been. Radiance's reminder that she had rescued Ben, and that it was better for Ben to have been rescued and to have known her, soothed the edges of her guilt, but that assurance could not heal her guilt, and it could heal the hole in her even less.

In the end, it was not her guilt though. It was the guilt of the dragon-slayers. Their crime was not hers. She had not killed Ben or neglected his needs. But she had ignored him and ignored his desires and thoughts, and that was the heart of her guilt. That she had not protected him was not guilt exactly, but it hurt no less.

On the day that they arranged to leave, Lavilor seemed extraordinary happy. At least, he acted a lot happier than Camilla had expected. She did not ask him why, though she guessed it had something to do with his friendship with Laoirn and had no idea what it could be, since she saw them hugging before she and Lavilor saddled the dragons, and she caught Lavilor waving vigorously, along with other gestures she did not recognize, out of the corner of her eye just before they took off.

A month or two more, and they would meet the Sha'adhri. They would meet dragons and riders who were born and lived free. They would meet dragons who were not tainted by the elven life-magic. Radiance was no less a dragon for that – she was as dragon as ever a dragon could be – but Camilla still hoped it would help them to learn things that would otherwise take them longer.

And, surely, there would be a place for Lavilor among the Sha'adhri, and then she could leave him in safety, where he could make friends and be happy and grow free, to pursue what maybe she should have done a year ago.

Sylvara's stomach seemed to be an empty space. After a moment, she realized Shimmer had stopped flying and was falling – only for a moment. They regained their wits and Shimmer's wing-beats steadied, though they were still a little scattered with excitement.

Whatever Nelexi and Flameheart had told them, Sylvara had not expected this. Shimmer must have, for he would have shared the images mind-to-mind as Nelexi and Flameheart had seen them – she had seen some of them from him – but it was just too much. It was not like *this*.

They flew past the shoulder of the mountain and the ridge-line dropped away below them and suddenly there was a huge, lush forest cloaking the sides of the mountains and a valley that turned blue and hazy with mist, leaving only the suggestion of huge, impossibly-sized mountains, to the north. But that was not what caused dragon and rider to almost fall from the sky.

It was the dots of every color in the rainbow, and a few white ones, that soared over the forest in the distance. A few of them were just close enough that Sylvara could make out their rough shape and see whether they were gliding or flying. And every one of those was a dragon.

The dragons were not on the verge of extinction at all. Sylvara could count hundreds of the dots, and there had to be far, far more. Dragons who weren't in the sky, dragons who were too far away, beyond where the forest's haze obscured them, and dragons who weren't in Dragonsong Forest at all.

Their freedom, the fact that she was *free*, struck Sylvara and Shimmer like it never had before, a wave of euphoria that felt as huge and dangerous as the ocean waves were to Sylvara. It could drown them or carry them away before they knew what it was. She had never before felt the full force of what it was to be free, a slave no more and never again, free from the shadow of the elves.

Then she saw a black dot.

Shimmer answered her thought before it formed. *"An obsidian dragon. Like Nelexi, but one who has not been born from the Volcano a second time."* An image entered Sylvara's mind. A dragon as black as Nelexi, but with tan wings and stripe instead of red, and much smaller, though still bigger than most dragons. Somehow, she knew that this dragon would never age, but that unlike Nelexi it could be killed by what one would expect to be able to kill something of that size and strength, and that unlike Nelexi it could not breathe lava, only fire.

They were here. They were finally here. They had come to the sanctuary of the Dragonriders. And they had come to the door-step of the Light Elves, the greatest mages of Areaer, from whom Sylvara might beg further training in healing.

The memories of distant ages informed Flameheart's feelings as the vale of Dragonsong Forest spread out beneath herself and Nelexi. These were her vale, her people, her dragons. She did not feel the shyness she expected, the shrinking from those who respected her as the Obsidian Guardian's Chosen, while dismissing her as one who could never be considered a true Dragonrider, since she had never had any experience of carrying for a hatchling dragon. She was still Flameheart, shy and reserved after a manner, but she did not feel the other shyness at all.

She could almost feel the currents of the lava inside her skin.

She knew the precise instant when the dragons noticed that the Obsidian Guardian was here, when their flight paths changed, a number of them angling to intercept the Obsidian Guardian, and a like number angling towards where they expected the Obsidian Guardian to land. Even in a forest with trees and clearings as huge as this one, there were not many good places for Nelexi to land.

When they landed in a clearing among trees so huge ordinary dragons could walk on their branches like birds, that cast down curtains of weeping foliage, the trees and the meadow were bright with dragons, so beautiful, so lovely, so treasured. Beside most of them, or sitting against their sides or chests, or astride their necks, were their riders. And in one corner stood the obsidian dragon Carnathan, with her two riders and their colored dragons.

Nelexi landed first and folded her brilliant red wings neatly. Shimmer hung in the sky behind her, while she took center stage. Then the small dragon landed neatly when the huge one had made room.

As he came into land, Flameheart felt the sudden, heart-breaking shift in the attitudes of the assembled dragons and riders. Up until now, Shimmer had been barely noticed at all, overshadowed by the presence of the Obsidian Guardian, who had been mostly absent from among the Sha'adhri for many decades, longer than most of those here had been alive. But now every dragon, and by extension every rider, saw Shimmer, met him, and knew him for an unnatural dragon, one of a breed changed over thousands of years by twisted magic, one who no longer thought like a dragon. At least to their minds.

Pity. Disdain. A thousand reactions. There were not a thousand dragons here, not even a thousand dragons and riders here, but one person could have more than one reaction.

Did you expect this? Flameheart asked Nelexi.

"I do not expect," answered the Obsidian Guardian. *"But that dragons and riders can be short-sighted, prejudiced, and arrogant I know. But I let them prove themselves, without the weight of expectations."*

Flameheart nodded, as Nelexi shifted slightly. *What now?* Nelexi did not rule the dragons. Many of the dragons and riders saw her as some sort of god, but she did not rule or reign over them. For the most part, she left them to make their own decisions. She would no more let them make her choose and think for them than she had been willing to do that for her own chosen rider, Flameheart. Yet she was their Guardian. She commanded their respect, without ever having to command. She wielded influence among them, influence she did not completely shirk.

"Patience, young one," said Nelexi with a chuckle. But Flameheart's question was answered, as she felt Nelexi extend a tendril of reassurance – reassurance that had Flameheart in it – to Shimmer. He stood taller and folded his wings with confidence, taking his time and doing it with a flourish.

This was so complicated it made Flameheart want to run into the middle of the Plains and never come back. It made the Sha'adhri's attitude towards her seem simple by comparison.

Gradually, the dragons and riders sorted themselves out. Flameheart felt it more than she saw it, somehow, since there was not much, and certainly not rapid, physical relocation. Yet there was physical relocation, and there was certainly shifting and settling of a thousand attitudes.

Flameheart climbed down Nelexi's shoulder to take her tiny, almost invisible place, in front of the huge dragon, momentarily distracting attention from Shimmer, as riders who had not been present when she had been in Dragonsong Forest before, approached her to greet her and Nelexi, sometimes physically accompanied by their dragons. From then on, the attention was divided between her and Nelexi, and Shimmer and Sylvara, with the attention of individual dragons and riders, or flights of them, shifting back and forth between the Obsidian Guardian and her rider, and the altered dragon from another continent and his rider.

Under the attention of the Dragonriders, Flameheart felt once more the shy child. She was distracted by their attitudes towards Shimmer by the sheer overwhelming weight and number of them, and by their attitudes towards her – and Nelexi. She could hear it in their voices, feel it from them, how some of them questioned whether she could possibly be an appropriate partner for the Obsidian Guardian, yet hesitated to really think it, because of their awe and respect for the Guardian. There were others who did not respect the Guardian much, but they would not greet her here. And then there were others, who had no such questions about her, maybe even no thoughts about her at all. It was all way, way too much and she could not process it. She could barely even respond and react, and that was only because Nelexi helped her.

Somehow, though, she noticed when Carnathan spread her tan wings, larger than those of any other dragon there except for Nelexi, though compared to Nelexi the difference did not matter, and flew away with her riders and their dragons. Flameheart had seen Carnathan before, but the obsidian dragon always kept her distance.

After a while, the stream of people and dragons stopped and settled away, though a dozen or so riders and dragons took up positions near to Flameheart and Nelexi. Some, Flameheart felt certain, were conversing with Nelexi, but Nelexi did not invite her into the conversation, and she felt too overwhelmed to listen anyways. She briefly entertained the idea of wandering off among the giant trees, but then sat down on Nelexi's paw. Somehow, it did not feel – *safe?* – to wander away. Yet the feeling felt wrong. These were their forests, their valley, their domain and sanctuary, from ages so old and so long ago Flameheart could not comprehend them, time so far removed from her it might have been the same time that the Sun-and-Storm-Chosen lived and Zharda freed her people from the slavery to the Old Ones. She knew this valley like her own hand, and it should be a sanctuary.

But something made her stay there, perched on Nelexi's foot.

After a while, most of those around her and Nelexi left, one by one, taking to the skies or meandering into the forests, mostly in one direction. Arm-in-arm with another Dragonrider, Sylvara wandered into the trees in the other direction, her silver dragon and presumably the other rider's gold and orange dragon accompanying the riders.

"Unless they violate the sanctuary, I will do nothing more, Flameheart," Nelexi answered. *"They know, or would if they thought, that I accept Sylvara and Shimmer, for I brought them. And, if they think for themselves, they know that it is not right to judge or condemn people for crimes committed against them before they were born. What would you like to do?"*

Flameheart stood up, balancing on Nelexi's slippery scales, and clapped her hands, thinking. "We could swim in the lake!"

"Very well. I will take you there."

A few days earlier, Camilla had first sensed the change in the wind. Before long, it became evident on the ground. Stream-beds, mostly dry from the summer, but still clearly stream-beds wandered through ground that sloped gently upwards, in a series of hills, to the north and east. Beyond, mountains rose against the sky, purple and blue, with only the smallest of white caps. It was far drier land than the forests of Ilesh had ever been, but far wetter and more forested than the plains they had just crossed.

Camilla knew what it meant: the mountains that guarded Dragonsong Forest were before them. Soon they would meet the Sha'adhri.

They were now being forced to rise higher, and Camilla felt the strain in Radiance's wings as she labored to fly at higher altitudes, as the mountains rose underneath them. Camilla would have liked to admire the view, especially after her realization at Eskeliae that she would like to create art. It would have been interesting to think about how to create an effect that was to these mountains as Eskeliae was to the sea. Their eyes were drawn to the ridges, the falls of the land, the valleys and the vales and the stream-beds, rocky cliffs and hillsides, and forested slopes, and to the patterns they wove. But the distraction of Radiance's pain, as wounds that had not healed quite right strained in the thinner air and mountain winds throbbed or protested what she asked of them, pulled their attention away from the mountain woodlands below them. As they ascended higher, the dragons started to struggle for breath.

When Sleet asked to land, Camilla and Radiance decided they had to. Radiance was of a mind with Camilla, willing, able, almost eager, to defy and press through anything, but she was weak and weary, and so was Sleet. But, while Radiance's aching body rested after she walked to cool off, Camilla climbed up what was almost a cairn of rocks at the top of a hill, and looked out over the mountains, blue-green with the leaf-color of the predominant tree species in this valley.

So close. So close. Of all the things to be slowed down and held back by, even if it was just a few more days.

Her eyes were drawn to a black speck circling, above them and to the east, between the shoulders of the rising mountains. As soon as Camilla thought it, she knew what circled there. A dragon. But she could not speak to this dragon or touch her thoughts. Somehow, she blocked Camilla out too well for that. Camilla could not even be sure that she was heard, though the dragon *had* to be aware of her presence.

Mingled emotions roiled in Camilla. *Should* that be what all dragons were like? Had the elves damaged them? Yet, here was proof, they *had* flown to the right place! There were dragons here. This was the home of the Sha'adhri.

So close. So close. And not there yet.

Radiance's wings and shoulders ached. They walked the pass. Camilla trudged beside her, her mind open to the intentions and presence of those around her, for she would not repeat the mistake that had caused Ben's death, but she walked with her head bowed, trudging through the snow, her feet cold. There was more snow than it had looked like there was.

And Ben was not here.

The weight of it crashed down on her, more of a burden than walking through the snow. He deserved to be here. He ought to be here. And she missed him more than anything. His warm voice was gone, stripped out of her soul. His thoughtful companionship left behind a void. She got used to it a little, in routine monotony, when there was nothing to say or do. She hardly thought, and she *felt* even less.

But they were almost there, and Ben was not. She could not, dared not, imagine his feelings, his voice, what he would point out or share, how he would encourage, or how she would encourage him. There was a void there too big to be touched, the edges of it raw with pain. It felt as if the winds of the pass, that beat against her wind-chapped face and Radiance's sore muscles, rubbed salt in a wound that could never be healed.

Radiance missed him, too. *They* missed him. A piece of both of them was left in him, gone with him.

Somewhere in the dimness that was almost despair, Camilla wondered if the loss of Ben affected them in a way the loss of her Mom did not, in part because Radiance had never personally known her Mom.

Past the despair that felt like it could crush the world, her determination only grew stronger. She *would* rescue Mom, she *would* defeat the Wizard-King, and there had to be more she could do! But first, she must make sure Lavilor was safe, and she must kill the Wizard-King. Nothing would be sweeter than to shred the very heart of the Northern Horror apart with that fire.

Camilla held out her hand and brought the flicker of a fire into being between her fingers. The whisper of the Heartfire soothed her, singing to her as if, even now, Ben's soulfire could touch hers. As if Ben's soulfire was there in the Heartfire, one with it.

She let it. *This* was what would destroy the Wizard-King. This was what would give her and Radiance the strength. She let it sing to her of more than she could know. Gripped in the song of the fire, the cold and the weariness was less a drain, though she still ached with it.

Their legs burned with weariness, and the burning did nothing to alleviate the dull sting of the cold, when a light breeze blew towards them, whipping Camilla's hair around her face. The dragons smelled it first, fresh and free, alive and rejuvenating. Radiance was so tired and aching that it took a few moments for what it meant to register: this had to be a breeze blowing from the valley of the dragons. They were so near the top. Even then, there was not much energy for the renewed vigor of that realization. They were so close, and they were so tired.

The ground started to slope down. Though it had done that before – there were valleys between the ranks of the mountains – this time Camilla was sure they were almost there. They had never sensed this breeze before, and now, weary as she was, her senses picked up something else, more indefinable than the breeze. It was more like the eerie feeling the wind from off the Guardian Isles had given her, the feeling that was a sense of the strange Fire Groves and Dark Woods tended by the Dark Elves of the isles. This feeling was not eerie, like that one, and she realized she had felt it for a long time, but had not noticed it over the flow of the fire she called. There was fire in it, dragonfire. She did not feel their minds, and she was too tired to tell, but she could sense the magic presence of thousands of dragons and something that felt so much like Nelexi, but she and Radiance were too exhausted to sort through her feelings about Nelexi. But it was not just dragons or fire. It was life, forests, forests so much different from those of Ilesh or the Guardian Isles, and healing, but healing that was not any more like the healing magic of Alian than these forests were like the Guardian Isles or the border enchantments of Ilesh. It was far more than she could untangle right now, but it did not frighten her. At least, it did not frighten her any more than her fire did.

Even with the breeze and the scent of magic, time did not seem to pass, even in a boring, painful trudge. Foot after foot, foot after foot. Drag foot out of the snow, drag foot out of the snow. Occasionally, Lavilor's whistling reached Camilla through the breeze. He and Sleet must be feeling amazingly well, if he felt like whistling. Then again, Lavilor rode on Sleet's shoulders, whereas Camilla walked to spare Radiance any additional burden. Even Lavilor's whistling she noticed distantly.

Suddenly, they stood on the side of a ridge. Camilla did not register it until Sleet whispered in her mind, *"Look!"*

She almost slid with surprise. Radiance dug her claws in deeper.

The mountains still cut off their view on most sides, but they could look straight down, through a narrow window between the shoulders of the mountains, these ones not clad with snow, towards a valley, indistinct with a slight haze. It was unmistakably the source of the magical breeze.

They were almost there, but Camilla was more happy that they were almost out of the snow. She and Radiance were too tired for excitement.

A sudden wind gusted Camilla, as Sleet spread his wings and launched himself into the air, roaring, while Lavilor shouted, his high, boyish voice cutting through the soft spots in the dragon's roar.

Radiance and Camilla thought together. They had to find a place to rest, soon. Camilla did not think she could scale this slope without sliding down it, not as tired as she was right now. But maybe Sleet could be convinced to carry her as well as Lavilor for a little while, and Radiance could follow. She and Radiance did not like it, but it might not be such a bad idea.

A little lee between two boulders would do. The boulders did not look like they were going anywhere soon, though smaller rocks had broken off, one by one, and fallen down hill.

As she stood there, cold and shivering, while Radiance tucked herself into a ball, trying to get her aching wings and shoulders warm, and Sleet arranged as much of his smaller body around her as he could, a spell came to Camilla.

It was an odd moment, and for a moment she mistrusted it. Yet if she was not to fear the fire altogether, she could not see why she should fear this. It was only that she did not know how she knew, and only half knew what she knew. But the song of fire was not the enemy. The song of fire had not killed Ben. Her foolishness in not listening, her pride and desire to escape Nelexi and Flameheart as much as Shimmer and Sylvara, had contributed.

Camilla opened her hand and a fountain of translucent fire sprang up. She held out her other hand below a stream of transparent fire, and a glowing half-transparent, clear as glass at the center, burning gold and opaque around the edges, formed. She let it fall into the snow at her feet, which hissed and let out a single note.

Half tripping in the snow, over her cold, muscles trembling with weariness, and her colder feet, Camilla walked a circle around the dragons, while Lavilor stood with a hand under Sleet's wing and watched her with curious, quiet eyes. She formed every ember to a different shape, one she saw, sensed, but did not fully understand, only that it seemed to fit the pattern of other spells she had seen before. It was a different pattern, a different rhythm, and a different kind of music than Lìarz's spell-craft, yet a similarity. As if it resonated on a different set of notes, in a different part of the world, yet some – not all – of the patterns were the same.

With every ember that fell softly onto the snow, a new note arose, and every note tied all the previous notes together, until they sang.

And in that moment, as Camilla laid the key of the spell and wove it in with a singing of fire, reaching a soft and stable climax, she saw it, and a moment later she felt it: in the circle she had walked, transparent fire rose up, and from all sides warmth wafted inwards. It was not strong, but it was definite, and it would soak in Radiance's chilled bones and tendons.

Tired, Camilla laid out the bedroll she had received from Lìarz against Radiance's shoulder that was not covered by Lavilor's body, and almost before she could lay down, she was asleep.

Dragonsong

Radiance flew low over the hills, and Camilla could hardly believe her eyes. There should be no way for trees to be this huge. She could not see how thick the trunks were, but the canopies covered hundreds and hundreds of feet, and some of the branches she glimpsed through them looked half as thick around as Radiance. The branches lower down had to be even larger than that.

A forest of trees that were to dragons as other trees were to birds.

But it was a forest that showed the advance of the year. Here and there, individual trees boasted leaves tinged or rimmed in orange, gold, or near-red.

But where are the dragons? wondered Camilla. She did not see any, and she did not *feel* any near, either. They had to all be both far away and hiding under the trees. But why? Did most dragons not enjoy flying? Why couldn't she see even one, soaring like a hawk or an eagle? Why didn't she see even a few darting over the canopy? A glint of shining, sparkling blue or yellow, red or purple. A sudden shimmer of white on scales or wings reflecting the light.

Radiance was certainly enjoying skimming over the trees. The air was a reasonable temperature that did not make the aches in her bones and wings worse. She felt small and light. Something about the air, or the huge trees, lifted spirits. Sleet was positively bouncing around, and several times Camilla heard an excited call from Lavilor on the wind.

She touched his mind gently. *You are having fun.*

"*Yes!*" There were definite undertones of Sleet in Lavilor's reply.

Have you or Sleet seen any dragons? I and Radiance haven't.

"No. Nor felt any." Lavilor answered carelessly, as if neither he nor Sleet cared.

Then again, Radiance did not seem to care either. Should she?

Did it really matter if this place was not as full of dragons as Camilla had been led to believe? That would mean there was more space for them. She pulled her mind away from that feeling. This place felt seductively like home, and she could not be home yet. She had to destroy the Wizard-King first, even if there was not anyone left alive to be saved, which she did not know, one way or another. But she had to make sure home was safe and would *stay* safe before she could feel at home. She must not get distracted again.

"*Just a little fun, Camilla.*" It was Radiance's voice, at once her own voice and separate from her.

But Camilla could never ignore the undertones. To fight the Nightmare, they had to have home, to carry it in their hearts. With this feeling around them, this peace, this joy and uplifting *fun* in their souls, could the Nightmare even touch their minds? No?

They had to know what they were fighting for. They had to keep it in themselves. That was even more important that knowing what they fought against. They had to stay separate. They had to stay themselves, whatever raged around or against them. And *this* was freedom from the Nightmare.

But Camilla was afraid to relinquish the anger and hatred. She was afraid that she would forget her purpose and find one excuse after another not to do what she must.

Find Lavilor a place to be as safe as possible, safer than she could keep him, so that she would not be going off and leaving him in danger. Whether he chose to take full advantage of the safety was another matter, but she had to do her best to offer it to him. And then go, destroy the Wizard-King and free his captives – anything that deserved to be free. Then come back and live here. It was odd to have a foretaste of what that would be, the – the freedom and happiness of it.

Then Camilla and Radiance felt a dragon mind, a little like Nelexi's, a little like the minds of the obsidian dragons Nelexi had fought over the fleet, the ones whose voices and words had resonated with Camilla so deeply, except that she was not quite sure how she felt about them. And they had suggested that she leave Radiance behind, and that was impossible and abhorrent. She and Radiance were one soul, and her choices were Radiance's, just as Radiance's were hers. Radiance was not something between her and the magic and immortality it might be hers to claim. But she was so confused, and she preferred not to remember them, especially after what had happened to Ben.

Between a gap in the trees, several hills ahead, a dragon rose up, black like Nelexi but much smaller, and with dark tan instead of burning red wings and stripe.

"*I am Carnathan,*" she said, and Camilla somehow knew that she could speak to humans and even elves, as well as dragons, like Nelexi could. Was that something all dragons ought to be able to do, and only the ones damaged by the elves couldn't? "*With me are my riders, Tessel and Alcovi, and the dragons, Math and Lalnaph. We are here to escort you to the presence of Nelexi, Obsidian Guardian, Guardian of the Dragons, Guardian of the Forest of Dragonsong, Wings of the Fire of Areaer.*"

I don't think so, said Camilla. She felt Radiance rise underneath her, bunching together, their attitude joined into one song of fire. They reached out and felt the others Carnathan had mentioned – farther than the black dragon, but still not far. They would hear Camilla's words as well, mind-to-mind, as dragons heard, and the riders as well. *I. Do. Not. Think. So.*

"*We were sent by Nelexi, the Obsidian Guardian herself.*"

Camilla was not sure whether she believed that at the moment, if it mattered, or if she cared.

We claim the same right to this valley that all dragons claim, and I do not think so. Defy us at your own danger.

The obsidian dragon rose also, matching Radiance. "*I, too, am a*

*guardian of the dragons. All obsidian dragons are. And there are two more
with me. I am here to escort you to the presence of Nelexi – not to cast you
from the valley or imprison you."*

We go to Nelexi when we please, not when you do, not when she does.

They were so tired, but also so enraged. This was supposed to be a
home-coming, and this was *no* home-greeting. What had happened? Had
Nelexi somehow poisoned this place against them?

"No, I have not." Nelexi's voice was red thunder of fire, and she was
not very far – though exactly how far she was, Camilla and Radiance did not
know. But Camilla did not know that after her voice abruptly cut off, she
continued speaking to Carnathan, words Camilla could not hear.

How did she know? Camilla asked.

Half-bold, half-defiant, Sleet answered. *"I spoke to her."*

It's okay, Camilla hastened to reassure him. *I don't hate her. My
feelings about Nelexi are just confused. I'd rather not think about her.*

How had she created a situation where her own brother and his dragon
were half-afraid of how she would react to anything that was not her own idea?
Had she really been that horrible, or done something else to contribute to their
fear? All she wanted was to protect them, even if she had done that horribly.

Even if that was not all she had wanted. If that had been all she had
wanted, Camilla somehow knew, she would not have fled from Nelexi. She
knew Nelexi was not a danger. But she had been confident in her own strength
and ability, and she had wanted other things, too. But she had never, *never,*
wanted those other things at the risk of the lives or well-being of those she
cared about.

Ben.

Camilla jerked herself back into full awareness of her surroundings,
and saw that Carnathan and her riders – whatever that meant, since Camilla
had no idea how a dragon could have more than one rider, though if a rider
could have more than one dragon she did not see how it was impossible for a
dragon to have more than one rider – and their dragons were flying away.

Radiance, why don't we angle there? Camilla noted a place in the other
direction than Carnathan was flying, and knew that Radiance had noticed it
with her. A small river flowed into a depression between hills and made a little
lake before flowing out again. It looked beautiful and peaceful, a fresh place to
recover and feast on the goodness of this land, and to think about how to deal
with it.

Clearly, there were some dragons here who were not very nice. This
was not going to be simple, but Camilla *hoped* it would be a safe place for
Lavilor and Sleet. She needed to find one so desperately, so that she could turn
her mind fully to her other goal.

Lavilor flung himself on Camilla, and she staggered back from his weight. "Don't do that!"

He cringed momentarily, then straightened. "I'm sorry. I forget – y'you're not as big as a dragon!"

Camilla laughed shortly.

"This place is beautiful! Look at the huge trees! Do you want to climb one with me?"

"Maybe later." *Why? There might not be a later ... not for a long time. I'm looking for a safe place. Then I go for vengeance and rescue.*

"Why not now?"

"Are you afraid? I don't think – the dragons might not be very nice, but I don't think they're going to hurt us."

Her heart twanged. Could she deny him? Or would that be another action she would regret forever?

"Sure. I will climb with you." Her heart betrayed her as she spoke.

Lavilor seemed to sense it, even though she knew she was not mind-touching with him. "You don't have to if you don't want to," he said, all exuberance gone.

"I do want to."

"You sure?"

"Certain."

Camilla looked over her shoulder to where the dragons stood, shimmering gold and silver in the fresh green twilight – and red. But there was no bulk of sparkling red scales and shimmering crimson wings, and there was no whisper of Ben's sedate yet playful thoughts rubbing against her mind. He was gone. He was not here. And a part of her was not here, and the wound did not heal.

"You sure? You all right?" Lavilor's voice drifted to her, insistent, caring.

"I – I miss Ben." His hand clutched hers and she felt it, and turned to face him. He had grown, and now he was almost as tall as she was. His forehead reached her chin. His dark brown eyes implored her, beckoned her.

"I miss Ben, but I'll be all right. Let's go climb."

The dragons stretched their necks and spread their wings behind them, wishing them well. They were too tired from the long flight to want to climb, and at least for now, they would rest better on the ground like they were accustomed, than in a tree.

They meandered to a large tree with dark green foliage and even darker smooth brown skin growing at the edge of the water. Camilla stood still, looking up at it, Lavilor at her elbow.

"Cam?" he said.

"Yes?"

"Can you make a – a step with your hands? I think I can reach there, then." He pointed to where the massive trunk split making a sort of saddle, about one and a half man-heights above the ground. From there, one trunk headed in a fairly sharp angle upwards, while another bent in a curving, serpentine shape above the ground.

"Sure." Camilla locked her fingers together and placed her hands across her thigh. She crouched a little and braced herself, as Lavilor scrambled into her hold. He stood there for a moment, one heel cupped in her hands, his hands on the tree. Then he lurched up, and Camilla half-stumbled. She recovered herself and looked up.

He was in the tree, scrambling into the saddle.

"Can you get up here if I help you?"

"I'm sure." She forced all other thoughts away and approached the tree. He reached a hand down towards her, and she reached up, until their hands met and clasped.

This was something they had never been allowed to do by the elves, at least not nearly as much as children should have. They might have managed to try and climb a tree once or twice when they were very young. Camilla felt Radiance move in her mind. Together they wrestled the thought down to the ground, squishing it between their combined weight.

It took several tries before Camilla got into the tree, wedged with Lavilor between the branches. She was not sure if she enjoyed it. It felt precarious, and not her idea of comfortable.

Lavilor did not seem to notice. He beckoned her onward, and went half-scrambling half-running up the serpentine branch. Camilla followed, testing her footing more carefully. She wondered if he had spent a lot of time climbing trees on the islands off the coast of Ellenesia, when they had been traveling with that Dark Elf. *No, don't think about that.*

They were slowly making their way up the tree, when Camilla stopped with her hand on an upright branch that sought the sky.

"It's pretty easy," said Lavilor, tapping the branch with his foot.

"Not that," said Camilla. "Dragons come this way."

He looked like he had swallowed something unpleasant. "Do you really *need* to get back to the dragons? Sleet isn't afraid, and he says Radiance isn't either. They're *dragons*. They might not be nice, but they're not going to kill or enslave our friends. We don't need to be there.

"A-are you okay?"

Camilla clenched her hand on the branch. Ben had died. Because she had not been vigilant. He was not here. He was not there. There was no whisper of him in her mind, telling her what he felt, what he wanted.

He was gone, because she had not been there for him.

"No! I need to get back!" Fire pulsed out from her. She felt the flickers of heat race across her skin, harmless but raging.

"No-no!" Lavilor screamed, his words turning from some sort of admonition into terror. Too many voices assaulted Camilla at once. Dragons. Assuring her they were not dragon slayers, they would never kill a dragon who did not threaten them, they had never killed a dragon in their life, they would never kill a dragon for his *scales*, they wanted to hunt and kill the men who killed Ben!

"Camilla!" Lavilor's scream, stark with terror, brought her awareness back to him.

He was walking away from her on the branch, backwards, hands held up as if somehow they could ward off the threat. She looked around, extending her senses, to see why he was afraid, briefly touched his mind, *knew*, saw!

The tree was burning around her!

The limitations of her own knowledge of magic struck her as heat never could. The damage was done. The tree was burning. She stepped away from the fire herself now, her feet dancing through flames. If she knew more, she could lower herself and Lavilor down to the ground, slowly, without harm, then deal with the fire.

But she did not!

She turned around and faced the fire, licking out from every place her body had been touching, eating leaves that curled into ashes and smoked, racing along the bark and blackening it, charing it, weakening it.

No fire. Back into me. I called you on accident. You are not needed. Come back. Return. Do not burn.

It seemed slowly, the flames flickered, dimmed, then winked out of existence. She felt their happy flickers darting through her veins, and then realized she was hearing the sound of dragon wings. Very close, now.

Feeling unbalanced and precarious on the half-burned branch, she extended only her mind, and felt Sleet angling up towards where Lavilor crouched in fear. She felt the branch vibrate when he jumped, and knew the moment he caught his arms around Sleet's neck. She knew when the dragon landed, and he rolled onto the ground.

But she had no idea how to get out of the tree now. She had no idea how much she had weakened it with the fire. She and Radiance had no idea if they could pull the stunt Lavilor and Sleet had, successfully.

Another dragon touched her – their – mind. Something like disdain lurked beneath the surface of a plan explained in images and feelings, memory and the thought of motion. This dragon had done this sort of thing. She had done it in far more challenging circumstances. She would glide over Camilla's head, between the branches of the tree, and pluck the human out of the branches with her claws. Then she could land on her her hind legs and drop down on one fore leg, to put Camilla down with the other.

Something in Camilla burned with fury, but she tamped it down. Radiance might be able to do this, too, if she weren't stiff from her injuries. If they had gotten to practice the sort of things dragons and riders ought to get to do to together.

But no. This would not help. Not now. She waited for the dragon.

Camilla let herself sink into the soft moss. Radiance curled despondently around her. She had lost control of her fear and grief, and she had almost caused a disaster. She had almost hurt her little brother.

She was not safe.

And the other dragons hated her. Maybe it was not hate, but it was nothing Camilla liked any better than hate. Pity. Disdain. Scorn. Something that could have been fear, but instead it was more scorn. Disgust. A great deal of disgust. Other feelings of that sort.

Ordinarily, she would not have cared. She would have met their scorn with more scorn, their pity with disdain, and their disgust with greater disgust. She was not sure that she cared, now.

Ben was dead. Ben was dead because of her, because she had not listened to the wants of others, because she had gone off on her own without Nelexi, because she had failed to be there for them and protect him. Her little brother had almost died, she had almost hurt her little brother, because she was there.

Radiance loved her, and she loved Radiance, but the other dragons hurt her. And they were together in their loss, their grief, their failure.

It was all because they had not been allowed to grow the way they should have been, and because Radiance and her ancestors had been abused and altered before they were even born. The other dragons did not think like Radiance, or else they did not think like the other dragons. The dragons' thoughts were all feeling, utterly primal, effortlessly precise with the exactitude of a single leaf among all leaves, not the sharpness of a knife's edge.

Camilla felt the approach of another fire, deeper than the earth. She sat up, and Radiance raised her head slowly, as the huge black and molten red dragon approached them, lumbering through the meadow grasses.

The molten flame caressed her, and she drew back as from a knife's edge, cold as a cloudless night in the high snows, as from fire licking the skin from flesh. Even as she knew it was meant to comfort, it was only torment to her despair.

Nelexi came to a halt, so near her wings almost covered them, her *presence*, deep as the earth, looming over them.

The fire reached out again, and Camilla and Radiance were torn between it, its touch like a hand on a raw bruise, yet like cool water begging to be splashed on a burning face. *"You are not conquered."*

Camilla straightened, defiance sparking. *Who are you to say that?*

"I am not. Is it true?" The fire flickered, a haze that taunted, reminding Camilla of the moment she had freed Ben, bringing to her soul the rush of that sea of molten flame that she could never forget.

Radiance's soft voice hummed in her mind, and it was her own, yet not her own, and the more hers because of that. *She is right. We are not.* It was soothing, comfort. Love. Pure, undiluted love.

They were one, and they were two. The love they shared, that they *were,* wrapped around Camilla like the antidote to all wounds. She loved herself. Another loved her. She was another.

We may not be conquered, but we have *failed.*

They felt the black presence draw back for a moment, as if considering – not far, still surrounding them, but not quite pressed against them.

"And you did not believe you could *fail, and so you feel conquered."*

Who are you to tell me that? Who *was* Nelexi to ask these things? To speak as if she were their conscience, their inner voice? As if they ought to – as if they could not help – confiding their deepest weaknesses to her?

For weakness they, apparently, had, even though it was not possible that such as they – *she* – were should have weakness.

Camilla got to her feet and beside her, moving in perfect synchrony with her movements, Radiance also rose. The fire was still there, the fire that had flowed forth in power from her soul freeing Ben and sweeping the Northern Horror away. Its power still burned, ready to embrace and ready to cleanse, ready to burn and ready to purge, ready to take herself into it, ready to consume, invincible, power as pure as the sharpest pain or love itself, undiluted, unbreakable, unstoppable. The fire was still there for her, and she felt its power in every drop in her veins, in every bit of her, from the greatest to the smallest.

And this same power was there for Nelexi.

She let it pour through her, filling every wound torn out of her by Ben's loss but not replacing him and overflowing, filling every empty reservoir inside of her with power that burned to *be,* pure sustenance to the root of her existence.

"Nelexi." It was two voices that spoke, or more, or only one. Radiance's voice burned through hers as perfectly as heat through flame.

The black dragon looked down on her with a molten, glowing eye.

"This fire is yours, as it is mine." Deeper, deeper, a whisper, not Nelexi's, but the fire whose voice always burned through Nelexi's. *As you are mine.* "Why did you not free my people? My race? *Are you Guardian of the Dragons ... or not?"*

It was as if they spoke to themselves. Nelexi was not stirred. Her eye stared down at them, like a window into the very fire that flowed upwards in Camilla's and Radiance's veins. *"There are limits to my power. And there are limits to my existence."*

"It is no excuse. There is no limit to the Fire."

"True – as you may mean it. But you are not the Fire. Yet." Was it Nelexi, speaking to her? Or the Fire, speaking to Nelexi – or them both?

"There may be no limits to the Fire, but there are limits to this existence. Nor, long as I have lived, was I present to prevent the atrocity which calls forth your rage. Neither do I explain myself to you. I live the Fire and I follow the Fire, Dragon-mage.

"I was not there to protect Ben. I am the Obsidian Guardian, but I am not there to protect all dragons."

Camilla felt as if fire rose up her throat. "Ben is with the Fire, now. Do not speak to me of death, in the face of that which death alone can end."

"Then you have answered yourself, Dragon-mage. Death can end it. I cannot.

"It is the same Fire, but the power which you have from the Fire is not the power I have from the Fire. And the Fire in me and the Fire in death are one Fire, but mine is the power of the Obsidian Guardian, not the power of the Death Guardian.

"I, Dragon-mage, am the Obsidian Guardian, not the Healer."

"I demand answers."

Something of the power in Nelexi veiled itself, still there, still immediately palpable to Camilla, but somehow less pressing, less overbearing. *"Answers you will have. Answers we all will have. But I have lived thousands of years, longer than you can yet understand, and I do not know all answers. Some answers it takes us a very long time to understand."*

"You are only making excuses for not answering me." *I believe it.* But was it *the truth?* The Fire?

This was the oddest experience of her life, and as the power dampened – though it was still there, a burning ember in her bones – some of the despondency flowed back around her, like water seeping out of the ground into the moat around a castle.

"You know that is not true. Or you could. Either way, it is not true. And there is much I may not tell you, for I cannot. I cannot even tell my rider."

"Tell me what you can."

Nelexi took a moment to settle herself and lay down in the meadow, her wing-tips resting in the shallows of the water. *"I have no power to reverse what the life-mages have done, and I have no power to break a bond – or if I did, it would be cruel to do so, and it would not heal the scars."* Her voice was one Camilla was not sure she had ever heard before, though Radiance recognized it. She had always seen the power, the Fire, and not the dragon – or rather, a dim reflection of the Fire in a twisted mirror. And it had been easy to do, for the Fire was ever present in Nelexi, as Radiance was in her, and she in Radiance. But though the Fire and Nelexi were one, they were also two, and their oneness was another thing from hers and Radiance's. She did not understand all of it, but she knew that much. It was more like something else she did not want to think about, and she wanted to think about less than ever because she had just experienced it.

"It would not heal the scars. The eggs must hatch, and hatch to riders. I have rescued eggs, and rescued riders. I have helped riders find their way out of Ilesh. But I could not free them all. Do you even know what you mean when you ask that? You do not, and you know it, but I will let you tell yourself what you know. You might not believe I have done this, because there are so few of those dragons left free, but you know already how the Wizard-King hunted and slaughtered them. And there is another thing you may not know: for some reason, outside of Ilesh, their numbers do not grow. Instead they dwindle. I cannot tell you the reasons why. And this is all that I can tell you for now.

"You may think that what happened in Ilesh is the greatest atrocity in the world and was my greatest responsibility to prevent, as Guardian of the Dragons. But you have seen only a tiny corner of the world and what is in it. You do not yet know what it means to fight, or to win, or to lose. You know only in a very small part what it means to live, to be. You do not know what I am. And you do not know what else I must guard and what else I must fight. It may be I can learn from you, but you too must learn.

"Be well, Camilla and Radiance, Dragon-mage. Live free. Love in full. Never despair. The Fire will transform all who are."

With that, the great black dragon rose to her feet, like a slumbering volcano waking – or what they imagined such a thing must be – and turned her back towards them. The earth shook and the wind shuddered as she took to the sky, her great red wings rippling and glowing against the green and the blue.

Camilla felt Radiance considering Nelexi and her departure. *What do we do now?*

Lavilor was safe. If he chose to be. And she might not make him any safer. *No. No.* Radiance's presence wrapped around her. She could not give in, could not give up.

They turned to face the west. Maybe this was their sign that they should fly west now, cross the sea again, and bring the Fire to the gate of the Northern Horror. Nelexi would not do it. Maybe she could not. Maybe she was a coward. She certainly would not give them all the answers or even acknowledge many of their questions. But *they* could, and *they* would.

It seemed now that all her choices went awry. Was that because she was not flying to scorch her enemy and the enemy of all freedom and all life from the earth? Or was it something else? There was a point when they had begun to go awry, was there not? She had freed Ben, and she had been fleeing then. What was it? What was it?

Would flying now to confront the Northern Horror be another choice that went awry?

No. NO. NO! The world tilted under her, like the deck of a Sea Elf ship on a great cresting wave, tilting first one way, then the other, too rapidly and chaotically for her to get her bearings.

NO!!

She chose. She must succeed. She would succeed. She willed to succeed. That was all. What was this horror?

That was all. That was all. That was *absolutely* all.

She needed time to process this, to understand what had just happened, but *that* was not an option.

Then, said Radiance, *we stay. A little while longer. For you.*

For you. For you. For you.

Radiance loved her. She loved Radiance. She was loved. That was freedom. She knew it.

The others are gone? She knew it now. They had left, perhaps before Nelexi came. And Nelexi had not judged her. The other dragons and riders had. For being different. For not thinking like a dragon. For burning the tree. For things Camilla could not define or name. But Nelexi had not.

It did not fit her vision of Nelexi. Or her memory of Nelexi.

But she still felt like her first day trying to walk the deck of a ship tilting erratically in a near-storm.

Camilla paced through the grasses, stepping over Radiance's lashing tail, and after a while something like thoughts began to take form.

Either her desire to be free was not as pure as she knew it was, or the world did not work the way that she knew it must.

This all started because she had failed Ben. She had failed everyone she loved. And she knew where she had failed Ben. She had not respected his freedom, because respecting someone else's freedom meant respecting their desires.

Everything about Ben, except for Ben himself, upset her. Maybe his desire for freedom was not the unstoppable fire that hers was, but it was there. It was real. And she and Radiance were what they were because they were together. The impossible possibility that they could not be together did not bear thinking. But Ben, however his desire for freedom compared to hers, had been captured and enslaved in the most horrible ways possible, one after the other, and she could not decide which one was the most horrible. Running over his desires, instead of nurturing his will and giving his desires the same consideration as her own, had been a failure on her part. Misunderstanding and negligence.

But he had been enslaved in the first place.

She stopped and ground her fists into the loose fabric of her trousers. Radiance tore up grass and dirt between her claws. The world was not the way it ought to be. No, it was worse than that, the world was not the way it was.

Or was she weak because she had failed? Would none of it have happened if she had respected the desires and freedom of others? But how did it help for those who were most committed to freedom to be made too weak to fight those who opposed freedom because they were not perfect in perceiving the needs of others, while those who cared nothing for freedom – like the elven life-mages and slave masters, or the Wizard-King – were strong?

Nothing made sense!

Her dragon-senses touched two minds, a dragon and her rider. Were these more who looked down on them for what had happened to them? If they were, she and Radiance would give them what they deserved.

But, no, that was not what she picked up from them. Not even pity, or not much of it. This was ... this was a desire to make friends. A desire to be friends. A thought that they could be friends to the new dragons and riders, and maybe make up for the fact everyone else did not like them. Camilla-Radiance could not be certain about all of it, but most of what pity she felt was for the others not liking them.

She certainly did not need any pity for the fact most of the dragons and riders so far did not approve of her, but that did not mean she had to scorn it either. She was not sure how she knew that.

A green dragon with white wings landed on the far edge of the meadow, and a light-skinned human with hair that glowed yellow climbed down her shoulder.

Camilla spared a thought for Lavilor, who was sleeping with Sleet in a tree they had found with a nook big enough for both of them between two branches, and stepped towards the new-comer.

The new human wore a dress of frills in soft colors that rivaled anything Camilla or Radiance had seen among the Sea Elves. She bowed in what they understood to be a formal greeting, and she and her dragon shared their names. Helarinth – the dragon – and Teladri – the human.

Hello, Helarinth and Teladri. We are Radiance and Camilla.

Teladri startled for a brief moment at their voice in her mind, but then relaxed. "I thought you might like someone to help you settle in here," she said shyly.

We don't really plan on settling in. We come from a far land where a great evil has destroyed many things. We came to find a safe place for our brother, and then we will return to destroy the Wizard-King and free any of our people who are still alive.

Teladri shifted nervously, and Helarinth curled around her slightly, protective but also nervous. *Why?* But they did not ask that question.

"I've heard you – you're a dragon keeper, and you lost a dragon."

That's what they call it? – We are, and we did. He was a friend. We rescued him from our enemy, the Wizard-King, and then I failed to protect him.

Teladri shied even farther, the ruffles on her sleeves and shoulders shimmering in the breeze. "I am – sorry to remind you. I do not want to hurt, and I do not know how to do these things. I and Helarinth are young and new here. But I know it is a terrible thing to lose a dragon." She paused and took a deep breath. Then another.

Camilla-Radiance did not know what to do. She nodded.

Teladri took a small, shy, nervous step forward. Helarinth raised her head and looked down on her with a whirling green eye that matched her scales, as if watching over her rider. "I wanted you to know, we will not all judge you for what happened, with the fire – in the tree. We – some of us understand. I – if I lost Helarinth, I wouldn't manage. Nor she without me."

Camilla stepped up against Radiance's neck. *We still have each other.*

"But I know it is still hard. And others do, or will, once they think. Once they learn."

It is okay. We do not need their approval. Or their understanding.

Teladri shifted nervously again, and Camilla felt her worry. She was about to say something, and she was not sure if she should, or how it would be received. Helarinth did not understand her worry – or her curiosity. "A-are … can you not speak?"

"No, I can speak." She said that in her language, though it was a language she hated as well. *But I do not speak the language you do. And when I and Radiance became one, I gained this ability, too.*

Teladri nodded, still nervous, but somehow relieved.

This is so awkward. This is so, so awkward. What is this about?

They did not know what it was like to interact with other people, just … well, at their leisure. Camilla had never had much of it. She certainly had not had it as a slave, or with the Sea Elves who looked at her as a curiosity, or injured with the Plains People.

"Umm," said Teladri, licking her lips again, "what happened to you? You don't have to tell me if you don't want to!"

Of course I don't have to tell you if I don't want to. Do free peoples not know that?

Teladri paled. And this time she did not put words to her thoughts and speak them out loud. She and Helarinth directed their thoughts directly to her and Radiance. *"Are you mad? – But you are not."*

We are not mad. I am … annoyed with this, not with your questions as you seem to be concerned. But I do not understand, and I am annoyed. Somehow, Teladri's questions were not like the curiosity that wanted to make her an object to be looked at that Camilla had experienced elsewhere. It was more like Lavilor wanting to know how she did things.

Teladri reverted back to normal human speech. "I am sorry. We will leave then. But –?"

"You want to know," Camilla found herself saying in Anerian trade speech. *I don't mind. For some reason, this is how I heal now. When I use too much of my fire, it burns me, and this is how the burns heal. I don't know if other wounds would, but those do.*

Teladri nodded. "All right. I will go now, and leave you alone. If you ever want company, or to understand something about the way things are here, or anything, speak to us."

"I will."

Teladri jumped onto Helarinth's shoulders. "You're learning how to speak our language! Well, actually, I had to learn to speak this language myself. Ever want to hear my birth language?"

Maybe. But I don't like my birth language.

Teladri smiled and waved, and Camilla felt a wave of – consideration – from Helarinth.

That was interesting …. And exhausting.

Choice

The tree branch cracked, creaked, and fell. A void formed in her stomach as she fell. She screamed in terror with no voice, and reached for the power. Fire roared from her arms, incinerating the tree above her. Her brother screamed, falling, burning. She could not stop the falling, only burn, burn, burn ...

"Camilla!"

She was bathed in sweat, her heart hammering. A nightmare. It was only a nightmare. A touch told her that her brother was sleeping peacefully, and Sleet was dreaming about eating glowing blue flowers that grew in the marshy shallows of a lake whose surface scintillated with rainbows, reminiscent of the blue-green colors that shifted across the backs of some beetles.

A nightmare. It was only a nightmare.

She took a deep, calming breath and wrapped her hand around Radiance's foreleg. *No, no, no.*

But she could not shake the feeling. The desperation. Falling. Unable to do what she knew she could, but did not know how, to do.

So. I will learn how.

The decision came before she knew it, like a blast of icy wind cutting through her clothing and wrapping around her neck.

Radiance affirmed it, as reassuring and true as the cold spaces between the stars. The dragon agreed whole-heartedly.

That was enough for Camilla. She was not going to take the risk of ignoring her friend's desires anymore. Let alone Radiance's. They were one, and they had to act like one.

I will. It felt like she was promising the dragon. She was not sure why. She was not sure how. She was not sure what had just happened.

But she knew what Helarinth's thoughts had felt like, and bits and pieces of the thoughts of the other, disdainful dragons. They might have things wrong – or just be startled; she remembered how she had felt about the were-dragons – but it was the way dragons *should* think. And this thought from Radiance was something like that. She could not challenge it because it was not the way she was used to; she had to nurture it, even if it did not make sense to her. She had to feel the sense in it, because Radiance did.

Radiance was not like the other dragons. She and her rider were not like the Sha'adhri. And there was no lack in Radiance because of what had been done to her. She was not lesser. Camilla would assure her of that, believe that for her and in her, as surely as she loved and assured Camilla through her own fears. She did not need to think like the other dragons, should not be asked to more than was natural for her, as she now was.

But Camilla also must never, never make it hard for her, lest she help to deprive her dragon of what she otherwise could have. She must never do to

Radiance what others had done to her before her egg was even laid: stifle the way the dragon thought, because it did not make sense to her or suit her.

Her choices must be Radiance's, as much as her own.

"Are you going back to free Mom and kill the Wizard-King?" Lavilor sounded a mixture of eager and regretful. Anxious. Almost afraid.

"Not just yet. I'm going to the Light Elves first, to learn a little more about using the magic I have." It felt so odd to say it. The words were like stones on her tongue.

His shoulders tensed and slumped at once. Something like accusation laced his tone. "Are you ever going to rescue them?" His voice was quiet, hopeless, and that hurt Camilla, but the accusation within it stung like acid on raw wounds.

"Yes, yes, I am," she said, balling her hands into fists. "I am, but Radiance thinks this is a good idea." She took a mental step back, retreated inside herself. There were lots of good reasons for what she was doing. Lots of them. "There might be obstacles I have to get the prisoners past. Mostly what I can do right now is fire, lots of fire. But I couldn't float somebody up a cliff. If I learn how, I probably can. I have to be able to get there, and get them out, and hopefully survive any fights. That will probably require more control and skill than I have right now."

He looked away, utterly un-reassured. "You can say that forever. And, in the end, if you even do decide you're ready before you're dead, it will be too late, and they will all be dead."

That was her fear, too. "I know," she said. "I know. And I promise. But I've gone so wrong already by ignoring the wishes of others. I can't ignore what Radiance feels: and tell me, would it be better for me to fail?"

He looked back towards with her with fire in his eyes. "What would *you* say to that?"

Lavilor stared at Camilla, held her gaze in a way he never had before. He noticed, but did not acknowledge, her barely perceptible flinch.

Where had she gone? Where had the sister he knew gone?

This was not like her. But he had to face it. She had not been like herself for a long time. She had just been denying it, and so he had been able to try to ignore it. But he had sensed it.

Somewhere, and he was not sure when exactly because it had been happening before Ben's death, she had lost what made her Camilla. Ben's death had not brought it out, it had just changed the way it expressed. She had lost her fire, her belief. She might have been annoying, but she had believed. And now, she might not admit it, but she had almost admitted it. She had lost the confidence that made her Camilla.

His sister was broken.

Whatever he had or had not liked about some of her moods, however he had or had not disagreed with some of her perceptions or actions, this was … wrong.

He turned and ran.

"I'm coming, Lav. You have me."

The desperation of love from his dragon freed the tears he had not noticed.

He had Sleet. No matter what happened to Camilla, he had Sleet. And Laoirn. They would visit, sometime, soon.

The dragon soared through the tree branches, and the boy clung to his silver neck. Sleet was deeply contemplative, and he was going to say something soon, but Lavilor was too distraught to appreciate the scenery while he waited.

"Camilla is trying. She wants you to feel loved and cared about."

I know, Sleet, but she's broken. Something inside her is ruined.

The dragon did not say anything. He shifted his wings and slipped between two branches, changing course slightly. An image slipped across their bond. Sleet was taking them to Nelexi and Flameheart. Lavilor got the sense that on some level the dragon thought they might be able to help. Or something. It was a vague, faint thought.

It was true. Camilla was trying to be thoughtful, aware of what others wanted, but it was because she was broken. She no longer believed that she only had to care enough, love enough, and she would win through whatever opposed her. And while Lavilor had not always liked the way she applied that belief, the belief itself was something he loved about her.

"I do not disagree."

I still love her. I want to bring her back.

"That is why we are going to the Obsidian Guardian."

Nelexi believed. Flameheart believed. And Nelexi had lived for thousands of years. She had been bonded to hundreds of humans. Well, maybe not hundreds, but Sleet did not know how many. She never told anyone. But she had known many, many humans, and many, many dragons. She had had experiences to tower over all their experiences combined as much as her wings outspanned Sleet's.

She might be able to help them.

Even Lavilor felt her presence before he saw it: the huge black bulk that felt like the earth itself. She rose above the tops of the gigantic trees, her red wings sweeping down and up. Sleet altered course to follow her, and they landed on a hill-top, a rocky spur of the mountains. He clung to Sleet's neck, not wanting to break that fragile comfort, while Flameheart climbed down Nelexi's shoulders and then onto her knee, to stand near the head that felt almost as big as all of Sleet put together. He let Sleet explain their concerns to the Obsidian Guardian. He was not ready to put anything more into words.

Nelexi's voice flowed like fire through their minds. *"Camilla does believe."*

– *She does?* –

"She does," repeated the river of rushing fire. *"She is bound, as I am, to the Fire. She believes. She knows. She must discover what that means when the world does not appear to be the only way she imagined it must be, and she is confused. But she knows the Fire, and she cannot deny it for long. You do not need to be afraid."*

But she's not doing what she –

"What you valued about her is not lost. It simply has a challenge to meet, and she is struggling. But belief will *win in time."* Nelexi paused, and Lavilor heard what felt like an echo of Flameheart's voice.

"She is not doing what she promised you. What you expected her to do. She is changing, and she must change, but she will find her confidence again, stronger than before .... Do you –"

Nelexi did not have to finish saying it. Sleet and Lavilor both knew. Did they want her to try to do what Camilla said she was not yet ready to try. Did they want to fly back across the ocean to fight the Wizard-King?

Was Nelexi offering to go with them, right now, if they asked? They were not sure.

"To rescue Mom, or for vengeance?" Lavilor thought it was Sleet's voice that spoke, not his, but even so, the voice, mental as it was, broke on the word 'Mom'.

"If she was captured, she does not live," said Nelexi.

Then. No. Vengeance did not interest either of them. Sleet would rather fly through the trees, and Lavilor would rather visit Laoirn.

The mood shifted. The conversation changed. *"I will also be going to the Light Elves shortly. You are free here, as free as any of the other Sha'adhri. You may come and go as you wish, and eat what you want. Many of the Sha'adhri may look down on you for the past, but they will not hinder you from living here as you please, and some will be friendly to you, if you find each other. Is there more you need?"*

Lavilor shook his head. Sleet sent his assent.

"I'll miss you, but we'll be back!" Flameheart called aloud, waving.

"Me too," he croaked, looking up from Sleet's head to wave at her.

When the Obsidian Guardian and her rider left, Lavilor sat astride the dragon's shoulders, looking at the giant leaves rippling in the breeze. *I think I will go and visit Laoirn, soon.*

Sleet hummed. That suited him, and he knew he could find the boy and his clan again. He liked the boy, too. And he wished, for Lavilor's sake, that they did not have that silly restriction about Dragonriders living with them.

I'm okay. I'm okay.

Nelexi!

There was no other black dragon so large or with a red stripe down her back and tail and red wings. She lay across the opening of the Riders' Passage, that they had to take to reach the Light Elves who could help them learn the magic they needed.

Did she intend to stop them?

White-hot rage curled in Camilla's mind. She knew what the other dragons and riders said: that no one and nothing could kill the Obsidian Guardian. But she was something that had never been before. If Nelexi stood in her way, by Fire, she *would* kill her.

"*I do not come to stop you. I come to guide you, for even dragons can get lost in caves. And I come to make sure you have enough food and water for the journey.*"

The fire drained away, leaving only emptiness behind. She was useless. She was a useless failure. This was the same mistake she had made before. She had not considered how hard it would be to find water on the plains, and that had almost killed them all, or it might have. She should have known better now. She should have known to consider the fact that caves might not have any food and water at all for her to find, and how to think about this.

This habit of not thinking was going to get her killed before she even begun.

"*I should have thought, too,*" Radiance whispered, the emotions far more reassurance than the words that flew beside them. Love. Caring. Belief. Radiance believed in her, in them, and the dragon would not let her despair.

She was not useless. She was not a failure. She was fundamentally and completely valuable, through and through. She was everything, life and love, wind and fire and light, day and night, to Radiance.

They flew on, and when they reached the opening they found that Nelexi had left plenty of space for them to land. But while wanting to kill

Nelexi had been the feeling of a moment and more of a reaction to her own fears and insecurities than anything else, and Camilla did not even want to refuse the black dragon's company after what had happened last time, her feelings were still conflicted. She scrambled out of Radiance's saddle, and hit the rock hard.

"Nelexi!" she called.

The great fire-striped black head turned to look at her. *She was not small!* "What did you tell my brother?"

Lavilor had been acting differently since she had told him they were going to learn magic before flying back to kill the Wizard-King, and Camilla *knew* it was something to do with Nelexi and her rider.

"Only that he did not need to be worried that you no longer believed the Fire must triumph," said Flameheart from atop Nelexi's shoulders.

Camilla nodded. She did not know what she thought about it. Any of it. She did not want to remember that strange confrontation with Nelexi, that she did not understand. She could not even remember why she had said some of what she did, but she knew that Nelexi's answers did not satisfy her as to why the black dragon had done nothing about the atrocities committed against her and Radiance's people.

She squared her shoulders and spoke with all the authority she could muster. "It is still early. Let us go on."

An odd, stale breeze flowed down the passage. Flameheart stepped over a knee-high boulder that glowed a gentle shade of rose and glanced behind her at Camilla and Radiance.

Camilla's face looked strange in the multi-colored light. The lines of iridescent gold-green dragon skin shimmered with all the different colors of the stone, green, aquamarine, cerulean, sapphire, violent, indigo, magenta, scarlet, and every other imaginable shade, while her bronze human skin remained mostly dark, now and then shimmering a gentle hue. She did not look human. She looked more like the painted carving of a demon or a demi-god Flameheart had seen among one of the peoples Nelexi had taken her to visit.

Right now, her face was set in a frown, her brows drawn up together, and she looked like she was steadfastly trying to ignore the wonders around her.

This was not Flameheart's favorite place in the world. She much preferred the night sky with its free winds on the gently rolling plains to these confined caverns. Though some of the Sha'adhri and Light Elves referred to the glowing stones as the stars in the earth, and she could understand the analogy, they did not really feel like stars at all. But they still evoked wonder in her, and she *knew* they evoked wonder in Camilla. She had seen the look on the Dragonrider's face a time or two, and she had felt the pure wash of it when they had ventured into the caves. Since then, even though she had made no comment, Camilla had contained her wonder, but it was strong. Flameheart knew it.

"*Leave well alone,*" Nelexi spoke to her. The black dragon did not fit in this passage and had taken a round-about way she could fly through. "*You won't be able to help Camilla figure this out, anyways.*"

Do you know that, then?

Flameheart wished she had asked to ride Nelexi through the passage. It was boring to be stuck alone with Camilla and Radiance.

"*I will remember that next time. And, no, I do not know that. Trust your heart.*"

Flameheart nodded, and flipped her lightstone between her fingers, admiring the webbing of white across the brilliant red. She took it off her neck and wound it over her head, then let it bounce on her palm as she walked.

They were going back to the Light Elves, and presumably they would be staying a bit longer than they had last time. She might get to learn some of those things Azayr-ren had wanted to show her.

She felt Camilla step up behind her. After a few moments, she turned her head. "Hello."

Camilla took a few moments to respond. When she did, her voice was half-grudging. "Hello."

She waited, trying to ignore the tension that poured off of Camilla in waves. She had lost a dragon bonded to her, and Flameheart knew that had to hurt. Maybe Nelexi was right. Camilla had grown a lot less hostile, but she was still hostile, and she had to be grieving. Crushed. It hurt Flameheart to lose Ben. She had no idea how it would be for Camilla. Devastating.

Still, it was not comfortable to travel with someone in the moods Camilla tended to adopt. But that did not mean it was wrong.

No, some of this was just her tension about being underground. Her people did not belong underground. She did not mind being with the Light Elves, but that did not feel like this. With the Light Elves, she could go outside whenever she needed to, but she would not see the sun or the free wind for weeks now.

"What's that?"

Flameheart held out her hand and felt Camilla's curt nod, reverberating through the pattern of her steps.

"It's a lightstone, one I chose. The Light Elves all have one like this, except they're all different colors, and most of them are plainer than this one… " She stopped short, at what sounded like an exasperated sigh.

Could Camilla just *say* what she wanted to know, and not get annoyed when Flameheart did not understand her perfectly?

"What do you want to know?"

"Go on."

Flameheart did not want to. She wanted to scream something at Camilla, she was not sure what.

"You don't have to talk if you don't wish to. Just be nice about it." Nelexi's voice flew through her mind, like a smaller dragon through the branches of the giant trees in Dragonsong.

"It's the same sort of stone as the ones all over these passages, just a small one."

"I've seen some small ones." Camilla suddenly sounded … nicer.

These mood changes bewildered Flameheart in a way the shifting winds of spring in the Plains never had.

"Would you like one?" Flameheart asked, desperately wanting to keep the pleasant mood.

Camilla shrugged, and some of the tension flowed back. "I don't see why I would need one. I can always make light of my own." She flicked her wrist, and a flame shuddered into view, shimmering through the whole range of colors, from sullen red to violet-blue, before it winked out of existence.

"I'm not a mage, so I don't know any more than this, but the Light Elves say if you find one that matches you, it can sometimes help your magic." She proffered the statement like an offering, almost shy but with more familiarity.

Camilla made a soft growling noise. The tension was there, but Flameheart did not feel it pooling like a stagnant puddle the way it usually did. "Then maybe I will look for it. See if there's any that get my attention."

Flameheart did not say anything. It did not seem there was anything more to say.

Camilla sat on a rock that glowed a wash of purple through blue-tinged green, shaped perfectly for a seat. She wondered if perhaps it had been, by generations of Dragonriders who used this passage. She rested her chin on the heel of her hand, and let her eyes rest on the refracted rainbow lights glancing off of Radiance's shoulders.

The dragon was asleep, she was awake, and she was depressed.

Walk, walk, walk. Sometimes the passage was big enough to fly, and then they flew. The caverns opened up sometimes, to vaults so high that it really did look almost like the night sky, and the lights were always changing, but it was ... it felt absolutely, utterly useless. It felt more useless than any step of the journey up until this point had felt, though she was glad it was easy on Radiance's joints.

Or maybe the feeling of uselessness had grown since Ben died. She did not know, but there seemed to be a particular uselessness to this trudging she was doing through this strange caverns.

It was the feeling of being without direction, without purpose. And every second, a part of her mind whispered to her that Lavilor's challenge was right.

But maybe it was not. Maybe her need to always be doing something that she could see directly taking her to her goal, to be always responding to and righting atrocities, did not leave Radiance room to grow. To be the dragon she should be. Because, as close as they were, they were two persons, not one person with two bodies the way that the were-dragons were. Radiance should be her first priority, and she should not expect Radiance to be ... well, to be what was most convenient for her other goals.

Life made no sense. Nothing made sense.

Lavilor? She reached out to the feeling of his mind, as present to her as if they were standing across a clearing from each other.

She felt his immediate response. He was half-asleep, but he knew she spoke to him.

If now is a bad time, that's okay.

"*It's not,*" he dreamily mumbled. Maybe he was half-dreaming.

I'm not abandoning you.

"I know." He did not seem a whole lot more responsive.

Sleep well. Nice dreams, to you and Sleet.

"Thank you."

She withdrew. He clearly was not awake enough to talk about anything, and she was not sure she needed to be talking about it, anyways. She hoped he understood, that it made him feel cared about that she checked in on him.

That she was still the sister he knew, the sister who loved and would do everything for him.

But she was sad, and she hoped she was doing the right thing, and she hated not having a sure way of knowing.

She crossed her arms on her lap, and bent over, resting her head on them. It was easy to talk about freedom. To insist you cared about and valued that above all else, and would do whatever you had to, to be free, and that would give you the strength to be victorious over whatever threatened your freedom, just as long as you held true to loving your friends and living free.

Or did she think it was harder to actually know how to love and respect the freedom of your friends, to know what she had done wrong and what she had done right and, most importantly, what the next right thing to do was, because her will to love and be free was not as pure as she believed it?

But how could it not be? That was everything she cared about. Everything she built her life on. The reason behind her every decision and motivation.

How could it be a lie? How could she ever go wrong that way?

Was she just too tired to think and too broken with the loss of Ben, his soul torn out of hers after they have been woven together, taking threads of her with him, so that now she was unraveling like a torn piece of knitting or a tunic with an unsewn hem?

How must that make Radiance feel, the golden dragon who was her soul and ought to be enough for her?

Yet Radiance would never judge her, never condemn her. There were times when that felt like the only thing she knew for certain. The only thing that kept her living.

Radiance woke her in the morning. *"Why didn't you sleep with me?"* she asked so gently it made Camilla ... happy, for a moment. Purely, simply happy.

The explanation did not require words. Radiance was everything Camilla could ever have imagined or wanted, and she loved her so much her heart would burst, would burn itself up the way her body did when she drew on too much fire.

If there was one thing she had ever done right, it had been being at that stadium to Recognize Radiance.

As the days passed, both dragon and rider's mental and emotional state suffered. Camilla felt Radiance's desperate itch to be above ground, to feel the sun on her back and the wind under her wings. They had always enjoyed flying together, and the little bit of flying they could do when the passage opened in a wide cavern only taunted them with the real thing. It could not break Camilla's depression, and it did little for Radiance's mood, which fell farther and farther towards that of her rider.

There were times when Nelexi would wake them in the morning, and Camilla wondered why she did not just sit there until she turned to stone. She never wanted to wake up, and she never got to sleep quickly either, when they decided to stop, no matter how tired she was. She spoke to Lavilor and Sleet only rarely, in part because she spent most of the time with her mind and will far away, but also because she did not want to share her depression with them. They seemed reasonably happy, but the longer she spent in contact with them, the more they would pick up on her misery.

So they walked on and on through the bright caverns as through an abyss of misery, until it seemed as if the free wind under their wings was only a memory and the alternation of day and night was less than that. There was nothing that Camilla could do, and no way for her to know whether or not she had made the right choice or the wrong one. She knew only that, while day and night had no meaning here, her misery alternated. Sometimes, all she wanted was to be doing something, to be flying or falling, fighting, winning, even dying was preferable to this doing nothing. Other times, she had no wants at all, and even eating, putting one foot in front of the other, sleeping were burdens strapped to her back that she felt she could not sustain for another moment. And, sometimes, she felt both at once.

She could not imagine how *she* of all people had ever come to be this miserable. But she did not ask to go back. She feared too much that Nelexi would say no, and would refuse to guide her, and that she would not be able to force Nelexi.

And she did not know if that was the right choice. Did it even matter any more?

She had waited too long, and by now everyone was surely dead. Did it even matter any more?

How long had it been? Was she doomed to travel here forever?

Sometimes, she would wake to something more than absolute misery, but then the lightstones shining above, so strange, would make her wonder:

what would have Ben thought? What would his reaction be? There was no way that she could know. She had never gotten to know him that well, never made that effort to really understand … anyone.

Not even Radiance, secure in the belief that she was Radiance, and Radiance was her, and so she did not need to try to understand.

Then, she woke looking up at an arrangement of lightstones that suddenly reminded her of her father's Dolphin. She owed it to everyone she loved, and everyone she had not loved, to try. She owed it to her mother, and her father who had died when she was little and of whom she had only the faintest memories. She owed it to Radiance, who was still with her and to whom she could make up her failures, and to Ben, whom she had failed in more ways than one. She owed it to Lavilor, whom she had failed in some ways but not in all.

She opened her hand and let the flames dance across her fingers. There was no excuse for *her* not to believe the Fire.

If things had gone wrong, and she did not have the strength to be victorious because of her own flaws and failure to respect and nurture other's freedom, then the first and only thing required of her was to change that. Which meant that she had made the right choice, this once. She owed it to Radiance to let the golden dragon choose just as much as she chose. Only then could they truly be together. They would be truly one when Camilla followed Radiance as much as Radiance followed Camilla, when Camilla encouraged Radiance to think and be her own, unique creature as much as Camilla herself was.

For what Camilla had been making of her relationship with Radiance was very much like the horror that she had detested in what the were-dragons seemed to be. That, and … no, no, that was unthinkable.

Unforgivable. And Camilla knew she was not that horrible. She did not want to violate other's freedom. Once she knew that was what she was doing, she stopped. No matter how much it seemed to cost her.

It did not make any sense. She knew she loved, and therefore her freedom should not be able to clash with the freedom of those she loved.

Was it possible she did not love perfectly? When she loved perfectly, would her freedom and Radiance's be the same thing? But how could she not love the dragon she was bonded to, with whom her soul was bound in such an intimate way as to make their souls one, perfectly and absolutely? It was not possible!

She felt Radiance watching her, observing her, and finally realized that the dragon was almost laughing at her, but in the kindest way possible.

What? She could not help the frustration that leaked through. How was it possible that there could be a thought of Radiance's that she did not understand?

She felt the dragon thinking, struggling, and then a thought clear, but incomprehensible. Almost *too* clear: it did not matter, did not make a difference, whether her love was perfect or flawed. The thing was to *love*.

She almost asked Radiance to explain what she meant, but she knew it was not possible. What the dragon shared *was* what she meant. It just did not make sense to her rider.

Had Camilla violated Radiance by trying to make her thoughts make sense to her? Perhaps. Now she would try to *understand*, to *accept*, to be Radiance and so to understand the dragon's thoughts without changing them. She had done some of that in the past, but perhaps not fully enough.

The dragon chuckled at her again. The thing was to love. The thing was to try. There was nothing else to be considered. Perfect or flawed, those were concepts without meaning. No regrets, and no shame. Only *love*, right here, right now, in the way before them.

And when they were fully two, then they would be fully one. When they were fully one, then they would be fully two.

"Let's try."

That conversation did not end her depression. To walk on and on, with no sense of time, no sense of the goal they were approaching, and no way to do anything, while her soul screamed at her that there were things that *must* be done, and that she had put off for far too long, was in ways the hardest thing she had ever done.

But something that she had put off for far too long was letting Radiance lead, and letting Radiance's way of thinking lead. It was hard, and she was not sure if she was really doing it even now, but she was fully committed. And that meant she had to let go of what made sense to her in order to understand what made sense to her dragon. It made her feel vulnerable and helpless, as if she had no armor against a threat and she did not even know what direction the threat would come from next.

One of the things this meant, that she understood and yet did not, was that she had to let go of her feelings about perfection and flaws. To Radiance and in the dragon's way of thinking, those were not even concepts, at least in as much as Camilla did not force her to consider them. What mattered was to try to love, to the best of one's present capability and understanding, or at least that was how Camilla understood Radiance's thoughts.

Had she even been able to give Radiance the freedom to develop much earlier? Maybe meeting the freed dragons had helped. But she thought it was more than that. Her own withdrawal into depression, and lack of energy to be constantly present in Radiance's thinking, had given her dragon space to have her thoughts, she thought.

Then, somewhat suddenly, Nelexi lifted off in front of them, and the wind from the black dragon's wings pushed Camilla back a pace and into a crouch. When she was able to stand again and look she saw something that at first she did not understand.

The caverns opened up in a space wider than any she had ever seen before, and for the first time what opened ahead and before them *did* resemble a night sky. Or had it only been that she had not seen a real night sky in so long she had forgotten what it looked like?

At any rate, the space was vast, with brighter lights, and smaller ones, and sprinklings of smaller ones yet that created an effect like that of the Path of Light across the sky, where hardly an individual light was visible, yet everything was just a little brighter. But the constellations were different, or mostly different. She saw no Dolphin here, at least not yet.

And … below them was something that faded into the distance, glowing with melded lights. It was not rock, and it was not one huge multi-colored lightstone, which was the first explanation that occurred to her. The light was softer, somehow different than that, and it rippled a little.

She responded to a thought from Radiance, and climbed onto the gold dragon's shoulders. A moment later they pushed off, following Nelexi. As the rock of the Riders' Passage fell away below them, she looked down and saw two lightstone boulders, and from between them something that flowed, rippling, into a channel that flowed downward to meet the sheet of melded lights.

Water! It was water! A vast underground lake that glowed with the hundreds and thousands of lightstones buried beneath its waters!

"The Spring of Nerya," said Nelexi, *"and the Lake of Light."*

A gentle breeze came from somewhere, stirring the air under their wings. It was not a breeze like the ones in the outer world, but it *was* a stirring of wind, however subtle. Camilla felt a smile stretch her lips, the first in weeks – in she did not really know how long!

Radiance roared and flamed, and the bright dragonfire reflected on the glowing waters below them, mingling with the muddled glow.

"This is a good place," continued the obsidian dragon. *"We will fly, and then we will land and drink."*

Sparkling joy flashed through Camilla, like the burst of dragonfire over the Lake of Light. It was not something she understood.

Radiance climbed higher and higher and higher, stretching her wings to their fullest extent, circling and twirling. Her rider leaned forward, the air rushing her hair past her cheeks, leaning into the wind. It smelled … fresher, here, too. Like something she could not quite name, a little like the feel of Dragonsong Vale, but different.

The lightstones above them grew larger and clearer, and then she could see distance, could see that the roof was not quite smooth. It had bumps and ledges and crevices, and along one of these they flew, the underground stars no more than a few dragon spans above their heads.

Then, when her wings shook with weariness, Radiance descended, gliding and circling, and flew along the surface of the lake, until Nelexi's black and red bulk loomed ahead of them on the shoreline. There they landed. Camilla slid down Radiance's shoulders, and the dragon turned to drink from the lake, taking in great gulps of the shining water.

Almost at once, Camilla felt her sated, to her own surprise. The water seemed to drain her thirst away and fill her with light. There was no pain and no grief. No regret. The tremors in her muscles soothed, and the aches in her joints faded. She straightened, her scales sparkling and her wings lifting, as if truly alive and free for the first time ever, happy and at rest. With a mental touch, she motioned her rider to step forward and drink.

Camilla knelt on the edge of the water and bent down to lap at the still waters, rippling gently from where Radiance had put her foot in them. She was not very thirsty to begin with, so the water did not soothe her thirst as it had Radiance's, but it flooded through her, like light in her veins.

She tapped a lightstone boulder and knelt next to it, to match it with the lightstone hanging around her neck. It was a lighter, pinker red, more like a sunset, and the veins of white were more faded, too, and chaotic, like a cloud pattern.

She straightened and sighed. She could feel the Volcano calling her, its voice resonating in the stone she wore over her heart and in her heart, and along every one of Nelexi's scales. Calling her, as it called the Obsidian Guardian who had emerged from its heart so long ago.

> Souls long born from the living flame
> Flames re-issued from the soul of fire
> A conflagration long due as time rolls by
> To enfold earths and souls in arms of heart's fire

She stopped suddenly, aware she had been humming it, or singing it, or something, she was not sure which. Feeling a presence behind her, she turned around.

Camilla stood, framed in the light of a gold and crimson boulder even larger than the one she had just been kneeling beside. She did not look like a demon now, but like something else, soft and severe, her head canted a little, as if she were about to ask a question. She almost looked like she could have stepped out of the boulder itself – or out of fire and the sky.

"Did I interrupt you?" she asked quietly, her voice echoing strangely in the huge underground chamber.

Flameheart shook her head, and for a moment she imagined that the hair that flew about her face and shoulders were strings of fire flying out from the Volcano. "I don't mind." She pulled herself up onto her boulder and made herself as comfortable as its rough, hard edges would allow.

Camilla was strange these days. She did not eat or sleep well, and she was looking like a ghost of her formal self. The outbursts of scorching anger with which Flameheart was so familiar did not occur, but a crushing grief, a sense of loss and purposelessness, poured out from her, one so overwhelming and undercutting Flameheart was profoundly grateful for the ever-present vision of the Volcano.

Otherwise, even with Nelexi, it would have been hard not to be swept away by it.

Right now, she did not feel that from Camilla. It was not raging forth, at any rate.

"I was just singing something. A song I sung before, after Nelexi drove off some nightmare creatures. Would you like me to sing it for you now?"

Flameheart. Her name was Flameheart. She had always been meant to see the Heart of Fire this way. What had happened – perhaps it had not been anything Nelexi did, but her inner self hatching.

Camilla sat down on the ground a few paces away, looking vulnerable in a way she had only begun to appear recently – very recently. "Please do."

Flameheart sang.

Only when she was finished, did she realize that she had sung in the language of the Plains, the language of her people, not the awkward elf tongue Camilla spoke.

But would it matter? Camilla heard as dragons hear. Surely, she understood as much as she was ready to understand. Even Flameheart only understood as much as she was ready to understand of her own song. She understood it better now than she had when she had first sung it – or perhaps she did not understand it better, but only understand different parts of it in different ways. And another time, she would find in it what she had found neither this time, nor the last time.

"When do we go on?" asked Camilla. It was not the voice of someone dismissing what she had just heard, but of someone seeking another topic because the song was too much to talk about, or even think about.

"Nelexi says this a good place to rest. We will go on when those of us who are still mortal have recovered our strength."

"Still mortal?" asked Camilla, with a smile to her voice.

"Not Nelexi," said Flameheart. "She is ready to go again, at almost any time."

Camilla stiffened, and Flameheart immediately decided she had said something wrong. She climbed up and slid off the boulder. She could not make things right, and she was going crazy in here, like a gazelle bound up in a tent. It made the back of her shoulders itch. *I'm as impatient as Camilla is,* she told Nelexi.

"You are, but if you, and more importantly Radiance, stay here to rest and drink again when you are ready, we will be able to fly faster and get where we are going sooner."

As soon as you introduce Camilla and Radiance to the Light Elves and there is no danger of her getting lost, we are going out for a real *flight!*

"Agreed."

Flameheart laughed, chuckling deeply. Nelexi did that to her sometimes. She whooped and jumped in the air. For a moment, she could *feel* that real flight, as if it were here, right now, waiting only for them to jump off a ledge, or even as if they were flying already, diving, wind and sky rushing past them.

She stopped on the smooth rock, worn with thousands of subtle ripples and striations, Nelexi had told her, by the rise and fall of the waters of the Lake of Light over tens of thousands of years. She stopped on the edge of the waters and swirled her fingers through them, letting the waves fold into complicated patterns that grew ever more complex as she stirred them. These waters felt a little like the Heart of Fire, no substitute for it, but something a little like it – and something that would not harm mortals, would sustain and refresh them while still allowing them to continue their journeys on the paths of mortals. That would not force them, not yet, into the Presence of the Fire, yet would give them a faint, far-off taste of it.

That was how these waters felt to Flameheart. Pale light, light, yes, but pale and thin, not like the Sun: burning and strong. Giving light and bringing growth, then scorching it. This place had neither the life and beauty, nor the harshness, of the Plains. It was not alive, and it did not kill.

Fire was both.

She bent forward, over the water, and placed both her hands under the water: just under it, so the top-line of her thumb was even with the surface of the water. Then she pushed them towards each other, creating a wave that rose up and flowed back over her rising hands. Again and again she did this, building the wave higher and higher, rejoicing in the sound of the flowing waters.

"You've been too long underground," said Nelexi when she wearied of her game. *"But we will remedy that soon."*

"We're almost there."

Radiance's voice was like warm light flooding through a tomb long cold and dark.

We are, she replied, leaning forward with a smile on her face, as if she could help Radiance fly faster that way, or as if she could somehow peer through the miles of rock and lightstone-lit passages still between them and their destination.

It made her feel immensely better to be able to do something – or at least to know that, very soon now, she *would* be able to do something. She needed to be doing, and being unable to do wore on her perhaps almost as much as the loss of Ben. And it made Radiance feel better, too, to be almost there, almost where she was going.

She smiled even wider as the irony of it occurred to her: this was what Radiance wanted to do, but it would be her rider who would be doing it. It would be Camilla who learned the magic. But that was what it meant to be dragon and rider. That Radiance's powers were at the service of Camilla's will, and Camilla's powers were at the service of Radiance's will. This was *right*. And the fact that she could finally *do* something made her feel so much better about it.

"*Silly,*" Radiance chided gently. "*It won't be just you who learn the magic. I will learn with you and for you.*"

Even better.

To Be Continued ...

In **Dragon-Mage Book Three**
HEALING OF FIRE

"A thousand considerations rose in Camilla's mind, but she ignored them all, not having the time for them. She held her hands out, palms placed together, in obedience to her magic that she now knew as her own body, and her mind and body vibrated with a single harp-like note. Fire erupted between her palms and shot out towards the self-styled Lord of the Dead.

The voice of the thousands of dead filled the hall. "Do you really think your magic poses a threat to *me?*" Fire swept out of the Wizard-King's eyes and formed a barrier against her flame. Radiance coiled on her tail, preparing to fight, and Camilla *wished* they were together."

Sign up to be notified about new releases:
https://books2read.com/r/B-A-OUYQ-HMXXB

Follow me on Goodreads:
https://www.goodreads.com/author/show/20243136.Raina_Nightingale

Follow me on BookBub:
https://www.bookbub.com/authors/raina-nightingale

Or, if you like weekly reviews, ramblings of all sorts, and occasional art posts, you can follow my blog:
https://enthralledbylove.com

If you liked Scars of Fire, please leave an honest review on your favorite book platforms. It really helps readers and independent authors to find each other. I would deeply grateful and encouraged.

See you again!

www.ingramcontent.com/pod-product-compliance
Lightning Source LLC
Chambersburg PA
CBHW052133170626
46812CB00004B/1386